JAN '17

11

6-20

11

THE PRODIGAL FATHER

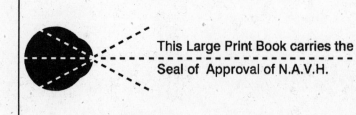

THE PRODIGAL FATHER

KARA LYNN RUSSELL

THORNDIKE PRESS
A part of Gale, Cengage Learning

GALE
CENGAGE Learning™

Detroit • New York • San Francisco • New Haven, Conn • Waterville, Maine • London

GALE
CENGAGE·Learning·

LIBRARY OF CONGRESS CATALOGING-IN-PUBLICATION DATA

Russell, Kara Lynn.
  The prodigal father / by Kara Lynn Russell.
    p. cm. — (Thorndike Press large print clean reads)
  ISBN-13: 978-1-4104-2815-8
  ISBN-10: 1-4104-2815-X
    1. Marriage—Fiction. 2. Down syndrome—Fiction. 3. Domestic fiction.
  4. Large type books. I. Title.
  PS3618.U754P76 2010
  813'.6—dc22   2010012063

Published in 2010 by arrangement with Tekno Books.

Printed in the United States of America
1 2 3 4 5 6 7 14 13 12 11 10

To all the caring, hardworking professionals in the Birth to Three programs all over the U.S., especially to Theresa. We'd never have made it without you!

CHAPTER 1

On the outside, Beth Lund was calm, collected, and in full professional mode. On the inside, her mind wandered. She was bored, bored, bored; another *routine* day in her routine life. But she maintained her smile as she led Mr. and Mrs. Palmer, an older couple with matching snow-white hair, from the showroom to the car lot where they could see the model of vehicle they were interested in buying.

She walked backwards so she could face the couple as she rattled off the features, warranty, safety rating, and other information she had memorized about the make and model. She didn't see the tall man who had already opened the dealership door and was about to step in.

Beth slammed right into a solid form and lost her balance.

Strong arms caught and supported her as she righted herself. She turned to apologize to the man and froze. It couldn't be *him,* she told herself.

She tried to breathe, but no air seemed to get into her lungs. The tanned face and brilliant blue eyes swam out of focus and Beth's knees buckled. Those same strong arms that had kept her from stumbling before caught her again and swept her up. He carried her into the showroom, past her stunned customers. She heard the familiar baritone rumble of his voice in her ear, but couldn't focus on the words. Closing her eyes because the room was showing an alarming tendency to spin, she felt herself being set down on a chair and then a gentle hand pressed her head down close to her knees.

Slowly, the dizziness receded and she found she could breathe again. She risked opening her eyes. The shiny new cars that surrounded her no longer wavered out of focus. "I'm all right now. I can sit up," she said.

He removed his hand from the back of her head and she straightened.

It was no hallucination; he was here. She surveyed him, from his spiky blond hair to his snug-fitting jeans. He hadn't changed. Scott Lund was as devastatingly handsome as he'd been three and a half years ago when he'd walked out on her and their marriage.

"What . . . what are you doing here?" she asked.

He smiled, and her heart contracted inside her chest. "Looking for you. I didn't actually expect to find you so easily. I didn't mean to startle you like that."

"What are you doing here?" The question was repeated but in stern male tones. Beth turned to see Scott's cousin, Jared, approach them, a scowl on his face.

Scott rose to greet his cousin, but instead of accepting the hand he held out, Jared punched him square in the jaw.

Scott lost his balance and was sent sprawling, taking down a large potted plant with him. Dirt sprayed across the linoleum floor.

Everything was happening fast, too fast for Beth to take it in. She watched as Scott sat up, touched his jaw gingerly and glared at his cousin.

"Gee Jared, it's nice to see you, too," he grumbled as he got to his feet.

She saw Jared's hand clench into a fist. When she realized he was going to hit Scott again, Beth jumped up and grabbed his arm. "Jared, stop it," she hissed. This commotion was sure to catch their boss's attention.

Scott was at her side in a flash. "Beth, sit down."

9

She brushed him away. "No, I'm fine."

"What did you do to her?" Jared glared at Scott.

"He surprised me, that's all," Beth said. "Calm down, Jared."

"I want to know what's going on." He stood with his hands on his hips now, not budging.

"I owe Beth an explanation, not you," insisted Scott, his stance mirroring Jared's.

Had she been complaining about her routine day? She wished she could take it back now.

Beth slipped in between them, facing Scott. "You have to go before your father. . . ."

"What's going on up there?" Hal Lund's voice echoed from the back of the building.

She groaned. Too late to get him out unnoticed. "Scott, just go, please."

"I want to see Dad, too," he said.

"No, you don't," insisted Beth as she pushed him toward the door.

"Hey, what about me?" whined Jared.

"You can clean up the dirt from the plant you knocked over," Beth snapped at him.

Scott balked. "I'll go on one condition."

"What's that?" She was desperate to get him out before Hal saw him.

"You come with me." He grabbed her

hand and pulled her toward the door.

What was she doing? She shouldn't be going anywhere with this man who'd broken her heart and then abandoned her. She was absolutely going to refuse. Then she made the mistake of looking at him before she spoke. The intensity in his blue eyes, the look of entreaty on his face did her in. Beth called over her shoulder to Jared, "Tell Hal I'll be back as soon as I can." Then to her potential clients, who were standing where she'd left them, she called, "I'm sorry Mr. and Mrs. Palmer. I'm sure someone else can help you."

Scott tugged on her hand and she followed him. After all, he did owe her an explanation.

He led Beth to a silver SUV.

"Nice," she commented, as he opened the passenger door and handed her in.

Getting in on the driver's side he looked at Beth. "Coffee?"

She nodded and they left.

A few minutes later they pulled up in front of a coffee shop.

"Scott," she started to say as he turned off the engine.

"Sshh," he hushed her gently, then leaned over and pulled her into his arms. Beth was too surprised to resist. He lowered his

11

mouth to hers and kissed her, his lips moving gently against hers. He pulled her even closer and deepened the kiss. She felt his heart beating against her chest and his arms felt strong and solid around her. Strong enough to hold off the real world for a little while.

It had been more than three years since she'd been held and kissed by him. Those years apart had done nothing to raise her resistance to the man. It just wasn't fair that he could still do this to her after so long.

The kiss was over too soon and Beth felt off balance. She leaned back in her seat and noted that her hands were shaking so she folded them in her lap.

"What was that for?" she asked.

"Because you haven't slapped me silly," he said. "Because you came with me. I didn't think you'd let me kiss you once we got inside and started to talk."

She looked away, blinking hard to hold back the tears. "I didn't *let* you kiss me. You just did it."

"I know, Beth."

"And if I slapped you, it would be because you deserved it."

"I know that, too."

"Then let's get some coffee."

He got out and came around to her side

to open the door. Normally she didn't wait for a man to open doors for her, but today, as shaky as she felt, she was glad to accept the courtesy, to feel his hand on her back, guiding her as they entered the coffee shop. So much for her routine life.

Scott's heart was light as he followed Beth into the coffee shop. In spite of his sore jaw and bruised behind, he thought things were going well. Actually things were going incredibly well, compared to what he had expected.

Once they were seated and had steaming mugs of coffee in their hands, he couldn't help pausing to savor the moment.

Sitting here together — him and Beth.

He'd spent the last three years dreaming about her. Why *had* he stayed away for so long?

She was even more beautiful than he remembered. She was tall; an elegant, willowy figure. Her long dark-brown hair was done in a neat French braid, very business-like he supposed, but he preferred it loose. The only thing that bothered him was the pain he saw in her eyes, pain he knew he had caused.

"Why did you come back?" Beth asked.

Scott shrugged. "It was time."

"Time for what?"

"Time to resolve things between us."

"Oh. You want a divorce." She dropped her gaze to the table, but he heard the bitter note in her voice.

"I didn't say that."

Beth sighed. "Then, what *do* you want?"

He wanted to reach out to her, to take her hands in his and reassure her that everything would be okay, but she was too tense. He'd caught her off guard with the kiss. It wouldn't happen again.

"Scott?"

"I want a second chance."

Her jaw dropped and he watched as she floundered for a moment. "What? Why now?"

"Beth, I finally have something to offer you."

"I don't understand."

"I've done a lot since I left. I've worked hard, and I have something to call my own now. I want to share it with you," he explained.

Beth was silent so he continued.

"I want to give you a choice. Either give me a second chance, or if you prefer, we can get a divorce."

"Scott, before this conversation goes any further, there's something I need to tell you." She was staring down at the table, so he couldn't read the emotion in her eyes. He shifted in his seat, no longer so confident that this was going well.

The door to the shop burst open. Scott's father, Hal, strode into the shop, Jared behind him.

"I'm sure that SUV is his, Uncle Hal. Look, there they are, back there," Jared said.

Beth murmured, "Oh no," and hid her face in her hands.

Scott watched as his father approached them. The man looked grim. He didn't expect his father would be happy to see him, but he hadn't expected him to be this *un-*happy either.

Hal stopped at their table, the annoying Jared still at his heels. He put a hand on Beth's shoulder. "Are you all right?"

"Yes," she replied, straightening to look at him. "Scott and I need to talk some things through."

Hal turned on his son. "You come back now? After more than three years of nothing. Not a phone call, not a visit, not even a lousy e-mail. Why?"

Scott refused to get sucked into an argument right now. "I'm sorry, Dad. You're right. I should have made some sort of contact but this is between me and Beth."

"Haven't you done enough to Beth already?"

What was that supposed to mean? Surely he couldn't still be blaming Scott for Beth's pregnancy. That was ancient history.

Beth was signaling for his attention. "Hal, I was just about to tell Scott. . . ."

"You left her. No job, no money. Nothing but a baby on the way."

Scott locked gazes with his father. "I left for her own good. And you know very well that Beth miscarried. There was no baby."

"Hal . . . ," Beth interrupted again.

"She miscarried the *first* baby," Hal informed Scott. "She was pregnant again when you left."

Scott was certain he couldn't have heard his father correctly. He looked to Beth for confirmation.

Hesitantly she spoke. "I didn't want you to find out this way, but yes, I was pregnant when you left. We have a daughter."

"But the doctor said we should wait at least. . . ."

"I know, but birth control isn't infallible."

"Beth, I'm so sorry. If I had known. . . ."

"Well, there's more. Risa, our daughter, . . . Risa has Down syndrome."

He leaned against the hard back of the booth as his brain tried to make sense of it all. Dimly he was aware of Beth speaking.

"Hal, I can handle this. Please go back to work."

His father's gruff voice softened as he spoke to Beth. "Are you sure? I can take you back with me. You don't have to see him if. . . ."

"Hal, it's okay. Please go."

Scott barely noted his exit, or that of Jared.

When they were alone silence covered them. Beth lifted her mug with a trembling hand and took a sip.

"Beth, I'm sorry."

She reached out and took his hand. "Don't be. You didn't know. I found out the same day you left. I came home from the doctor to tell you . . . but you'd already gone."

"Talk about bad timing." His stomach twisted and lurched as he realized he'd made a mistake — a mistake of gargantuan proportions. He realized that Beth was speaking again and forced his attention back to her.

"As you can guess, your parents sort of took me in. They've been great to me these last three years. Your mother looks after Risa for me while I'm at work."

"Risa." His mind latched onto that small detail. He could handle that much. "That's a pretty name. How did you choose it?"

17

"I got it from a baby book. It means 'laughter'."

He nodded in approval. "I like it."

"Her middle name is Jane, after my grandmother. I hope you don't mind."

"No, I don't mind." It seemed ridiculous that she should even ask. He'd left her to raise their child alone and she was worrying that he wouldn't like the name she picked out.

He'd been so sure of what he wanted to say to her. He had seen this meeting going several different ways, but never in his wildest dreams did he imagine Beth telling him he was a father. "I'm afraid I need some time to think. This changes some things."

Her hands tightened around the mug in front of her. "I understand."

After Scott dropped her off, Beth worked furiously all day at the car dealership. It was a slow day, so she did a little spring cleaning. She sorted through the various piles on her desk, recycled outdated brochures, caught up on her filing, anything to keep her mind off Scott. By the time quitting time rolled around, she was ready to lend a hand to the car washers if it could keep her too busy to think.

Hal came into her office and closed the

door behind him. "Okay, Beth," he said. "You haven't said a word to me all day. What's going on with Scott?"

Beth toyed with the pencil on her desk. She wished she hadn't cleaned so ruthlessly. She needed some papers to shuffle while she stalled for time. Finally she said, "He said he wanted a second chance and that if I didn't want to give him one, that he wouldn't contest a divorce."

"And?"

"Before I could say anything, you came in and spilled the beans about Risa. After that, he said he needed time to think."

Hal's mouth tightened. "Now what?"

"I don't know, Hal. That was some pretty shocking news."

"It shouldn't have been news. He should have been here all along."

Beth sighed. "You realize that this is your son we're talking about. Shouldn't you be on his side?"

"I haven't been on 'his' side since the day he walked out on his responsibilities," snapped Hal. "I have some paperwork to catch up on. Tell Margie I'll be late, will you?"

"Sure."

Beth's mood lightened as she drove to pick

up her daughter. Risa was definitely the light of her life. She couldn't wait to hear what the toddler had been up to all day. Margie kept her well-informed. She felt good knowing Risa was with her grandmother, being loved and cared for. It allowed Beth to appreciate that she could work to support them, instead of feeling torn between making a living and caring for her daughter. Not that she *loved* her job, exactly. There was satisfaction in knowing that she was good at it, and it kept her from having to lean on Hal and Margie any more than she already did.

When Beth pulled up to their house, she was surprised to see Scott's SUV parked there, too. What was he doing there?

Her heart pounded as she hurried up the walk. She entered the house by the side door, walking into Margie's cozy kitchen.

Her mother-in-law had a huge grin plastered on her face. She motioned for Beth to be silent and led her to the living-room doorway. Beth gasped at what she saw.

Scott was sitting on the floor with Risa. They were building a tower with blocks. Risa watched him solemnly as he piled up the blocks. He was talking to her, but so softly that Beth couldn't make out what he was saying. When the tower of blocks began to wobble and fall, Risa laughed. Scott joined in and hugged her.

She wondered what Scott thought of their daughter. Risa was small for her age, with light-brown hair, a shade between Beth's dark-brown and Scott's blond hair, cut into a short bob. She had Beth's brown eyes and a heart-melting smile.

Did Scott see these things or did he just see the typical features of a child who had Down syndrome?

Margie wiped a tear from her eye. "Isn't it wonderful?"

Beth wasn't so sure. Was Scott going to stick around for Risa? She walked into the room and the moment Risa saw her, she was up and heading toward Beth, arms outstretched.

"Mamma," cried Risa, as Beth swept her up into a fierce hug. The little girl settled into her mother's arms.

Scott stood up, too. "You're here."

"Yes, I'm here. What I don't understand is why you're here."

He looked at her blankly. "Where else would I be?"

"When you said you had to think things over, I thought. . . ."

Scott's eyes widened. "You thought I'd run out on you?"

21

"Not exactly. I thought maybe you'd go for the divorce option and forget about the second-chance thing."

"That's not what I meant!"

She hid her face in Risa's shoulder. "Now what?" she asked hoarsely.

"I think it might be a good idea if Risa stayed with Mom a little while longer so we can finish sorting things out."

"Really?"

"Yeah. I'll take you out to dinner."

"I think that's a wonderful idea," said Margie, coming into the room to join them.

That reminded her. "Hal said he's working late, Margie."

"All the better. Risa will keep me company," Margie declared, taking the toddler from Beth. Risa put her arms around her grandmother's neck and hugged her.

"If you're sure," said Beth. She wasn't sure herself that she wanted to be alone with Scott again. If he stole another kiss she'd be in trouble.

"Of course. You two go and have supper. Take your time and work everything out," Margie declared, obviously excited about Scott's return.

Scott stooped to kiss his mother's cheek. "Thanks, Mom." He kissed Risa's cheek, too, and brushed her bangs from her eyes.

"I'll be back," he told her.

The tenderness she heard in his voice as he talked to his daughter caught Beth's attention. Just when she thought she'd figured out what was going on, Scott surprised her again.

Out in the SUV, Scott asked her where she wanted to go. Beth named a chain restaurant nearby. She wondered if she should assert her independence by insisting on driving, but with her emotions skidding out of control, she figured it was just as well she wasn't behind the wheel.

"Risa is a beautiful little girl," said Scott. "You've done a wonderful job with her."

"Thanks," Beth said rather stiffly. "Your mom and dad have helped a lot."

"I noticed they seemed friendlier to you now, especially Dad."

Beth looked at Scott sharply. Did it bother him? Things had never been easy between Scott and his father. When they'd first married, his parents didn't like her at all, not that she could blame them. But they'd really come through for her after Scott left.

He pulled into the parking lot of the cozy family diner Beth had chosen. After they'd been seated in a vinyl booth by the window and had placed their order Scott asked, "You work at Dad's car dealership now?"

"Yes." Beth decided she may as well confess it all now. "I took your job."

His eyebrows lifted in surprise. "How did that happen?"

She drew in a deep breath. It took Beth a moment before she could continue. "It was a bad night for me after you left. I don't think I slept at all, I was so scared. I hoped you'd be back the next morning, but when I saw your stuff was gone I knew you wouldn't be. I realized that I couldn't afford to be scared anymore. I had a baby on the way and she was my responsibility. So I got up, got dressed and marched right down to your dad's office. I told him you had left, and I needed your job."

"Dad has never hired a woman as a salesperson before," commented Scott. "I always thought he was kind of old-fashioned that way."

"He didn't want to hire me at first," Beth confided. "But I kept at him for a few days until he agreed to give me a chance. As it turned out, I'm a pretty good salesperson. By the time he found out about Risa, I was already established."

Scott laughed. "I can't believe it. You used to be so shy. I wish I could have seen my dad's face when you asked for my job."

"I guess that being all alone taught me to

stand on my own two feet," Beth admitted.

"I never expected you to still be around. I went to the dealership to ask Dad if he might know where you were. I thought you'd have finished college and be starting your music career by now."

Beth felt a little stab of pain. She'd given that dream up a long time ago. "What about you? What have you been doing?"

He ignored her question. "You didn't go back to school, did you? I thought once your parents knew you were . . . um . . . unencumbered with a child and a husband they would pay for your tuition again."

"I never told them. They turned their back on me when they found out I was pregnant and we'd gotten married. They didn't care what happened to us or the baby. I guess I didn't want anything from them after that."

"Do you mean you haven't talked to them since . . . ?"

"Since the day we told them I was pregnant, no." Beth hated thinking about that scene. Her mother and father and both of her stepparents, all staring at them disapprovingly as they'd stammered out the news that they were married with a baby on the way. Her mother blamed her father, who put the blame right back on her, while her stepparents gloated, knowing that the wayward child from the past, that unwanted complication, had finally messed up.

She shook her head. "I'm better off without all of them. Margie and Hal and Risa are my family now."

"What about me, Beth?" Scott looked into her eyes as if searching for answers in them.

She swallowed the lump forming in her throat. "What did you have in mind?"

"I want us to try again, to make our marriage work."

"Scott, it's been over three years. I don't think we can just pick up where we left off."

He reached across the table and took her hands. "I know that. We need to get to know each other again. I need to get to know Risa."

Beth considered. "So, how will we do that?"

"Spending time together, how else?"

"How long will you be in town?" she asked. "You do have a job, don't you?"

"Of course I have a job. You didn't think I came back just to sponge off you, did you? It's not our busy season right now. I can take a couple of weeks off."

"A couple of weeks!" That seemed like too little time to make a decision. But at the same time it seemed way too much. She could fall in love with him all over again in a couple of weeks, and there was no guarantee that things would work out any better than the last time.

"And then maybe you can come and spend a couple of weeks with me."

She needed a little space so she could think. More space than the cramped booth provided. She pulled her hands away. "Where do you live?"

"Up near Rhinelander, in a small town called Spruce Point."

"What do you do up there?" Maybe she could keep him talking for a while and she wouldn't have to give him an answer right away.

Scott ducked his head, but she saw the glint of pride in his eyes. "I manage a resort. Actually, I own the resort."

Beth's mouth dropped open. She was about to ask how that happened when the waitress returned with their dinners. Her mouth snapped closed.

"It's a long story," he told her. "I'll save it for another time."

The waitress set down a plate with a burger and huge pile of fries in front of Scott and one with a chicken stir-fry in front of Beth. There was a pause in the conversation as they tasted their food. After a few minutes Beth asked, "Where are you planning to stay for those two weeks?"

"I thought I'd stay with my folks."

Beth eyed Scott. "I don't think that's a very good idea."

"Why?"

"You really have no idea how angry your father is, do you? In his eyes you failed to live up to your responsibilities," she explained gently.

"So what's new there? I've never lived up to his standards before." Scott's voice was bitter.

Inside Beth's heart, a battle raged. Did she want Scott back in her life? Could it possibly work out this time? Or would she be better off turning him down flat and saving herself the heartbreak?

"Scott, maybe we'd be better off if we just got a divorce. Then we could both start over again."

"Beth," he whispered, "when I said Risa changes things, I meant that divorce was no longer an option for me."

She blinked in surprise. "Oh."

"I intend to be a part of her life and do what's best for her. I think it's best for her mom and dad to be married, don't you?"

"I . . . I don't know." The pain of her own parents' divorce made her want to say yes, but this was a totally different situation, wasn't it?

"Come on, Beth," he coaxed, taking her hand again. "Give us a chance. I never would have left if I'd known you were pregnant. I only left in the first place because I thought it would be best for you."

"Best for me? What do you mean?"

"I thought you could get your life back on track. I felt like I was . . . holding you back."

Scott's thumb was making tiny circles on the back of her hand, causing shivers up her arm. She forced herself to focus on what Scott was saying.

"You were so depressed after the miscarriage. I thought if I left, you would have nothing to stop you from getting back into your family's good graces and going back to school."

"That's what you thought I'd do?"

He nodded solemnly. "I wanted you to be happy again."

"But the night before you left, we had that huge fight." She hadn't wanted to bring this up, didn't want to remind him of what she'd said that night, but she had to be sure of what he was thinking.

"Yeah, but that wasn't why I left. I'd been thinking about leaving for a long time."

Beth's mind swam, her dinner barely touched, she tried to take in what he'd said.

Was he telling the truth? Or was it just his daughter he wanted? Did it make a difference? Shouldn't she be glad he was willing to stick around for Risa's sake? There were lots of men who would resent being tied down with a child, never mind one with a disability.

But then again, look what he'd done? He thought he was some sort of martyr, leaving her for her own good. He hadn't given her a choice, hadn't even asked what she wanted. What if someday he decided that she and Risa would be better off without him *again?* Then what?

He was looking at her with such a tender expression, threatening to take away all her defenses.

"So what do you say, Beth? Will you take me back?"

Part of her wanted to shout *no* and run away as fast as she could. But another part of her was reminding herself that they were married. They had made promises to each other, promises that she took very seriously. She didn't want to be like her parents and throw her marriage away without really working at it. But on the other hand, could three years' separation really be seen as just a bump on the road of marital bliss?

She didn't know what to do.

CHAPTER 2

When he'd left, Scott thought he'd done the right thing. It was his fault she'd had to drop out of school and give up her dreams. It was his fault she was stuck in a marriage that her family disapproved of. There was nothing he could have done about the miscarriage itself, but it was his fault she'd gotten pregnant in the first place.

His father thought so, anyway.

Leaving Beth had been the hardest thing he'd ever had to do. He loved her and he couldn't stand to see her unhappy, wasting away day after day. He'd tried as hard as he could to make her happy. He couldn't do it, so he'd left, hoping *that* would make her happy.

How was he to know what a mistake it would turn out to be?

"Beth," he asked abruptly, "are you seeing anyone?"

"What? You mean, like dating?"

"Yes."

"No. Are you?"

"No. There's been no one since you," he told her truthfully.

Beth picked at the food on her plate. "I haven't really had time to think about romance the last few years. My whole focus has been on Risa."

"Then is there any reason we shouldn't try to make our marriage work?"

"There are a lot of reasons."

"Name one?" he asked.

"How about trust?" she snapped.

"We can build that again. What else have you got?"

She was silent, so he pressed on. "We have one very good reason to try again: Risa."

"You just found out about her today. How can you be so sure you want this? You don't really know what's involved with having a special-needs child like Risa."

"Yes." Reaching across the table, he took her chin in his hand. He looked her straight in the eye. "Yes, I'm sure I want Risa, and I'm sure I want you. I told you I wanted a second chance before I knew about Risa."

Still, she said nothing. So Scott asked, "Don't you think Risa deserves a father?"

Tears glimmered in Beth's eyes. "Yes."

"Then what's the problem?"

She pulled away from him. "I just need to be sure we can make it this time. I don't want Risa to get attached to you and then. . . ."

"Beth, you know I never would have left if I'd known about her." She should believe that even if she couldn't trust anything else he said.

She nodded, but he could still feel the hesitation in her. What did he have to do to convince her he was sincere?

"Tell me about your resort."

Scott knew she was deliberately changing the subject, but decided to let it go. Pressing her hadn't done him any good so far. "It's a small resort. We mostly get fishermen and families there. I've recently renovated and added some space for meetings. I'm hoping to get some corporate clients from that."

"How did you end up owning the resort?"

"I inherited it," he said quietly.

Beth's eyes widened. "Inherited it? From who?"

Scott leaned back in his chair. "It's sort of a long story. Are you sure you want to hear it now?"

"Sure. Go ahead."

He closed his eyes and gathered his thoughts. Where to start? He supposed he'd have to go all the way back to the beginning.

"On the day I left, I didn't know where I was going. I headed west until I got to Wausau. There was a pickup truck pulled off to the side of the road with a flat tire. I stopped to see if the driver needed any help.

"The driver was an elderly man so I offered to change the tire for him. His name was Henry Greenbaum. After I changed the tire, he thanked me by buying lunch. While we were eating, he told me he had just bought a resort and was remodeling it. I needed a job, so I told him I had experience with building things. I was hired on the spot and followed him up to the resort.

"We spent the next two years remodeling the cabins. He hired a crew to redo the lodge, but we did all the cabins ourselves. Henry and I got pretty close.

"After the remodeling was done, he asked me to stay on as business manager. He was technically retired and had bought the resort as sort of a hobby. He and his wife had stayed there on their honeymoon and on vacations many times over the years. It was their place. After she passed away, he went back and found the place had gone downhill considerably."

"So he just decided to buy it and reopen

it as his own? That's pretty ambitious for a retired guy," said Beth.

Scott nodded. "I'll say. But Henry had a lot of energy in him for a guy in his seventies. That's why we were all so shocked when he . . . he died." Scott had to swallow the lump that suddenly filled his throat.

"I'm so sorry, Scott," Beth murmured.

He waved away her sympathy. "Not too long after that, a lawyer showed up and told me Henry had left the resort to me. It turned out he owned considerable property in Chicago and all that went to his family. But he stated in his will that he wanted me to have the resort, because I put so much time and effort into it."

"Wow," said Beth. "Were you surprised?"

He laughed. "That's an understatement."

"This morning you said you came back because you finally had something to offer me. Did you mean the resort?"

"Yes," he replied, "and no. I also meant that the person I am has more to offer you. And even in the little time I've spent with you today, I can see you've changed, too. You aren't the timid little thing you used to be."

Beth blushed. "Thanks, I think."

"We were too young before," Scott insisted. "We've matured. We can make it work now."

"We're still pretty young." Her eyes sparked and he sensed that in spite of the calm façade she'd shown him, she was angry. And how could he blame her?

He promised himself he'd make it up to her later. He had to convince her to give him a second chance now, before she came up with too many reasons not to. "Don't we owe it to ourselves to give it a chance? And to Risa?"

Beth stilled. She closed her eyes and Scott knew she searched her heart. He watched her for the first sign of an answer. She was wearing a tailored red suit, a huge contrast to the jeans and T-shirts she'd worn in college. But even then, red had always been her favorite color. Unusual, he thought, for someone as shy as she was. His eyes dropped to the table and he noticed something he hadn't seen before.

"You still wear your wedding ring." He hadn't had the money for a diamond then. He'd put a plain gold band on Beth's finger when they'd said their vows. He still had his ring but he'd put it away when he and Henry had started on the cabins. After a while, it just seemed easier to leave it off. There were no awkward questions then from the people in his new life. Only Henry

36

knew about the wife Scott had left behind.

Her eyes popped open. "So?"

"Why are you still wearing it?"

Beth looked away. "It's good for business. People trust a woman with a family to sell them a safe, dependable car."

He took her hand and stroked the back of it with his thumb, his voice quiet. "I've loved you since the moment I first saw you, Beth."

She laughed. "The moment you saw me? I think you're exaggerating."

He was, but not by much. "Do you remember that, backstage in the university theater? When you weren't on stage, you liked to stand in the wings and watch."

She nodded. "I never noticed you until that night."

"And you were so beautiful, I was afraid to even talk to you."

She laughed again. "Beautiful?"

"Yes. Beautiful." He slipped out of his seat and moved over to her side of the booth. He put his arm around her and pulled her close to him. "Please," he said softly. "Please can we try this again."

She was weakening, he could tell.

"This is not a decision I want to make in a hurry," Beth protested, pushing him away.

Of course it wasn't, but he didn't have the

time to let her deliberate. Once his vacation was over, he'd be tied to the resort again. There wouldn't be a lot of time to come down to Green Bay and court her.

"Let's compromise. Give me the two weeks at least." If he could get her to agree to that, he should be able to convince her that they should be a family. He'd have to.

He held his breath while she deliberated, then let it out with a whoosh of relief when she answered, "All right. Two weeks."

Triumph sent a jolt of energy through him and he pulled her close again, intending to kiss her, but she pushed him away again. With a stern look, she told him. "I'm not making any promises."

He backed off and returned to his own seat. "I know," he said. But Scott couldn't stop a small smile that twitched his lips as they finished their dinners.

As they headed back to pick up Risa, Scott said, "If you really don't think I should stay at my folks' house, I'd better find a motel."

"Did you see your father's face in the coffee shop today?"

"I guess you're right." Scott sighed. He wished just once his dad would cut him some slack, listen to his side of things. But it had always been like that. Why would he expect him to change now?

"You could . . . ," Beth hesitated and then said, "you could stay at my place."

His face must have shown how surprised he was because she hurried to explain. "I have a spare bedroom where you can stay. You don't need to spend money on a hotel. But I'm not ready for us yet, Scott. I want to take it slow."

This was more than he had expected. Spare room, but still. "You wouldn't mind?" he asked.

"It will give you a chance to spend more time with Risa," Beth explained.

She was right. He did need to spend time with Risa. He had no idea how to be a parent.

When they pulled up in front of his parents' house, Beth got out. "I'll run in and get Risa," she said. "You wait here. You can follow me to my place."

He frowned. "I'm not trying to avoid my father."

"Scott, please. It's late and I don't want Risa upset by a scene."

"All right," Scott backed down grudgingly. "But he's going to have to talk to me sometime."

"I know. Just not tonight."

Beth ran into the house and came back out a few minutes later carrying Risa. She went to her own car and buckled Risa into the car seat in the back. Then she got into the driver's seat and pulled out into the street.

Scott followed her to a nearby neighborhood and up to a small Cape Cod–style house. Even in the dark he could tell the grass was shaggy and the porch light showed that the trim needed to be repainted. Otherwise, it looked solid and taken care of. He parked by the curb. Beth eased a sleeping Risa from the car seat and carried her up the porch steps. He took the toddler from her so she could unlock the door more easily. They went in the side door that opened into the kitchen. Beth led him through the dark house and up the stairs to a small bedroom done in pink and yellow. She pulled down the covers of the toddler-sized bed and Scott laid their daughter down. Beth tucked Risa in while he looked on.

He was unprepared for the emotions that seeing his sleeping child evoked. This was *his* child. He marveled at her tiny fingers and the sweet expression on her sleeping face. He didn't know it was possible to fall in love so fast. He hadn't even fallen for Beth this quickly.

He made a silent promise to always be there for Risa. To always love her and take

care of her. It was a moment before he realized that Beth was staring at him as hard
as he was staring at Risa.

He cleared his throat and looked away.
"I'll just go out to the car and get my stuff."

Scott got his duffel from the car. Back
inside, she led him to a small room at the
back of the house. "It's really kind of an
office-slash-guest room," Beth explained
apologetically. "But at least it's free."

Scott noted the computer chair and desk.
The room also contained a small, two-
drawer filing cabinet, a book shelf, an end
table and a futon.

"I'll get some sheets and pillows," Beth
said, slipping past him and back out of the
room. "The downstairs bathroom is just
next door here," she said, her voice muffled
as she pulled linens out of the hall closet.

Scott flattened the futon, changing it from
couch to bed. She walked back in the room
and chattered as she spread the sheets over
it.

"I have to be at work by nine. I'm usually
up between seven and seven-thirty. I leave
at eight-thirty and drop Risa off at your
mom's."

"You won't have to do that tomorrow,"
said Scott. "I can take care of Risa."

Beth straightened. "I'm not so sure that's

a good idea."

"Don't you trust me?"

"You don't have any experience with toddlers as far as I know, and you definitely don't have experience with a child like Risa."

He supposed that was true. "I'll take her to Mom's house then and spend the day there."

Looking relieved, Beth agreed. "Yes, I think that's the best plan."

She went back to the closet to get blankets and a comforter. "I hope you don't mind if I go to bed, Scott. It's been a long day."

"Go ahead and get some sleep. Is it okay if I sit up and watch TV?"

"Sure, please make yourself at home. And help yourself to anything in the kitchen." She made a small smile.

"Thank you."

"You're welcome."

They stood together, suddenly awkward and unsure of how to end the conversation.

Beth took a step back. "Well, if there's nothing else you need. . . ."

He wanted to say *Just you. I need you,* but stopped himself. It was too soon, their connection too fragile. He had to keep things light or he would scare her away.

He settled on "How about a good-night kiss?"

Before she could voice the protest that he knew was coming, Scott set his hands on her shoulders and kissed her forehead.

She looked surprised and uncertain and — possibly — disappointed.

"Good night," he said.

She blinked. "Yes . . . good night." After another moment she left, closing the door behind her.

Beth jerked awake as the alarm on her clock chimed. Usually she was waiting for it to ring in the morning. She must have slept soundly last night. Rolling over, Beth slapped at the clock and the noise was silenced.

She snuggled back under the covers, hoping for a few stolen moments of calm before the day began. The sound of the shower running brought her fully, instantly awake. Scott was here.

Although she'd gone to bed early the night before, it had been a long time before she'd slept. Questions and memories had run through her mind, refusing to be ignored or put off. No wonder she hadn't woken before the alarm went off.

She waited until she heard the shower

turn off and the bathroom door opening, followed by the sound of the guest-room door closing. Then she got up, slipped into the robe she seldom bothered with and grabbed her towel. She rushed to the bathroom and locked the door behind herself without encountering her house guest.

What had she been thinking last night, Beth asked herself. Why had she agreed — no, offered — to let him stay here? How would she ever be able to think clearly about their relationship with him under her very own roof?

She showered and then made another swift trip back to her room without running into Scott. Beth leaned against the door and took a deep breath. She could handle this.

Fifteen minutes later, she was dressed in a lightweight cotton sweater and a slim skirt. She brushed out her hair and swiftly braided it. Glancing at the clock, Beth realized that she was running behind. This was definitely not a day that she wanted to attract Hal's attention by coming in late.

She hurried into Risa's room to wake her and found her bed deserted. Risa rarely woke before Beth and if she did, she usually came straight to her room. Hoping her daughter hadn't gotten into anything she shouldn't have, Beth made a quick trip downstairs to find her.

Risa and Scott were in the kitchen together. They hadn't heard her and Beth paused to watch them.

Risa sat at the table in her booster seat, still wearing the clothes she'd fallen asleep in. Scott was opening cupboards. He took out cereal, crackers, and bananas and showed them to her. Risa shook her head at each one. She made the sign for milk, squeezing her tiny hands together like someone milking a cow.

Scott obviously didn't understand the sign and kept looking for something to give her for breakfast. Beth couldn't hold back the smile. The scene was so endearing, her nervousness over Scott's presence temporarily abated and she stepped into the kitchen.

"She usually has milk and a cereal bar before we go to your mom's house."

Scott looked relieved. "I didn't think I'd ever find the right thing. She definitely knew what she wanted, but *I* didn't. Doesn't she talk at all other than the few words I've heard her say?"

"Yes," Beth replied as she pulled a box of cereal bars from the cupboard. "She can say a lot of words, although no sentences so far. Her speech therapist has taught her

45

some sign language as well."

"Speech therapist? Risa has a speech therapist?"

After handing the unwrapped bar to Risa, Beth grabbed a plastic cup from the cupboard and filled it with milk from the fridge. "Yes. She also has a physical therapist, an occupational therapist, a teacher and a service coordinator."

Scott's eyes widened. "Seriously?"

She nodded. "Your mom will fill you in. Right now, we have to get going. I'll grab some clothes for Risa."

"Don't worry about us. I can find my way back to my parents' house. I haven't been gone that long."

Already halfway up the stairs, Beth called over her shoulder, "All right, but you'd better transfer Risa's car seat to your SUV."

In short order Beth helped Risa use the potty and dress, then checked the car seat to make sure Scott had secured it properly in the SUV.

"I really don't want to be late," Beth told him. "I'd better go. I'll meet you both back here around five-thirty." She stooped to kiss Risa's cheek and headed toward the door.

"Hey, what about me?" protested Scott. Beth hesitated, turned, and blew him a kiss as she left. She climbed into her car and backed out of the drive.

It had been fast thinking, blowing Scott a kiss instead of actually giving him one, or worse, arguing about why she wasn't going to kiss him. And it served him right after that peck on the forehead last night. The Scott she knew would definitely not count that as a proper kiss.

She made it to work a few minutes before nine, but it didn't matter. Hal was waiting for her anyway.

"I want to talk to you, Beth," he said and led her to his office. Stepping behind the huge, battered desk, he motioned her to take a seat. His own battered chair squeaked loudly as he settled himself into it.

"What happened with you and Scott last night?"

Beth willed herself to be calm. She could handle Hal. "We went out to dinner and talked."

"And?"

"Scott's on vacation from his job for two weeks. He wants . . . he wants to spend that time with me and Risa."

Hal leaned forward on the desk. "And you told him to get lost, right?"

"Not exactly."

"Then *what* did you tell him?"

"He's Risa's father, Hal. He has a right to

47

see her, and get to know her."

"Not the way I see it. If he wanted to be a father, then he should have stuck around for you. He should have been here."

"I know. But . . . but he didn't know about her. Scott says he wouldn't have left if he'd known and I . . . I believe him." That was the truth. What she didn't know was whether or not their marriage would have worked out even if he'd stayed.

"What happens after the two weeks is over?" asked Hal.

"I don't know," Beth admitted.

"You're setting yourself up to get hurt again."

She shrugged. "Sometimes you have to take risks." She wasn't about to admit to Hal how frightened she was that Scott would break her heart again. If it hadn't been for Risa, she didn't know how she would have survived before.

But she found the idea of divorce equally abhorrent. Perhaps it was her own childhood experience with her parents' breakup, but she knew she did not want to go that route.

"Yes, but think about it," said Hal. "You aren't just risking your own heart this time. You're risking Risa's."

Beth knew this. She didn't need her

father-in-law to tell her. She clenched her hands in her lap and made an attempt to get a handle on the anger and anxiety that rose within her. Raising her gaze to meet and hold his, Beth told him, "You didn't like me at first, but you took a chance on me and look where we are now."

There had been a time when Hal had intimidated Beth to the point where she couldn't be in his presence without becoming tongue-tied. Now she was well aware that his gruff manner hid a soft heart. She wouldn't back down from him anymore.

Hal stood abruptly, his chair rolling into the wall with a crash. "Where is Scott, now?"

"I . . . I think he's with Risa and Margie . . . at your house." So much for not being intimidated.

"He must have gotten up early for a guy on vacation. Where's he staying?"

"I invited him to stay with Risa and me." Beth steeled herself for Hal's response.

"What?" Hal let out a string of words that made her cringe.

She was sure everyone within the building heard him, and hurried to explain. "He stayed in the guest room."

Her father-in-law had already grabbed his jacket from a hook behind the door and was putting it on.

Beth jumped up, placing herself between him and the doorway. "Where are you going?"

"I'm going to talk to my s— your husband."

"No, I can handle this."

Hal reached out and moved her aside, but she grabbed his arm and hung on.

"Please, don't do this. You're angry. You're not thinking straight."

"Beth, let go."

"Hal, don't start a fight in front of Risa. She'll be frightened."

That made him pause. He would never do anything to hurt his granddaughter. "I won't do anything to upset Risa," he promised.

Beth let him go, realizing this was the best she could accomplish right now. As soon as the dealership door closed behind him, she headed to her own office, planning to phone Margie and Scott. At least she would warn them that Hal was coming.

She didn't realize she wasn't alone until she had punched in half the number. She jumped and dropped the phone when she saw Jared lurking just inside the door.

"J-Jared," Beth sputtered. "What are you doing?"

50

"I'm sorry, Beth. I was just worried about you."

Her expression softened. Jared might be annoying and have a painfully obvious crush on her, but he meant well. It was hard to stay mad at him.

But not impossible.

"I agree with Hal," Jared told her bluntly. "Scott gave up his right to be Risa's dad when he walked out on you."

Beth ground her teeth and prayed for patience. "Jared, Scott didn't know about Risa when he left. Now if you're done delivering your judgments, I have work to do."

"I'm just saying, you need to be careful."

Setting the phone down, she escorted him to the door. "Thank you for your concern. I'll keep that in mind." She closed the door firmly behind him and hurried back to the phone.

Margie answered the call.

"Is Scott there?" Beth asked, trying to keep the anxiety she was feeling from creeping into her voice.

"He just got here, Beth. He forgot Risa's busy bag, so I sent him back out to his car to get it."

"I just talked to Hal. He's really upset with Scott."

"Yes, I know." Margie sighed. "I had to listen to him rant about it last night."

"Well, you're in for another earful. He's on his way over to talk to Scott."

"Oh."

"Oh, what?"

"Hal just pulled up behind Scott. I can see him from the window."

Beth groaned, imagining the scene the neighbors were about to be treated to.

"Don't worry," Margie told her. "I can handle those two."

Beth hoped she could.

CHAPTER 3

Scott closed the door to his SUV, the bag with Risa's toys in hand. As he turned he saw his father's car pull up into the driveway. Hal stepped out of the vehicle and stood, glaring at Scott.

"Hi, Dad." He tried to keep his voice neutral.

"So, you *are* here."

Scott took in his father's red face and narrowed eyes. "Yes. Should we go in or would you prefer to yell at me in front of the whole neighborhood?"

Hal ignored his son's suggestion and crossed to where Scott stood by his SUV. "How did you talk Beth into letting you stay with her and Risa?"

Scott folded his arms across his chest. "I *did not* talk her into it. I mentioned I needed to find a hotel, since she didn't think I'd be welcome at your house —"

"She got that right," snarled Hal.

53

"And then Beth suggested I stay with her. You can ask her if you don't believe me."

The two men glared at each other for a moment, and then Hal asked, "Why did you come back?"

"I felt it was time."

"What is that supposed to mean?"

"It means I felt like I finally had something to share with Beth. I worked hard these last three years and it's paid off."

"How so?"

"I own a resort up north, Dad."

Hal's eyebrows rose. "A resort?"

"Yes, a hotel resort. I came back to ask Beth to give me another chance, or, if she preferred, I'd divorce her. If we divorced, I'd make sure she got a fair settlement. But now that I know about Risa I wouldn't agree to a divorce. A child needs a family."

"This child has a family — a mother, a grandmother and a grandfather. She doesn't need you. When things got tough before, you took off. Why should we think this time is any different?"

Scott closed his eyes and pinched the bridge of his nose. He tried to collect his thoughts. As much as his father's attitude hurt and angered him, it would serve no purpose to lose his temper.

"Dad, why don't we sit down and talk this

through?"

"Sit down with you? I don't think so." The contempt in his voice was obvious.

"Don't have a few minutes for your son?"

"Not anymore. When you walked out on us, you ceased to be my son."

Scott took a step back. It took a moment to absorb the meaning of the words his father had thrown at him. They had been butting heads for years, but this was a deeper cut than those his father had formerly delivered.

Hal advanced on him, possibly taking his retreat as a sign of weakness. "I will do everything in my power to convince Beth to divorce you," he growled.

Once again, Scott squashed down his hurt and anger and managed to answer in an even voice. "If that's the way you feel, Dad, I guess there's nothing else we have to say to each other."

Hal's voice rose. "Don't call me Dad. I'm not your father anymore. Are you going to give Beth a divorce?"

Scott planted his feet and looked his father in the eye. "No."

The color in Hal's face deepened and he opened his mouth to speak again, but the sound of the kitchen door opening stopped him.

"Hey, you two," Margie called, "stop yapping and bring Risa's bag in."

Scott saw that she held Risa in her arms. He knew his father saw her, too. Margie came out, letting the door slap shut behind her. Risa bounced with happiness, eager to see her grandfather.

"What are you doing home at this time of day, Hal?" asked Margie. She handed Risa off to him without asking.

Scott was amazed to see his father's face soften as he gathered his granddaughter into his arms. Risa snuggled up to him and Hal rested his cheek on her head. "I just needed to talk to Scott," he answered, his voice gruff but soft.

"Why don't you come inside? It's chilly out here."

Hal handed Risa back to her grandmother. "That's all right. I think we're finished." He threw Scott a contemptuous glance. "Apparently we have nothing left to say to each other."

Scott met his gaze. "No, I don't think we do," he answered. They stared at each other for a few moments, and then Hal turned and stalked back to his car.

Scott exhaled slowly as he watched his father drive away. His stomach churned with the emotion he'd held back. He tried

56

to think of what Henry would say to him now.

Henry had been more of a father to him in the last few years than his own father had been in a lifetime. But now Henry was gone, the victim of a stroke, and his real father was more hostile and distant than ever.

"Let's go in," Marge urged. "It really is cold out here."

"You go ahead, Mom," said Scott. "I'm going to . . . take a walk around the block . . . see a little bit of the old neighborhood."

She frowned, concern evident on her face. "Don't let him bother you. He'll come around in time."

Scott doubted it, but he didn't want to hurt his mother's feelings. "I'll just be a few minutes."

"All right, but not too long. You don't even have a jacket on."

That made him smile. "Mom, I'm not a kid anymore."

She sniffed. "Oh, so that means you don't get cold?"

He shook his head as she turned and went back into the house. Risa, looking over her grandmother's shoulder, waved "bye-bye" to him. Her gesture brought him a measure of comfort and he raised his hand to wave back at his daughter.

When the door closed behind them, Scott set out on his walk. He didn't really care about seeing his old neighborhood. He just wanted a few moments alone to think about what had happened with his father.

He wasn't exactly surprised that his father was angry with him, but the level of his hostility was unexpected. His gentleness with Risa was another surprise. Obviously Hal loved his granddaughter, disability and all. Scott guessed that she would never have a problem living up to his father's expectations. Was it because she was his grandchild and not his child? Because she was a girl?

As he turned the corner, the wind brushed his face and he shivered. It *was* cold out here. The early spring sunlight was too weak to warm him up. He walked faster, hoping the exercise would keep the cold at bay.

Hal had been an involved father, coaching his sons' basketball team, attending PTA meetings and chaperoning youth events at church. He'd always demanded his sons give one-hundred-and-ten-percent effort to whatever project they worked on.

When Scott was in high school everything changed.

He'd always looked up to his brother Dave. His brother was a star athlete and an honor-roll student. He was popular, a leader in his class. No one was surprised when he was offered a basketball scholarship at Michigan State.

Unfortunately, Dave never got a chance to play for them. That summer, he and some friends had gone water-skiing on Lake Michigan. A drunk boater had crashed into Dave and killed him.

His brother's death was a heavy blow to his family. It changed all of them, but his father seemed to be the most affected. With only Scott left to focus his attention on, he went from encouraging to pushing, from advising to criticizing. Soon Scott felt there was nothing he could do to please his father.

The little scene they'd just enacted was proof that nothing had changed in the years he'd been gone.

He felt a little better by the time he'd circled the block and come back to his parents' home. Stepping into the kitchen, he inhaled the smell of his mother's chicken soup. She was adding carrots to the pot when he walked in.

She stirred the soup and put the lid on. "There, that's finished. Now it can simmer until we're ready to eat lunch."

"That smells fantastic, Mom. I've really missed your cooking." He leaned down and kissed her cheek.

Her face flushed with pleasure at the compliment. "Thank you, dear."

Risa was sitting in a high chair playing with a stuffed animal. Scott sat at the table next to her and was rewarded with a dazzling smile from her.

Margie sat down at the table across from Scott. "We might as well enjoy the morning," she said. "It's going to be a busy afternoon."

"Why? What's going on this afternoon?"

"Didn't Beth tell you?"

"She said something about Risa seeing a therapist. No, several therapists."

"She's in the Birth to Three program," Margie explained. "It's a federal- and state-funded program to help children with disabilities or developmental delays. Through the program, Risa receives physical therapy, occupational therapy, and speech therapy."

He was impressed. "I had no idea a program like that existed."

"Oh, yes," Margie told him. "We were certainly glad of it. They helped us right away after Risa was born. Beth was so lost after we got the diagnosis from the doctors."

Scott felt his breath catch. "Did she have a hard time dealing with it?"

"A little. Not more than could be expected. But really, Scott, you would have been proud of her. She handled everything beautifully."

"I wish I would have been here."

"I wish you had, too." Abruptly, she stood and walked to the counter. "Coffee, Scott?"

"No, thanks. Are you all right, Mom?"

She poured a cup of coffee for herself and sat back down at the table. "I told myself I wasn't going to ask you about anything. I wanted to wait until you were ready to tell me on your own."

"Tell you what?"

"Everything! Why you left. Where did you go? Why didn't you call or write? I was worried sick about you."

More mistakes. More regrets. "I'm sorry, Mom. I thought maybe you'd be happier not knowing. You and Dad were pretty upset with me, remember?"

"And I'm sorry if our being angry with you led you to believe that we didn't love you anymore. That's not why you left, is it?"

"No, not really. It just seemed like the best thing to do. I felt my absence would solve a lot of problems."

He explained to his mother about thinking that Beth could get back into her parents' good graces.

"Then I guess you were really being noble. I always believed you loved Beth. I knew you wouldn't just take off and leave her for no reason." A triumphant look lit her face. Scott had the feeling she'd be saying "I told you so" to someone soon.

His mother's understanding was doubly precious after his father's harsh judgment.

"While we're trading confidences," Margie continued, "I must admit, I always felt a bit guilty over the whole thing myself."

This surprised Scott. "Guilty? Why?"

She blushed. "Well, we weren't exactly very welcoming to Beth when you told us that you'd eloped and she was pregnant. If we'd been more supportive maybe things would have been different."

"I doubt it." Scott thought about the dark days that followed the miscarriage. That was what had really done them in. "But you helped Beth after I left, didn't you, Mom?"

She nodded, still showing her embarrassment.

"I'm grateful for that. I never thought she'd refuse to go back to her own family," he said. That had shocked him.

Margie shook her head. "I don't know what happened there, but I think they hurt her very deeply. She won't talk to me about it."

Scott knew Beth and her parents were not close, but he didn't realize the rift between them was this bad. He wondered if he should ask her about it. Probably, but not until she was ready to trust him again.

A squawk from Risa broke into his thoughts. She'd dropped the toy she'd been playing with.

"Oh, Risa," cried Margie. "I forgot all about you. She must be bored sitting there. Lift her down, will you?"

Scott lifted Risa's tiny body out of the high chair, set her on the ground and offered her the toy.

Instead of taking it, she toddled off to one of the cupboards. The effort needed to tug it open sent her down on her bottom. Unconcerned, Risa pulled out several pots.

Margie got up and stirred the soup. Scott decided it an excellent time to change the topic of conversation. "So who is coming to see Risa today?"

"Let's see." Margie consulted a calendar clipped to the refrigerator with a magnet. "Today she sees Monica for speech and Bill for occupational therapy."

"Do we have to go to a clinic or something?"

Margie came back to the table and sat down again. "No, they come to the house.

The idea is that it's best to work with a child in her everyday environment. That way they can understand her unique needs and challenges."

"Sounds like you memorized the brochure," Scott teased.

"No, but I've become very familiar with all of this. Too bad it will end soon."

"What do you mean?" Scott found himself raising his voice to be heard over Risa's banging on the pots and pans.

"It's the Birth to Three program, Scott," Margie shouted back. "Risa will turn three soon and she'll be too old for the program."

"Is there a Four to Six program or something?"

"Something like that. It's called Early Childhood. Now why don't you take Risa in the living room and play with her while I get a few things done."

He grinned. "What, you don't like the concert she's giving you?"

"What she's giving me is a headache. Besides, you and Risa need to get better acquainted."

Scott couldn't argue with that. "Come on Risa." He scooped her up from the floor. "Let's go play."

"There are toys in the wicker chest," Margie said as they left the room.

Risa was only too happy to show him all her toys. She brought them to Scott one at a time and waited for him to exclaim over them before hurrying back to the toy box to get another one. When the box was empty, Scott gathered up all the toys and put them away. Then the game started all over again.

The tension he'd felt from the confrontation with his father began to melt away. Whatever else happened, he would always be thankful he'd come back. Otherwise, he'd never have met his daughter. She delighted him with her quick smile, her sweet face and abundant hugs.

The morning passed quickly. Lunch was delicious, although it turned out that soup was pretty messy when a two-year-old was involved.

"I'll just take our little lady to freshen up before her afternoon engagements begin," Margie said, leading Risa away.

Meanwhile Scott cleaned up and put the dishes in the dishwasher. Margie came back with a freshly dressed and washed Risa just before the doorbell rang.

The speech therapist was a pleasant middle-aged lady named Monica. There were a few moments of awkwardness as Margie explained who Scott was, but if she felt any surprise Monica hid it well. Scott sat with her and Risa on the floor in the living room. Margie was close by on the couch. Monica explained to Scott that she and Beth had been working on teaching Risa some simple sign language. "It's not meant to replace speech, but rather to reinforce it. Many children learn to speak words faster when they also know the sign."

Scott remembered how Risa had held out her hands and made squeezing motions with them that morning. He tried to repeat the gesture for Monica.

"That means 'milk.' Risa was asking for milk."

Scott grinned. It was like miming milking a cow. "That makes sense."

Monica and Risa also showed him the signs for "eat," "drink," "cracker," "juice," "play," and "all done."

Then the therapist did some exercises with Risa that would help her strengthen her facial muscles. They blew a cotton ball across a tabletop and made faces in front of a mirror. As Monica finished up, Margie opened the door to let in Bill, the occupational therapist. She introduced Scott and again explained who he was. Bill also took the sudden appearance of a father in Risa's life in stride. Scott wondered what other family situations the therapists had seen that made this seem so unremarkable.

The introduction over, Bill quickly got down to business. He explained that while a physical therapist worked with helping children develop the use of large muscle groups, occupational therapists worked on helping children develop their small-muscle skills. He had Risa put window clings on a mirror, then pick up pennies and drop them into a container.

Picking up pennies was difficult for Risa. After she'd done a few, she made the sign for "all done." Bill encouraged her to keep going, but after each penny she signed "all done" again. He let her quit after a few more. "There's no sense in letting her get too frustrated," he explained to Scott.

Then Bill blew bubbles for Risa to pop. "This helps with eye-hand coordination," he explained.

After about forty-five minutes, Bill started to pack up his things.

"How often do you see Risa?" Scott asked.

"Twice a week. But Beth works on these same things at home with Risa. I believe you do too sometimes, Margie, right?"

Margie nodded. "We work a little every day. We have exercises from you, Monica, and Pam, the physical therapist. Risa sees all of them twice a week."

"It was nice to meet you, Scott," said Bill, as he stood. "Will I see you again?"

"Definitely," Scott replied, wishing he was as sure as he sounded. He wanted to be a part of Risa's everyday life, but he didn't know how this was all going to work out.

Margie said good-bye and closed the door behind Bill. Then she turned and asked Scott, "What did you think?"

He struggled to find the words. "This is all . . . amazing. I can see how this is all much harder for Risa than for other children. But . . . she works so hard, I can't help but be proud of her." Scott pulled his daughter up on his lap and hugged her.

"Risa, you sure taught me a lot today, kiddo."

She giggled and hugged him back. Scott's heart overflowed.

With a sigh, he came back to reality. Hal would be home soon and he didn't want his father to be angry with his mother for having him over. "Risa and I had better go, Mom," he said. "Beth will be done at the dealership soon. And so will Dad."

"Don't be too discouraged with your father," she urged. "He'll come around."

"Sure," said Scott, but he didn't believe it.

Beth had had a hard time concentrating at work. Fortunately, it was busy and she showed a lot of cars.

Hal hardly spoke to her all day. She knew he was angry at her for giving Scott a second chance, but she didn't feel she had much choice at the moment. In time she would see if it had been a bad decision to let him back into her life, and hopefully she'd be strong enough to deal with it.

At lunch, she went out to eat just to get away for a while. But sitting alone at a restaurant gave her time to dwell on the situation. Yesterday she had been too surprised by everything to really examine how she felt about Scott. Today, her emotions all seemed to be screaming at her for attention.

How *did* she feel about Scott's return? She wished she could say she was happy. But if it was any kind of happy it was a cautious kind. It was happy paired with fear. Fear that she would mess everything up again. Fear that she couldn't succeed at a marriage.

Beth's parents had divorced when she was eight. The memories of their arguments made her heart ache. Her mother and father had assured her that the divorce would be for the best and that everyone would be "happier."

Well, her parents had been happier, that much was true. Both of them had remarried within two years of the divorce. They had started new families. Beth was constantly shuttled back and forth between the two houses. But neither of them was home for her.

Fortunately, she had Grandma Jane. Her father's mother invited Beth to spend time with her frequently. By the time she was sixteen, she lived there more than she lived with her parents. Grandma Jane's little country home had been her refuge.

Beth shook her head, bringing herself back to reality. Now there was Scott and there was Risa. If she didn't make her marriage with Scott work, where did that leave Risa? She didn't want her daughter to be in the same position she'd been in while growing up. Beth vowed to herself that if things didn't work out between her and Scott, she wouldn't remarry. She would never allow Risa to be the outsider within her own family.

But what if it *did* work out with Scott?

For a moment, Beth allowed herself to

dream. He said he'd left because he thought it would help her. That he still loved her. He was happy about Risa. Her disability hadn't fazed him at all.

And if she were going to be honest with herself, she'd admit that the breakup of their marriage was her fault, not his. She'd practically driven him away.

So this time she would have to be very careful. There was too much riding on it for her to make another mistake.

Once they were home, Scott asked Risa, "Why don't we take Mommy out to eat tonight? Should we get you dressed up?"

Scott thought about giving Risa a bath, but he didn't think he was comfortable doing that alone yet. So he settled for helping Risa change into a pink dress he found in her closet. The early spring weather was a little chilly so he dug out a white cardigan for her to wear over it. Then he combed her hair, and washed her face and hands.

"Beautiful," he announced, and Risa smiled.

"Can you play with your toys while Daddy gets ready?" Scott went into the bathroom to shave, but left the door open so he could still see and hear what Risa was up to. He was wiping his freshly shaved face with a towel when he heard Beth pull into the driveway. His heart gave a little jump at the thought of seeing her again.

When he'd decided to find Beth, he hadn't been sure that his feelings for her would be the same. Yesterday he discovered there was still a powerful attraction between them. Now he was anxious to spend more time with her and get to know her again. She'd changed since they'd been apart.

He'd changed, too, and hoped she'd see him as a "new and improved" Scott, ready to take on the challenges of marriage — and parenthood — and succeed.

He heard the front door opening and took a deep breath to calm himself.

CHAPTER 4

Beth felt strange going straight home from work. In truth, she missed seeing Margie and having a cup of coffee with her before taking Risa home. But it was only one day, she told herself. If only it wasn't the one day that she really needed to talk to someone.

On the other hand, maybe it wasn't the best idea to discuss romance with your mother-in-law. She put her hand on the door and took a deep breath. When she opened it, she was greeted with a shout of "Mommy!" Risa toddled right into her arms and Beth picked her up and hugged her tight.

"Did you and Daddy have a good day?" she asked her daughter.

Risa nodded enthusiastically, then plucked at the bodice of her dress. "Pretty," she said.

"Yes, honey," Beth agreed. "You look very pretty. Why does Daddy have you all dressed up?"

"Because he's taking his two best girls out tonight," answered Scott, stepping out of the bathroom, wiping his freshly shaven face with a towel. He had a clean shirt on, but it was still unbuttoned.

Beth gulped. She could smell the woodsy scent of his aftershave and see the contours of his torso. All that construction work at the resort had kept him in shape. Butterflies started a riot in her stomach and she hid her face in Risa's shoulder to hide the emotions that must be plain on her face.

"What's the occasion?" She winced at the squeaky sound in her voice. She hoped he couldn't tell how he was affecting her.

"It's Friday night. Date night."

"Date night? And you need two dates?" she asked, widening her eyes in an attempt to look innocent. It was best to keep things light between them. She could handle that.

Scott winked. "Try not to be jealous."

Beth wrinkled her nose at him. "Don't worry."

He laughed, and stepping forward, hugged both her and Risa. "How was your day?"

Just when she thought she had a handle on things, he had to go and touch her. She managed to answer, "Terrible. Thank goodness it's Friday."

"Dad wasn't giving you a hard time, was he?"

"Not really," she fudged, not wanting to contribute to the feud between Hal and Scott. "Where are we going?"

"Where do you want to go?"

Beth considered. Risa would prefer the local pizza place, but she was a little overdressed for it. It seemed like Scott was determined to treat them, and she didn't want to disappoint him. She suggested a nice family restaurant that was close by.

"Just give me a few minutes to freshen up," Beth said as she headed up the stairs. Once she was safely in her bedroom with the door closed, she collapsed on the bed. Last night she'd agreed easily to Scott staying here, to giving their marriage another try. It hadn't seemed real at the time. But today he was still here. He was here in her house and he looked great and he smelled wonderful. He was attentive and loving to Risa. He was being sweet. It would be *way* too easy to get used to this.

With a sigh, Beth heaved herself up off the bed and over to her closet. She took off her skirt and hung it up, changing into a more casual jean skirt and peasant blouse. She shook her hair free from the clip it had been confined to all day and brushed her hair. It hung in thick, dark waves around her face. Finally, she added a touch of lipstick and slipped into a pair of soft brown shoes.

After a quick glance in the mirror, she hurried back down the stairs. Scott was reading a book to Risa. She paused on the stairs to watch them. Risa was sitting on Scott's lap as he read from the pages. Risa reached up and touched his cheek and Scott stopped reading, smiling down at her. It was a tender moment between father and daughter that brought a tear to Beth's eye. Then Scott noticed her standing there.

He looked up with a smile for her, too. "Ready to go?"

Her breath caught in her throat and she nodded, not trusting herself to speak.

At the restaurant they settled into a booth and Beth asked the hostess for a booster seat for Risa. As she settled Risa into the seat, she noticed Scott watching them, a strange look on his face.

"Do I have dirt on my face?"

Scott shook his head.

"Then, what?" she asked.

He looked embarrassed. "You're just such a good mother. I love watching you with Risa."

Beth felt her face grow warm. "Thank you," she said, and slid into the booth next to her daughter.

"I'm sorry about Hal hunting you down this morning." Beth continued, "I feel horrible that he's treating you this way."

He reached across the table. His hand felt warm and strong on hers. "It's not your fault. You know the problems between Dad and me go back way before you and I were together. Don't worry about it."

Well, she did worry about it, especially since Hal might not be so hard on Scott if she'd told him the whole truth when he'd left. But she was scared and desperate and feared that he would have thrown her right out of the car dealership that day instead of giving her a chance. She had promised herself she'd tell him as soon as her job was secure. The longer she put off telling him the truth, the harder it became to own up, even when her conscience pushed her to do so. But she should tell him now.

There was no use in dwelling on it now. Beth picked up her menu. "What do you want to eat, Risa?"

Risa made the sign for "eat."

"Do you want chicken nuggets?" asked Beth. Risa shook her head. "How about spaghetti?" She shook her head again. Beth

77

consulted the kids' menu. "Macaroni and cheese?" Risa smiled and nodded.

"What do you want to drink?" asked Beth and Risa signed.

"Milk," announced Scott with a triumphant note in his voice. "She wants milk."

Risa clapped her hands and laughed.

"You must have learned something from Monica today," said Beth.

"Yeah. I learned quite a bit from Monica and Bill. I'm amazed at it all. Risa works harder than I do." There was no mistaking the pride in his voice.

Beth nodded. "She does. I don't think I would have put up with all these people fussing over me and making me do things at that age."

"My mom told me that you work with her at home, too. She told me a lot about you and what you've done for Risa since she was born. You're a great mother and I'm proud of you, Beth."

"Oh." Overwhelmed, Beth felt the tears slip down her cheeks. An outburst of emotion was inevitable after the events of the last two days, but it would have been nice if it had happened in a more private place.

"Don't cry, Beth. It's okay."

"It's just that I still can't believe that you're here, and you love Risa, and you're being so sweet and . . . it's just too much."

Scott got up and switched sides, crowding her and Risa. "I'm sorry, sweetheart. I should have been here all along, but. . . ."

"Scott, I don't blame you for leaving. I don't know how you put up with me for as long as you did."

"Don't say that. It wasn't your fault." Scott pulled her close and Beth let her head drop onto his chest.

"We're making a scene."

"I don't care."

Beth took a swipe at her face. "I'm fine now."

"Mommy cry?" asked Risa, a look of concern on her round face.

"I'm okay, honey," Beth reassured her daughter.

Scott returned to his own side of the table though he continued to watch her. "I've been kind of surprised at everything that's happened, myself. This certainly wasn't what I envisioned."

"What do you mean?"

Before Scott could answer, the waitress came to take their order. Only Risa was ready, but rather than send her away, Scott and Beth quickly made their selections. Once the waitress had gone, Beth repeated her question.

"What *did* you think would happen when you came back?"

"Well, first of all, I didn't think you'd still be around. I expected it would take a while to track you down. I certainly didn't think you'd be at the car dealership.

"And secondly, I didn't expect you to actually want to talk to me. I fully expected to have to get down on my hands and knees and beg you to listen to me.

"Third, if you did listen to me, I thought you'd most likely opt for a divorce. I had my doubts that you'd be unattached."

Beth widened her eyes in surprise. "You really thought it would be that bad?"

He nodded.

"Why bother then?"

"Because I had to know if there was still anything between us. I couldn't move forward with my life until things were settled between us."

"And now that you've seen me, what do you think?"

"I think I want you back. Our marriage deserves a second chance, Beth."

There was a spark of determination in his eyes. She knew that when Scott wanted something he went after it. For the second time in her life, that "something" was her. Was it a good idea to give in to him again?

Did she even have a chance of resisting when he turned that ice-blue stare on her?

She felt the prickle of tears and closed her eyes to hold them back. "Scott, I'm going to cry again."

She felt him grab her hands and opened her eyes to see the alarm on his face.

"Don't cry. I didn't mean to upset you."

Beth sniffled. "I'm crying because I'm happy."

"Then smile at me and quit crying," he coaxed. "You'll upset Risa."

Beth gave him a watery smile.

"Well, what a surprise, running into you two here."

She turned her head and saw Jared approaching their table. She groaned. "Jared, what are you doing here?"

"I'm eating dinner, of course."

Beth raised an eyebrow in disbelief. "All by yourself?"

He shrugged. "A man's got to eat. Hello, Scott."

"Hi, Jared," Scott said warily.

"I see you're doing what you do best. Making Beth cry."

"They're happy tears," insisted Beth quickly. The last thing she needed was for Jared to provoke a fight with Scott.

"Not like the ones you shed three and half

81

years ago when he deserted you." The accusation in his tone was unmistakable.

"Jared, is there something you'd like to say to me?" Scott spoke calmly, but Beth sensed his anger. Her shoulders tightened.

Jared threw back his shoulders and planted his feet. "Yes, as a matter of fact there is."

Scott remained seated, his posture relaxed. "Is this something you want to say in front of Beth and Risa?"

"Yes, it is. I want you to know that someone is looking out for Beth and her interests."

"And who would that be?"

Couldn't Jared hear the dangerous undertone in Scott's voice? Why was he doing this? Beth wondered.

"Me," he answered. "I'm watching you, Scott, and I intend to make sure you don't hurt Beth again."

"Jared," interrupted Beth, unable to stay silent any longer. "I don't need you to look after me. *Please* leave us alone."

He ignored her request and continued to taunt his cousin. "You should have seen her the day she came in to beg Hal for your job."

"I didn't beg." Shut up Jared. Just shut up.

"She's come a long way since then. Beth is Hal's top salesperson. She's doing great.

She doesn't need you to come back and screw up her life again."

Scott switched his attention from his cousin to Beth. "Really? You're Dad's top salesperson? I can't believe it. I hated that job."

"I know. Remember, I helped you memorize everything about the different models of cars. That's how I figured I could do your job when you left," Beth said, glad that this had diverted his attention from Jared. Scott wasn't normally the type of person to lose his temper and make a scene, but Jared was pushing him pretty hard. It would serve him right if Scott pushed back, but she didn't want that to happen in front of Risa. And she didn't want their evening spoiled.

"You must have been very convincing. Dad never hired a woman, except as a receptionist, before you," Scott told her.

Jared cleared his throat to remind them that he was still standing there.

Beth glanced up at him, anger rising in her. "Did you want anything else, Jared?"

"Yes," he replied. "Can I talk to you alone, Beth?"

Scott looked like he was about to protest, but Beth slid out of the booth. "I think that would be an excellent idea."

■ ■ ■ ■

Scott watched as Beth led Jared to the lobby area of the restaurant. He figured if Jared were smart, he'd take one look at her face and let the matter drop. He turned his attention back to Risa, who was beginning to squirm restlessly in her seat, but kept an eye on Beth.

When had his cousin become such a pain? Jared, his mother's nephew, was about four years younger than he was. His dad had died when Scott was about twelve and Hal had taken the boy under his wing. They had gotten along well when they were kids, but he had often sensed jealousy on Jared's part. Scott supposed it was because Hal was his father and not Jared's.

A thought occurred to Scott. *Was Jared interested in Beth?*

When they reached a quiet spot in the lobby area, Beth turned on Jared. "What do you think you're doing? Following us?"

Jared shrugged. His belligerent attitude was gone. "I'm just keeping an eye on you and making sure you're all right."

"Why? I'm fine."

"Well, because . . . because I'm worried

about you."

"Did Hal put you up to this?"

"Um, not totally."

"Go tell Hal that I'm a big girl and I can handle this myself."

Jared gulped. "Yeah, but. . . ."

"But what?"

"But if you divorced Scott. . . ."

"If I divorced Scott what?"

Jared shook his head. "Never mind."

Beth decided to let it go. "Fine. I'd like to get back to my family."

Jared nodded.

Beth turned and walked back into the dining area. The rest of the evening was uninterrupted, but the fun seemed to have gone out of their little party. After dinner they went home.

Beth gave Risa a bath and put her to bed. When she came downstairs Scott was on his cell phone. He quickly finished his call when she appeared. She sat down beside him on the living-room couch. "Is everything okay?"

He nodded. "I was just checking on how things are going at the resort. It's a quiet time now, too late in the year for snowmobiling and cross-country skiing and too early for fishing and swimming. The staff can handle things for a little longer."

"Good," Beth snuggled closer. "I'm glad you can stay for a while yet."

"Want to see what's on TV?" asked Scott, putting an arm around her.

"Sure."

He picked up the remote, turned the TV on and began flipping through the channels. They found a romantic comedy to watch.

The sound of gunfire and squealing tires snatched Beth from a deep sleep. Confused, it took her a moment to realize that the sounds were coming from the television. Why was she sleeping on the couch? Abruptly the fog cleared from her brain and she became aware that she and Scott were snuggled up together. The movie was over and a rerun of a popular police drama was running.

Scott was still sound asleep, undisturbed by the burst of noise. Beth sat up and shook his shoulder. "Hey, sleepyhead, it's time to wake up and go to bed."

His eyes opened slowly and a teasing grin slid across his face. "Now that's an interesting suggestion."

Beth laughed. "To your own bed. Alone."

Scott yawned and stretched. "I can't believe I fell asleep. I guess chasing after a toddler all day wears you out."

She nodded her head in agreement. "You can say that again."

"I guess you'd know. What do you have going on tomorrow?"

"Saturdays are usually pretty routine. I clean the house and do the grocery shopping," Beth said.

"I'll make a deal with you," offered Scott. "You do the shopping and I'll stay home with Risa and clean house."

"Hmmm," considered Beth. "The idea of being able to do the shopping by myself is tempting. But I remember your housekeeping skills, or should I say lack of housekeeping skills."

"All right. How about Risa and I head outside and start getting the yard in shape for summer. You and I can split the house-cleaning chores."

"Really? You really want to spend your vacation doing my chores?"

"No," he replied. "I want to spend my vacation finding out what it would be like for us to live together again. Like it or not, chores are part of the bargain."

A smile twitched at her lips. "Unfortunately so. So if you're really willing, then" — Beth held out her hand for him to shake — "it's a deal."

He took her hand, but instead of shaking

it, he pulled her to himself for a long, slow kiss that made it hard to remember why they were sleeping in separate beds.

She gathered her self-control and pushed him away. "Don't start that, Scott."

"Why not?"

"Because we need our sleep if we're going to tackle all that tomorrow."

"We just had a nap," he reminded her. "I'm not tired anymore." Then he pulled her back for another kiss.

Beth was lost. It was wonderful, the feel of his lips on her, his weight pressing her into the soft cushions of the couch, the smell of his aftershave.

He nibbled on her ear and kissed his way down her throat. Beth dredged up the last bit of self-restraint she had. "Please stop."

Scott lifted his head. "Stop?"

"Yes, Scott. We went too fast last time. That's how we ended up pregnant and married before we finished college."

He sighed and moved away from her. "You're right."

She needed to make him understand so he didn't just think she was rejecting him. "Not that I don't want to be married to you. I just really want it to work this time. I want us to be together for the right reasons, because we love each other. Not because we lust after each other and. . . ."

"I would have married you anyway," Scott interrupted. "Not as soon, but Beth, I knew you were the one."

She nodded. "But things got so mixed up. Let's just take it slow this time."

Scott drew in a deep breath and released it. "Okay. There's no hurry. I'm not going anywhere."

"Well, I'm going to bed."

He grinned. "How about a good-night kiss first?"

"No!" Exasperated, Beth grabbed a couch cushion and whacked him over the head. Then she took off, hoping to make it to the stairs before he caught her.

No such luck. He grabbed her around the waist after she'd gone only a few steps. They tumbled to the floor, laughing, and he tickled her. Then he kissed her again.

The kiss was sweet, but Beth could sense his restraint. He wasn't going to let it go any further again. He'd really heard what she'd said about waiting. Her heart filled to bursting and she wanted to tell him that she loved him. But she didn't say it. She couldn't do it yet.

Scott got up and pulled Beth to her feet after him. He cleared his throat. "I guess I'll go see if there's anything else to watch on TV."

"All right. I'll see you in the morning."

"Good night." One more quick kiss, his lips just barely brushing hers for a second and then Scott turned around and starting hunting for the remote.

"Good night," echoed Beth as she fled up the stairs while she could still will herself to go.

CHAPTER 5

Saturday was pleasantly domestic. Scott did the yard work as promised while Beth did the shopping. He fixed a couple of cupboard doors in the kitchen that weren't latching correctly. He helped fold laundry and wash dishes. Risa followed him around wherever he went and he loved it, even when she got in the way.

Saturday evening he sat out on the deck behind the house and blew bubbles for her to pop, like her therapist had.

Beth opened the sliding doors on the patio and brought out a platter of hamburger patties. "Having fun, Risa?" she asked as she walked over to the grill.

Risa giggled and made the sign for "play."

"Yes, Daddy's playing with you," Beth replied.

Daddy. It had been a long time since Scott had thought of that word applying to him. He'd barely had a chance to get used to the idea the first time Beth was pregnant when it turned out that he wasn't going to be a daddy after all.

"What are you thinking?" asked Beth as she transferred the hamburgers to the grill.

"I'm thinking how much my life has changed since last weekend," he admitted.

"Yes, life is funny that way."

Scott paused to blow another bubble for Risa to catch. "Then how come you aren't laughing?"

She merely smiled and shrugged. "Do you want to go to church tomorrow?"

Scott thought about that. The three of them together in church made the idea that they were a family seem a bit more real. "I think I do," he said.

There was a hint of summer in the air as they stepped out Sunday morning. Risa was adorable in a pink dress, frilly socks and classic Mary Janes. Beth wore a red sweater and a black skirt. Scott had on a blue shirt, navy-blue dress pants, and a tie with swirls in shades of blue.

They arrived at the church with time to spare before the service started. Once they entered the sanctuary, Risa ran ahead of her parents. She went straight to Grandma and Grandpa and gave them both a big hug.

Scott stifled a groan. He hadn't thought about his parents being here. Well, it was unlikely that his father would start something at church.

Beth greeted Hal and Margie while Scott hung back a step or two. "Risa, honey," said Beth, "come and sit with your daddy and me."

"Oh, don't be ridiculous. There's plenty of room for all of us in this pew," insisted Margie, drawing Beth down to sit next to her. "Move down, Hal, and make room."

Hal was holding Risa on his lap. He gave Scott a hard stare, but reluctantly moved down. Scott slid in next to Beth. At least his father was on the opposite end of the pew.

While the pastor greeted everyone and began with the announcements, Scott took the opportunity to look around him. The place hadn't changed much over the years. Stained-glass windows portraying scenes from the life of Christ ran the length of both sides of the sanctuary. The banners on the wall were the same ones that had been used since he was in high school.

They rose for the opening hymn. Caught not paying attention, Scott was late in standing up. Fortunately Beth offered to share her hymnal. He hadn't even looked at the bulletin to see what they were singing.

But even the hymn was old and familiar. He'd sung it often inside these walls. Today, it couldn't hold his attention. He kept remembering other times, other circumstances when he'd been here.

Memories overwhelmed him and he fought to stay focused. But during the sermon, the pastor's droning voice couldn't hold his attention and the past rushed over him. He remembered sitting in this beautiful church with his parents and his brother Dave when he was younger. Dave always tried to make him laugh and get him in trouble.

He remembered standing at the altar for many Sunday-school Christmas programs. They always re-created the nativity in some way. Every year there were children dressed as angels and shepherds. The small children were always sheep, wearing wooly hoods with floppy ears. One year, when it was time for him to recite the innkeeper's lines, Scott froze. He couldn't remember a word of his part. Dave had saved him though, whispering the lines to him.

He remembered a time when he could sit next to his father and he would put his arm around Scott while they listened to the sermon. Scott leaned forward slightly and glanced at his father's face, tense and stony.

Obviously those days were long gone. He didn't even want to be in the same pew as his son now.

His brother's death had changed everything. He didn't want to think about it, but it was impossible not to while he was stuck sitting here. He couldn't leave without causing comment or worrying Beth and his mother.

Scott drew in a deep breath and willed himself to relax. He tried and failed to focus on what the pastor was saying. The memory blotted out everything else. Even now after years had passed, it seemed more like a nightmare than reality. If only he could dismiss it as easily.

He remembered the suit he'd worn was slightly too small and too warm for a summer day, but there'd been no time to buy a new one. Stepping into the church, he was hit by the overpowering scent from the dozens of flower arrangements. He tried not to look at anyone but it was impossible to miss the girls from their high school huddled together, crying on each other's shoulders and Dave's former basketball teammates trying hard to be tough and not break down. He escorted his mother to the family's pew at the front of the church. She was so encumbered with grief that he had to hold her up. He barely felt strong enough for this himself. The heat in the room and the smell from the flowers became overpowering and his stomach churned. He clenched his jaw to keep himself from vomiting.

His father had been much like he was now — as hard and still as stone. He betrayed no emotion at all as his eldest — and apparently most loved — son was laid to rest.

It was one of the worst experiences of Scott's life. The only other one that compared was the night that Beth had miscarried their baby. His life had taken a turn for the worse after both events.

Scott shook himself of the memory and saw Risa was making the sign for potty. He was quick to whisper, "I'll take her. I'm on the outside."

Relief rolled over him as he left the sanctuary. His brother had died years ago, and, since then, he'd been to church here more times than he could count. Why had it hit him so hard and so unexpectedly today? Was it because he'd been gone for so long? Was it a side effect of the current tension between him and his father? He didn't know and he wasn't inclined to examine it further.

After the service, Beth found Scott in the

hallway near the nursery. "What happened to you two?"

Scott shrugged. "Risa seemed restless so I took her to the nursery."

The grim expression in his eyes told her there was more to his escape than that but she decided to let it go. Instead, in an attempt to draw him out of his mood, she said, "Do you remember our wedding?"

He laughed, a low and humorless sound. "It wasn't much of a wedding. The two of us and our roommates for witnesses."

"You bought me roses, white and pink ones," she said with a smile.

"The bride has to have flowers."

"Yes, but roses seemed so extravagant."

Still frowning, he replied, "There wasn't much else I could give you."

"The roses were enough. To tell you the truth, I was thinking about not going through with the wedding. Something my mother said once kept coming back to me."

"And what was that?"

"She said that if a man marries a woman because she's pregnant, he'll always end up hating her. I was going to tell you I'd changed my mind about getting married until you gave me the roses."

Scott looked puzzled. "What difference did that make?"

"It made me feel . . . I don't know. Like you were marrying me because you loved me, and not because of the baby."

The sadness in his eyes finally retreated. He stepped closer and took her hands in his own. "I did really love you. I do. You were a beautiful bride."

"I didn't even have a real wedding gown, just the dress I bought for recitals."

"You were still beautiful."

He leaned down to kiss her forehead and Beth found herself moving closer to him, almost against her will. For the first time since he'd returned she admitted to herself just how much she'd missed him, how, for her, no one else could ever take his place.

"Mr. and Mrs. Lund?"

Beth jerked back, startled by the interruption. The nursery volunteer, a young woman, was there, Risa on her hip.

"Are you ready to take your daughter? All the other children have been picked up."

"Yes, thank you." Scott took Risa from the woman. "Sorry we were late."

A smile brought out the woman's dimples. "I could see you were otherwise occupied."

Beth felt her cheeks grow warm with embarrassment. Before she could say anything, make an attempt to explain, the woman was gone.

When she looked at Scott again, it was obvious that he was amused by her reaction and trying not to show it. Annoyed, she turned on her heel. "Come on, let's go home." She didn't look back to see if he was following. If she did, Beth was quite sure she'd see a big stupid grin on her husband's face.

As soon as they stepped into the narthex, Margie came over to them. "Why don't you three join us for brunch? We're going to that new buffet place."

Scott glanced over at his father, who looked like a brooding storm cloud. "Are you sure this is a good idea?" he asked his mother.

"You two have to talk to each other sooner or later," Margie said.

"We've already talked. It didn't go well," Scott said.

"He can't hold a grudge forever," Margie insisted. "What do you think, Beth?"

Margie was right. Hal and Scott would need to be together if they were ever going to work things out. "Sure, let's go."

The restaurant was crowded and noisy, bustling with the after-church crowd. It took some time for everyone to get their food and gather at the table, but finally they were settled. Risa was at the head of the table in a high chair. Margie and Hal sat on one side of the table while Beth and Scott sat on the other.

"So, Scott, tell me about your resort," prompted Margie.

Scott put his fork down. "What do you want to know?"

"Where is it? How big is it? What's it look like . . . ?"

"Whoa, hold on Mom," Scott interrupted. "I can only answer one question at a time."

"All right," Margie agreed. "Where is your resort?"

"It's northwest of here, near Rhinelander. The resort is on Emerald Lake. It's called that because the reflection of all the pine trees make the water appear dark green."

She continued with her interrogation. "That sounds like a beautiful setting. Now tell me what the resort is like."

"We renovated everything when I started there. Henry, the owner and I, redid all the cottages ourselves. They're like log cabins, only with better facilities. We let the professionals handle the lodge and they did a great job. It's a beautiful building."

"What's the name of the resort?" asked Margie.

Scott grinned. "It's kind of corny but we like it — the Pine Away Inn."

Beth and Margie giggled. "That is corny," agreed Beth, "but I like it."

"That was the resort's name when Henry and his wife stayed there for their honeymoon. After the resort changed owners in the eighties, the name was changed to the Tall Pines Resort. When Henry bought the place, he changed the name back."

"Who's Henry?" asked Hal, suddenly breaking into the conversation.

"Henry was the owner of the resort. He hired me to do the renovations. When it was completed I stayed on as business manager."

"You ran the place for him?" Hal had put his fork down and was clearly listening now.

Scott nodded. "When he passed away we found out that Henry was a very wealthy man. The resort was sort of a hobby for him after he retired. He and his wife loved the place and had vacationed there often.

"Most of his property went to his family, of course. But in his will Henry left me the resort. He . . . he said I'd put so much work into it that I should have it." Scott's voice betrayed him on the last bit, wavering for just a second before he finished. It was difficult for him to talk about Henry. He'd only known the man for three years, but Scott felt closer to Henry than to anyone else in the world. His loss still stung.

Hal nodded and didn't say anything more.

"Well, I think that's wonderful," said Margie. "Maybe we should take a vacation there, Hal." When her husband didn't answer she directed a stern look at him.

He must have gotten the message because he grudgingly replied, "Maybe."

"You're welcome to come anytime, no charge," Scott offered.

"A free vacation," joked Margie. "That's my favorite kind."

"Risa would love it up there." Scott paused to wipe a bit of potato from his daughter's face. "We have a playground on site and she could swim every day, Beth."

Margie clapped her hands. "I know. We should have Risa's birthday party at the resort. She turns three in July."

Beth sighed. "Don't remind me."

"Why?" questioned Scott. "What's wrong with turning three?"

"She won't be eligible for the Birth to Three program anymore," Beth replied in a flat voice. Scott noticed that her shoulders had tensed as soon as Margie brought up the subject of Risa's birthday.

"Does all her therapy end then?"

"Well, yes and no. We could enroll Risa in the Early Childhood program at a public school or in the Head Start program, and then she'd get the same services."

"So what's the problem?"

She shrugged and attempted to smile. "I guess it's just that I'm used to the people who work with her now. It'll be like starting all over again."

"There's no way she can stay in the program?" he asked.

"It's called Birth to Three for a reason, Scott. I'm sure it will be fine. Risa will adjust."

Scott noticed Beth was quiet for the rest of the time they spent together. On the way home, he tried to get her to talk about it a little more.

"So, tell me again, what happens when Risa turns three?"

"She'll have to transition into another program. Her service coordinator and I have been looking at the Early Childhood program at our local school."

"Then you're already planning for the transition. That's good."

Beth stared steadfastly out the window, but, in her lap, her clenched hands betrayed her feelings as well as her expression would have. She didn't say anything else all the way home.

Scott decided to leave the subject until later.

That evening, when Beth came down from putting Risa to bed, he asked her to come and sit with him in the living room.

"Do you want to watch some television?" she asked, sinking down on the couch next to him.

"No, I want to talk. Tell me what's bothering you about Risa's transition."

Her relaxed manner disappeared and a wary look entered her eyes.

"Why do you want to know?"

"I'm her father. I want to be part of this."

She leaned back against the cushions. "All right. Ask away."

She clearly wasn't happy that he'd brought it up, but at least she was willing to talk. "You said she was going to attend the local school. What do you know about it?"

Beth frowned. "I was supposed to tour the school next month, but I don't know if I should anymore."

"Why not?"

She seemed to struggle for words for a moment and then burst out with "Because . . . because . . . of you."

"Because of me? I'm not following you, Beth." He tried to put his arm around her, intending to calm her, but she pulled away from him.

"Scott, what's going to happen if . . . if we

decide to stay together. Where will we live?"

Now he got it, but he wasn't so sure his answer would make Beth happy. "I guess I was hoping that you and Risa would come and live with me at the resort. I'm sort of tied there."

"And Risa and I are gypsies? We have ties, too. What about my job?"

"You wouldn't need to work. You could stay home full-time with Risa."

"What about your parents? It would kill them if you took Risa away from them."

"I'm not taking her away. They could visit anytime for however long they wanted, I promise."

"It wouldn't be the same. This is never going to work." She rose from the couch and took a few steps away, standing with her back to him.

Scott's jaw dropped. He thought things were going well. He'd already been envisioning his life at the resort with Beth and Risa and that wasn't something he was willing to give up on so easily. Rising, he went to stand behind her. He almost rested his hands on her shoulders, but stopped himself, remembered how she'd pushed him away before.

"Let's calm down. We don't have to decide anything right now. It's only been a few days." He kept his voice soothing and steady and was rewarded by a slight lessening of tension in her shoulders. Seizing the opportunity, Scott turned Beth and put his arms around her.

She released one shuddering sigh and relaxed against him. "I don't know if time is going to change anything. Our circumstances will still be the same."

"Just let it go for now," he advised. "Everything will work itself out."

"I don't believe you," she grumbled, but she didn't argue anymore.

The next day when Beth went into work, Jared was waiting for her in her office. She stifled a groan. Usually she got along with Jared, but lately he was becoming very annoying.

"Good morning," she said, trying to sound cheerful.

"Morning, Beth. Do you want some coffee?" he asked.

"Not right now, thanks. I think I'll just dive right into work."

Jared lingered outside her office door.

"Was there something else you wanted?" She tried not to let her irritation creep into her voice. She'd known about Jared's crush on her for some time, and had believed that if she ignored it, he'd lose interest and find someone else. Since Scott had returned he'd really stepped over the line and she had no more patience with him.

He shuffled his feet and looked uncomfortable. Then he seemed to make a decision, stepped into the office and shut the door. "I wanted to talk to you about Scott."

Beth narrowed her eyes. "What about Scott?"

"I was just wondering if . . . if maybe you were going to stay married to him because you wanted to stay in the family."

"What?" Where was this coming from?

"Well, I know you're not on good terms with your own family and you've gotten really close to Aunt Margie and Uncle Hal."

"That's true," Beth conceded.

"But if you divorced Scott, you could still be part of the family." Jared was smiling at her like he'd just figured out the secret to world peace. Was he saying what she thought he was saying?

"Jared, let's just consider your suggestion for a moment. Forget that I took my wedding vows very seriously, or that Scott and I have a child together. What are you hinting at?"

Jared stared at the floor and mumbled something.

"Can you repeat that?"

"You and I *could* get married."

Beth sighed. As unpleasant as it might be, she needed to be brutally honest with him. "Jared, I'm sorry. I don't love you and I won't marry you."

"You could learn to love me. I could be a good father for Risa."

"Risa already has a father."

"Yeah, but for how long?"

Beth felt her jaw tighten and forced herself to relax and stay calm. "Scott has always been a good person. Just because he made one mistake doesn't mean he's not trustworthy. The two of you grew up together. How can you go behind his back like this?"

Jared's face went red. "I just don't want you to get hurt again."

"Don't worry about me. I can take care of myself." Beth pulled out a folder from the stack on her desk and began to read through it. He left without another word and she sighed in relief.

But having to defend Scott brought up new doubts. Scott was dependable. He did take his responsibilities seriously. But did he only come back because he felt it was his duty to share the windfall of his inheritance with her? Was he only insisting on staying because of his duty to Risa?

No, she was sure he loved Risa. She could

see it in his face. But what about her? Maybe it was Risa he really wanted, and not her? She remembered how he told her he loved her yesterday at the church. He couldn't look her in the eye and say things like that if he didn't mean them, could he? The Scott she remembered wasn't that kind of person. Had he changed?

At home, Scott took care of Risa. He helped her dress and fed her.

The sun was shining, daring everyone to think that summer had come already. Scott knew better than to expect summer in May, in Wisconsin, but there was no reason not to take advantage of the sunshine.

He put Risa in her stroller and they went to the park a few blocks away.

She wanted to go on the swings right away. Even though she was close to three years old, Risa was still tiny enough to fit in the baby swings.

The park was busy, filled with parents and children who had decided to take advantage of the warm weather. Scott watched the other children play. He watched as they climbed over the playground equipment. A man was helping a little girl — probably his daughter — learn to go hand-over-hand across the monkey bars. It was then that it hit him. Really hit him. Risa was not like the other children.

For the first time since he'd found out about his daughter, he wondered. Would he ever be able to do that with her? What would she be able to do as she matured? What things would she miss out on?

He looked down at his beautiful daughter and could see Risa was tired of the swing. When Scott lifted her down she toddled over to the sandbox. He continued to smile and play with her, but in his heart, a heavy weight had settled.

That afternoon Risa had an appointment with her Birth to Three teacher, a woman named Emily. They met at his parents' house again.

"I'm happy to meet you, Scott," said Emily. "I didn't know Risa's daddy was . . . um . . . around." She wrinkled her nose. "Sorry, that didn't come out right."

"That's okay. Beth and I have been . . . estranged. I didn't find out about Risa until last week."

"It's good to have you on board. Do you have any questions for me?"

Scott had a million questions. He didn't know where to start. He hugged Risa close as she sat on his lap. "What will life be like for Risa as she gets older?"

"That's a big question, Scott. I can't see into the future, but I can give you a few ideas. People with Down syndrome can have a wide range of abilities. While a few have severe cognitive delays, most are in the moderate to mild range."

"Where does Risa fall in the spectrum?" he asked.

"I think she's in the moderate range, perhaps mild. We'll see as she gets older. But I would anticipate that Risa will be able to read at a basic level, do simple math and be responsible for her own self-care."

"Will she ever be able to have a job or live by herself?"

Emily shrugged. "That's too far out to say for sure. When she gets into school it's important to find a program that teaches life skills as well as academics. Then, after school, it may depend to some extent on what programs in the community are available to her. Unfortunately, those programs can change from year to year based on funding."

Scott sat back in his chair. "That's a lot to think about."

"It can be overwhelming at first. But Risa's not going to grow up overnight. We'll just take it one step at a time."

"I understand that she will be leaving the

Birth to Three program soon."

Emily nodded. "Beth and I have been looking at Early Childhood programs in the area. We're trying to find the best placement for Risa."

Scott let the conversation go at that so Emily could work with his daughter. He went into the kitchen to get a drink of water. Margie was taking cookies out of the oven. As she transferred them to a baking rack, she said, "I'm going to pack some of these up for you to take home after they cool. They're Risa's favorite — snickerdoodles."

"Thanks, Mom," Scott said absently.

Margie smiled at him. "Don't be discouraged, Scott. Risa's going to be just fine."

"I know. I guess it just hit me that she's different from other children."

"She has some differences, but she's mostly the same. And she means the world to me and your father."

"What if Beth and Risa move up north with me?"

She frowned. "That would be hard."

"I'm sorry, Mom."

"But you should do what's best for Risa," insisted Margie.

"What *is* best for Risa?" Scott wanted to know.

"You and Beth will have to figure that out.

But I know it's best for her to have a daddy."

"Is it?" asked Scott. "Even if it means taking her away from the only home she knows?"

"Families move all the time. Risa would adjust," his mother assured him.

"What about Dad? Will he adjust?"

"What do you mean?"

"If I take Risa away, will he ever forgive me? Will I lose any chance that things will ever be right again between us?"

Margie took the now-empty cookie sheet to the sink and checked on the next batch in the oven before answering. "Of course your father will forgive you."

But to Scott, it didn't sound as if she believed her own words.

CHAPTER 6

Beth noticed how quiet Scott was all that evening as they made supper, cleaned up and got Risa ready for bed. Once Risa was asleep and all the household chores were done, they settled on the couch in front of the TV. Scott held the remote, but didn't turn the set on.

"Do you want to watch something? We could do something else if you'd rather," offered Beth.

Scott shook his head. "No. TV's fine. Unless *you* want to do something else. We used to be pretty competitive at Scrabble as I remember."

"I haven't played that game since . . . since we last played."

He didn't answer. Beth felt that although his body was next to hers, his mind was a million miles away.

"What's wrong? You seem preoccupied tonight."

"Yeah, I've been thinking about a lot of things." He recounted his conversation with Emily.

"I guess I was so happy that you were willing to give me another chance, and so surprised about Risa, that I didn't think about any of this. Today I took a step back into the real world. Things don't seem so simple anymore."

"What do you mean?"

"Beth, you know what I would really like to see happen, is for you and Risa to come and live with me at the resort. But now I'm not sure if that's the best idea. I don't know what sort of school programs or therapy would be available for Risa there. And I'm worried about how it will hurt my parents if I take Risa away from them."

"You could sell the resort and move here," Beth suggested.

"No, I can't." Scott ran his hands through his hair in a gesture of frustration. "Henry left me the resort because he knew I'd take good care of it. I can't just walk away."

"You *have* been thinking." She wished she had an easy answer for him that would wipe away the troubled set of his face. But he was right. Things just weren't that simple.

"I'd sell the resort if it was what was best for Risa. I want her to have the best help possible. Today at the park I saw a little girl learning to cross the monkey bars and . . . ," Scott told Beth about the other children he saw and how it got him thinking about Risa's future.

"I've only known Risa a few days, but she is my daughter. It hurts to think of all the things she may never be able to do."

Beth scooted over to Scott and put her arm around him. "I know. It was hard for me at first. I didn't know anything about Down syndrome and I was so scared. If I hadn't had Emily and the therapists to guide me through everything, I don't know what I would have done."

"I'm glad you weren't alone."

"You aren't alone in this either, you know."

He hugged Beth to him and rested his head on hers. "I know." His breath tickled her skin. It occurred to her that being with Scott would take some of the burden of making decisions for Risa off her shoulders. That was just one more reason why she could get used to having him around.

And that scared her. Her past had taught her that when you depended on someone you usually ended up regretting it. She'd depended on her parents and eventually, they both let her down. Then she'd turned to her grandmother and everything was good again until Grandma Jane died. Then she'd found Scott. . . .

When Beth got home the next day, Scott was on his cell phone. She picked up Risa and gave her a hug while listening to his half of the conversation.

"Are you sure it's that bad? No, I know, I know. I'll be there."

"What's up?" asked Beth as he clicked the phone shut.

"That was Ben from the resort. He and his wife Cindy run the restaurant there. Ben is pretty much my second-in-command. He called to tell me there was an early storm at the resort. A tree fell on one of the cabins and there's some wind damage to the other buildings."

"I'm sorry, Scott."

"It's nothing I can't deal with. The problem is, I have to go home to supervise the repairs and handle the insurance claim."

Beth's heart sank. Last night they had acknowledged that the real world was going to intrude into their lives soon, but she had thought they could avoid it a little longer.

"When do you leave?"

"I can wait until tomorrow morning. I want to spend one more night with my girls." He gave her a smile, trying to make light of the situation, but Beth could tell he was as upset as she was.

Still holding Risa in one arm, Beth hugged him with the other. He hugged her and Risa back. They stood that way for a few seconds, and then he broke away.

"Hey, I have an idea," said Scott. "Why don't you give Risa her bath and I'll get takeout. We can have a nice quiet evening at home and no dishes to spoil it."

Beth attempted a cheerful tone. There was no point in spoiling their last night together. "That sounds good. What do you want to eat?"

"How about Chinese?"

"That's fine with me. I know a place not too far from here." She frowned. "But Risa won't appreciate it."

"I can go through the drive-through at the burger place and get her a kid's meal."

Beth tickled Risa's tummy. "Did you hear that? Daddy's going to get you some chicken nuggets and fries. How about that?" She didn't want the little girl to pick up on her parents' less-than-positive emotions.

Risa clapped and laughed. Beth gave him directions to both the Chinese restaurant and the burger place. Scott grabbed his wallet and car keys and set out on his mission while she headed upstairs to change out of her work clothes and put Risa in the bath.

It was a nice evening. They stuffed themselves with takeout and played with Risa on the living-room floor long after her bedtime. When the little girl's eyelids started to droop, Scott scooped her up and carried her off to bed. Beth let him tuck her in alone, so he could say his good-bye to her.

He stayed with Risa a long time. Beth knew he was waiting for Risa to fall asleep.

When he came down, she had the Scrabble game set up on the dining-room table. "Are you ready to get beat? For old time's sake?"

He grinned. "You're on."

The competition between them was fierce. It was a close game, but Scott came out the winner. "You've gotten rusty," he taunted her.

"Can I help it if I haven't been able to find a decent partner since . . . ," her words trailed away.

"Since I left?"

She nodded. "I'm glad you came back." After the last few days there was no doubt in her mind that she loved him as much as she always had.

"Me, too. I'm sorry I can't stay as long as I'd planned."

"Where do we go from here?" asked Beth.

Scott reached across the table and took

her hand. "Will you and Risa come to the resort?"

She nodded. "I'd love to see it. But I can't commit to living there yet."

"That's all right. We don't have to decide everything at once."

"Some couples live in different places and see each other on weekends," suggested Beth, willing herself not to cry.

He was quick to dismiss that idea. "I've already missed out on too much of Risa's life and we've spent too much time apart. There's no way that would be enough for me."

She couldn't hold back her tears any longer. How would they ever work this out, she wondered as sobs shook her body. Scott got up and scooped her into his arms. He carried her into the living room and sat in an arm chair, cradling Beth against him.

"Don't cry. We'll make things work out."

"What if we don't? What if we can't?" she gasped between sobs.

Scott put his hands on either side of her face, forcing her to look at him. "Beth, I promise you we'll be together."

"How can you promise that?"

"I can promise that because I want you and Risa and me to be a family."

He kissed her and when he would have

pulled away, Beth threw her arms around his neck and brought him back to her, deepening the kiss. She pressed herself against him as her hands slid down his shoulders to the buttons on his shirt. She wanted them to be together like before.

This time it was Scott who put a stop to things, sliding out from under her and leaving her alone in the chair. He ran his fingers through his hair and took a shuddering breath. "Beth, we've got to wait."

"Why?" She didn't mean for that word to come out sounding so small and pitiful.

"Our relationship needs to be on firmer ground before we take this step."

"You just promised we'd be together. Didn't you mean it?"

"I did mean it," Scott knelt down next to her and stroked her cheek. "That's why there's no need to hurry. I want to make love to you, but not just because I'm going away and you're afraid."

Neither of them wanted the evening to end. They ended up curled up together on the couch, wrapped in an afghan. It wasn't long before they fell asleep, holding on to one another.

The next morning Beth woke up, wondering why she was on the couch instead of in her bed. Then she remembered. Scott was leaving.

It was early. The sun wasn't even out yet. Beth got up and wandered into the kitchen where Scott was filling a travel mug with coffee. When he saw her, he put the mug down and held out his arms.

Wordlessly, Beth went to him and held him tightly. She knew he wasn't leaving like last time, but she was still scared. Scott rested his head on top of hers.

"I'll miss you," he said.

She didn't reply.

"I'll call you tonight. And then, when the repairs are done, I'll come back and get you and Risa, okay?"

"When will that be?" she mumbled into his shoulder.

"Let's say the weekend after next?"

That would be plenty of time to arrange vacation leave with Hal. "All right."

Letting go of her, he went to gather up his things. He took them out to his SUV and came back in for his coffee.

She tried to smile. "Drive safely."

"I will." He kissed her, his unshaven face tickling hers. "Why don't you crawl into bed and get a couple hours of sleep yet?"

Beth nodded.

"Tell Risa I love her." He kissed her again.

"I will."

"And I love you, too, Beth."

A lump rose in her throat and she couldn't answer. She hugged him as hard as she could and hoped he understood. One more kiss and he was gone.

Beth contemplated calling in sick, but she knew if she did, Hal would be at her door in a heartbeat. So when her alarm went off she dragged herself out of bed and through her normal routine. She waited as long as she could to call her mother-in-law and ask if Risa could come over. Luckily, Margie didn't have any plans. "I was just getting used to sleeping in," joked Margie, "and now I'm back on duty. Where's Scott? Taking it easy today?"

Beth explained about the problems at the resort and Scott having to return.

"Oh, honey, I'm sorry," said Margie, drawing her into a hug. "But take it from me, when you own your own business those things come up."

"It's okay. I knew he would have to go back soon anyway." She wished she felt as nonchalant as she sounded.

"Are you and Risa going to visit him soon?"

"Scott is coming back to get us the weekend after next if I can arrange some vacation time with Hal," answered Beth.

"He'd better, or he'll be sleeping on the couch and eating TV dinners," Margie exclaimed. "If you have any trouble with him, you can tell him I said so."

She attempted a laugh. "I will. Thanks for taking Risa."

"It's no problem. I've missed my little helper."

Beth was running slightly behind schedule by the time she left Risa and headed for work. With a groan she remembered the morning was supposed to start with a staff meeting. She would have to walk in after it already started.

Quickly, she parked, and hurried into the building. She wished she'd taken the time to braid her hair this morning. She arrived, breathless and rumpled while Hal was in the middle of his usual pep talk.

Beth apologized and took her seat, as gracefully as she could. Hal pierced her with a penetrating gaze. After a moment he looked away and started speaking, smoothly picking up where he left off.

After the meeting, she tried to gather up her things and slip out unnoticed, but Hal said. "Beth, stay."

She sat back down.

One of her coworkers joked, "Does she roll over or fetch the paper?"

There were a few chuckles from the other guys, but the look on Hal's face stifled any general hilarity.

When the room was empty, he rounded the table and stood by Beth's chair. She kept her eyes focused on the legal pad on the table in front of her, afraid to look him in the eye. She could almost feel the disapproval like an aura around him as she waited for him to speak.

"So," he asked her, "when did he leave?"

CHAPTER 7

That evening when they got home, Risa seemed anxious to get into the house. As soon as she unlocked the door, the little girl rushed in. She toddled from room to room as if looking for something or, Beth realized, someone.

Risa came back to Beth and looked up at her puzzled.

"Daddy had to leave." How do I explain this to a two-year-old? she wondered. "We'll see Daddy again soon."

Risa nodded. Beth helped her get out crayons and a coloring book. She sat Risa at the kitchen table to color while she made supper, keeping one eye on Risa to make sure the crayons didn't go in her mouth. It was difficult for the toddler to press hard enough to make a mark with the crayons, but practicing built her hand strength.

Later, after Risa was in bed for the night, Beth went to her closet and dug out a box.

She would never think of throwing it away, but she rarely opened it.

She sat on her bed with the box in front of her and the phone next to her, for when Scott called.

Beth lifted the lid from the box and stared down at her precious collection of memories — memories of Scott.

On the top was a theater program — *Pirates of Penzance.* That was from her sophomore year in college. The beginning of that school year had been one of the loneliest times of her life.

During the summer between Beth's freshman and sophomore years of college, Grandma Jane had had a heart attack and passed away.

Back in school for the fall, Beth looked for something to distract her from the loneliness she felt. She had been a music major and when she saw the announcement about auditions for *Pirates of Penzance,* she decided to try out. Her need to forget her loneliness overcame her shyness.

Beth earned a role as one of General Stanley's daughters. The operetta worked as a distraction and helped her meet new people.

Jeremy Fletcher was cast as the Pirate King. He certainly had the macho swagger to pull it off. Beth didn't really like him, but her new friends did and so she allowed him to flirt with her a little.

One night after rehearsal, Beth remembered, she was getting ready to leave and couldn't find her script. She searched for it all over the green room, where the cast gathered every night, and by the time she realized it wasn't there, everyone else had gone. She had thought she left it in the theater. Walking down the aisle between the empty seats, she tried to remember where she'd sat to watch the scenes she wasn't in.

"Looking for something?"

Beth jumped. "Who's there?" Her eyes scanned the dark theater.

A single light on the stage flickered on and Jeremy swaggered out. "Looking for this?"

She sighed with relief. Now she could go home. "Yes, I guess I forgot to pick it up."

Beth climbed the stairs to the stage. As she approached him, Jeremy backed away. "You didn't forget. I grabbed it when you weren't looking."

"Why would you do that?"

Leering, Jeremy answered, "Because I knew it would bring you to me."

Great. Flirting with this macho idiot was the last thing she wanted to do tonight. "Jeremy, it's late and I'd like to go home.

May I please have my script?"

He held it out and when she reached for it, he pulled away and climbed up onto the pirate ship the stage crew had been building.

"Stop it Jeremy. I just want to go home." Frustration and anger made her voice sharp.

"Then come and get your script," he taunted.

"Forget it. I'll get it another time." Beth turned to go.

"Wait. I'm sorry, Beth. I was just teasing you. Here. Here's your script."

He was leaning down and holding out the script. Would he give it to her this time? He must have sensed her hesitation, because he added, "I won't pull it away again. I promise."

She really didn't want to leave the script behind, so Beth walked over to the ship. As she reached up for it, he grabbed her hand and pulled her up onto the ship and into an embrace.

Beth gasped. "What are you doing?"

"Come on, relax," he laughed. "Won't it be fun to do it on the set of the pirate ship?"

She tried to push him away. "Jeremy, stop. I don't want. . . ."

"Loosen up, Beth. Why not have a little fun?"

They were all alone in the dark, window-less theater. Keeping a short reign on her emotions, she said in a firm voice, "Jeremy, stop. I mean it."

He laughed at her. "But I'm the Pirate King. The Pirate King always gets what he wants."

"Not this time. Let go of me!" she screamed.

"All right, all right." He loosened his hold but didn't move away. "Give me a kiss first."

"No." She took a step back, relieved when he let her go.

"Come on, just one kiss. That's not too wild for you, is it?"

"I don't want to kiss you."

"Then *I'll* kiss you."

Beth backed away. "No, you won't."

Jeremy followed her until he'd backed her up against the railing of the fake ship. "Yes, I think I will."

Her heart beating fast, panic was beginning to take hold. Suddenly another figure stepped in between them, pushing Jeremy back.

"No, I don't think you will." It was one of the stage hands. Beth had almost cried out with relief.

Jeremy had backed off quickly when confronted. "All right, all right. Geez. Some people are so serious." He shuffled off the stage and into the wings. A few seconds later they heard the heavy stage door bang closed.

She was alone again, this time with a stranger, but right now she trusted him a sight farther than Jeremy.

"Are you okay?" he had asked.

She couldn't seem to catch her breath. His hands on her shoulders, he guided her to a bench built into the ship. She forced herself to take long, slow breaths. Her heartbeat returned to normal and she felt she could speak again.

"Thank you," Beth told her rescuer.

"It's all right," he responded. "How are you getting home? Do you have a car?"

She shook her head. "I'll be all right. I just have to walk back to the dorms."

He hesitated, then said, "Would you like me to walk with you? Jeremy may still be lurking somewhere."

"Oh, I'll be fine." Beth tried to exude a confidence she didn't feel. Just because he'd saved her once didn't mean she was helpless.

"If you're sure."

"I'm sure. . . ." On the other hand, she wouldn't mind getting to know this guy a little better. Would it be so bad to let him walk her home? "But if you don't mind. . . ."

He smiled. "No problem. I have to put a few things away. I'll meet you by the stage door."

Beth didn't wait long. She studied him as he walked toward her, pulling on his coat. He was a stage hand, but he could easily be a leading man with his height and build. Those gorgeous blue eyes wouldn't count against him either.

"I really appreciate this," Beth told him as he opened the door for her. "What's your name?"

"Scott Lund." As they headed out into the night, she noticed he walked with a slight limp.

"My name is. . . ."

"Beth Carlisle, I know."

He must have noticed her surprise because he added, "The crew knows most of the actors' names."

Beth was embarrassed that she couldn't say the same about the stage crew. To cover her discomfort she asked, "What do you do?"

"I'm a carpenter and I help run the show behind the scenes. It's my work-study job."

"I didn't know you could get paid for that sort of thing."

He shrugged. "It beats washing dishes at the cafeteria."

"I'll bet it does," she agreed. "This is my first show, but I like it. It's fun."

"You have a nice voice," he told her.

Beth felt her face warm. She wasn't used to compliments. "Thank you. Piano is my main instrument."

"I'd like to hear you play sometime."

"Really?"

"Sure."

Don't read too much into it, she told herself. He's probably just being polite.

They had reached the dorm area and Scott asked which building she lived in. Beth told him and they turned toward it.

"I'm really glad you were still around tonight. I think Jeremy would have eventually realized that I meant it when I said no, but. . . ."

He stuffed his hands into the pockets of his jeans and looked uncomfortable. "I've worked with him before. He has a tendency toward 'leading lady syndrome.' But he's not playing the lead this time, so I guess you were the lucky candidate for this show's affair. He isn't used to being turned down."

"Oh." She digested that little bit of news. "I thought he was just a flirt."

"You couldn't have known," Scott assured her.

"But" — Beth was turning this over in her

mind — "you knew. Did you stay behind on purpose?"

He looked embarrassed at being discovered, but admitted, "I heard him telling one of his friends what he was planning. I didn't think you were the kind of girl who would go along with it. But if you did, I figured I could just slip out."

Beth felt her gratitude increase a notch. "I don't know what to say. I've already said thank you, but I wish I could do more."

"Don't mention it." Scott opened the door for her. He walked her to the stairwell entrance and said good night.

"Good night," Beth replied. Then, not wanting to let it end at that, she asked, "Will I see you at rehearsal tomorrow night?"

He smiled, and her stomach did a little flip. "I'll be around."

She couldn't think of anything else to say to keep him, so she watched him leave and then went upstairs to her room.

Soon after, there was a knock at the door, and Mindy, one of the other girls from the floor, bounced in.

"What's up?" asked Beth looking up from the textbook she'd just pulled out, though she doubted she'd be able to concentrate any more tonight.

"That's what I was going to ask you. Did

I see you with Scott Lund earlier tonight?"

"Yes, why?"

"Why?" her eyes widened. "Don't you know who he is?"

She shook her head.

Mindy let out an exasperated sigh. "Do you live under a rock, Beth? He was a big star on the basketball team."

"Basketball team? He's a stage carpenter for *Pirates of Penzance*."

"So that's what he's doing now. Last year he blew out his knee. He couldn't play anymore and lost his scholarship."

"That's too bad. He's such a nice guy." A really nice guy, she added to herself.

"Not to mention gorgeous!" exclaimed Mindy with another bounce. "Are you going to see him again?"

"Well, sure. We're working together on the operetta."

Mindy rolled her eyes. "No, I mean socially."

"Well," admitted Beth, "we weren't actually on a date. He just walked me home because one of the other guys was . . . giving me a bit of trouble."

"If you're not dating him, can you introduce me?"

"I'm not dating him." But to herself she added, *yet*.

Beth put the theater program back into the box. At the next rehearsal she'd made a point of talking to Scott, and at the one after that he'd asked her out.

She'd fallen hard and fast for him, and she guessed her feelings hadn't changed since then.

The phone rang and she answered it immediately.

"Hello."

On the other end she heard Scott's rumbling laugh. "Were you sitting by the phone?"

Beth was glad he couldn't see her blushing or know how glad she was to hear his voice. "I guess I was. How was your trip back?"

"It was okay. Things are a mess here, but we got a lot done today. I'm sorry to call so late, but we had to sort through everything and deal with insurance, and. . . ." He cleared his throat. "And I don't want to waste this phone call talking about all that."

"Is there much damage to the other cabins?"

"No," said Scott. "Mostly missing shingles to replace. How was your day?"

"I talked to your dad today. My vacation is all set up," she told him, glad to have good news.

"That's great. I can't wait to have you here." He really did sound excited about it, Beth thought. They talked about Risa and about what vacation things to pack. Finally Beth noted that it was getting late and reluctantly suggested they end the conversation.

"Will you call again tomorrow?" she asked, hoping she didn't sound too pathetic. The last thing she wanted was to come off as needy.

"Sure. I'll call earlier so I can talk to Risa, too."

"That sounds good. She was so disappointed when we got home tonight and you weren't here. She looked all over the house for you."

There was a long silence on the other end of the line. "She really looked for me?"

Beth smiled at the hopeful note in his voice. "Of course. I wouldn't make that up."

"I can't wait to see you both again."

She was still hesitant to reveal too much about her feelings, but ventured, "We miss you."

"I miss you, too. Kiss Risa for me."

"I will," promised Beth.

"And Beth. . . ."

"Yes?"

"I love you."

Her breath caught at his declaration. "How can you be sure?"

"I wasn't sure when I decided to come looking for you. Once I saw you again, it didn't take long for me to figure it out."

"I wish I could say the same. I just don't know, Scott." Actually she did know. She just wasn't ready to take another chance, not with Risa's future at stake.

"Then I'll have to work harder at convincing you." There was more than a hint of stubbornness behind his words. It scared her a little . . . and thrilled her, too.

"It's late. I have to go," she choked out, overcome by her warring emotions.

"All right. Good night, Beth."

"Good night." She listened for the click that indicated he'd hung up before she pressed the button to disconnect. Setting the phone back on the bed, Beth lifted a small tulle bag from her box. It was filled with dried rose petals — white and pink.

Early the next morning Scott knocked on the door of the cottage next to his. Most of the employees didn't live on site, but Ben and Cindy, who had been running the resort's restaurant for years, did. They'd raised their family here at the resort. Their oldest kids, twins Shaun and Sam, were away at college but their daughter, Shannon, would start her senior year of high school in the fall.

Shannon opened the door. "Good morning, Scott. What are you doing here so early?"

"Looking for coffee. Don't you have school?"

She smiled at him. "Leaving right now, sir. Don't call my parole officer, okay?"

"Very funny. If you're late for school, I'll demote you from waitress to dishwasher."

She stuck out her tongue at him as she slid past him out the door. He had little say about how the restaurant was run, but Scott couldn't help teasing her. She was like a niece to him.

He wandered back to the kitchen where he found Cindy, a middle-aged woman of ample proportions, already pouring coffee into a mug for him. Ben, her husband, who towered even over Scott, was sitting at the kitchen table, his thatch of red hair still uncombed. Scott accepted the mug with thanks and took a seat at the table. They had become good friends to him and he felt at home here in their cozy, very-lived-in kitchen.

"Are you hungry, Scott?" asked Cindy, standing at the stove. "I've got some pancake batter left."

"I didn't come over to mooch breakfast off of you," he replied, "but since you're offering. . . ."

She smiled at him. "Do you want bacon, too?"

"Only if it's already made. Don't go to any trouble."

Ben put down the newspaper he was reading. "How was your vacation? We were so busy yesterday I never got a chance to ask you."

Scott took a sip from his mug and sighed in satisfaction. No one made coffee like Cindy. "It was great, actually. I was sorry I had to come home."

"What did you do?" Cindy asked, as she poured some batter onto the hot griddle.

There was no way to break this news without shocking them. Henry had been the only person he'd confided his secret in. Scott took a deep breath and plunged ahead. "I looked up my wife and asked her to take me back."

Ben's mouth dropped open and Cindy turned from the grill to face him. "Your what?" they both asked.

"My wife. I was married before I moved up here. It's a long story, but anyway, Henry always told me I should see her again and settle things between us. After he died. . . ." Scott paused to clear his throat, suddenly thick with emotion. "After he died, I got to thinking about it and decided to follow his advice. So I found her and asked her for a second chance." Scott felt a huge grin spreading over his face. "She said yes. Hey Cindy, are you burning my pancakes?"

With a little yelp Cindy turned around and moved the griddle off the flame. She started scraping off the burnt batter. "It serves you right," she grumbled. "Giving us news like that while I'm cooking."

"So what does this mean?" asked Ben. "Are you leaving us?"

Scott's grin fizzled. "I don't know. I want her to come here and live with me, but there's a complication."

"What's that?" Ben asked, giving Scott his full attention.

"We have a daughter. I didn't know about her."

"Scott!" cried Cindy, putting down her spatula and throwing up her hands. "Oh my goodness, I think I'm going to have to give up on cooking and sit down. You don't have any more surprises like this, do you?"

"Only a little one, I think. The problem is Risa, our daughter, has Down syndrome. I don't know if she can get the kind of help she needs up here."

"Well, we'll research it, honey," said Cindy, joining the men at the table with a small plate of somewhat crispy pancakes.

Their slightly charred appearance didn't worry Scott. He began adding butter and syrup to them. "Thanks, Cindy, but I need you to help me with something else."

"What's that?"

"Risa and Beth — my wife's name is Beth — are coming for a visit. I'm going to pick them up the weekend after next. Could you help me get Risa's room ready? I need a toddler bed and some toys, I guess. And anything else that little girls need."

"Oooh, shopping. Now those are the kind of favors I like doing. Maybe Shannon and I can go after school."

Ben rolled his eyes. "Make sure you take Scott's credit card."

Cindy jumped up and went back to the stove. "I'm so happy for you, Scott."

"Thanks, Cindy."

"Yeah, me too," added Ben. "If there's anything I can do. . . ."

"Actually," said Scott, an innocent smile on his face, "I did have something in mind."

CHAPTER 8

The next two weeks flew by and finally it was Thursday. Scott was coming to pick up Beth and Risa today for their visit to his resort. Beth was leaving work at noon, but that half day seemed longer to her than most full working days.

Just before it was time for her to leave, Hal called her into his office. "So, you're going," he said.

"Yes," Beth replied. "It's been a long time since I've had a vacation."

"Are you coming back?"

"Well, of course."

"Coming back to work, or just coming back to pack up your things and give notice to your landlord?"

"I want to come back," Beth told him. She knew it was a lame thing to say, but it was all she could come up with.

"I know you have a couple of weeks' vacation coming, but here's the thing, Beth.

Don't come back until you're sure it's for good. You're one of my best salesmen — salespeople. I'll always have a place for you. But it won't work for you to be running back and forth between here and the north woods. So you take all the time you need. But if you do come back, you'd better be certain that you're staying."

She nodded. "I understand, Hal. I know you took a chance on me when you hired me and I appreciate that."

"It paid off."

An uncomfortable silence grew between them.

"Well, I guess I'll be going now," said Beth. She turned, but Hal called out for her to wait. Turning back to him she saw tears in his eyes. "What is it, Hal?"

"Risa means everything to me. Whatever happens, I don't want to be left out of her life." His brusque businessman persona was gone. This was Risa's grandfather speaking, not the owner of Lund Motors.

Beth rushed around the desk and put her arms around his shoulders, squeezing him in a hug. He'd done so much for her, and she'd never really thanked the man. Now she tried to make up for that in a single squeeze. "I would never let that happen, Hal."

"You wouldn't?"

"Hal," said Beth, looking him straight in the eye. It was best to be blunt with him. Beating around the bush never worked with her father-in-law. "You know how important family is to me."

It occurred to Beth that this could be the right time to tell Hal the whole truth about Scott's leaving, about the huge argument they'd had the night before, about the terrible things she'd said. She was going to tell him, Beth decided. Then maybe there'd be a chance that he and Scott could repair their relationship.

But Hal's next words took her completely off guard and changed the direction of her thoughts.

"It seems to me you've cut your own family out of your life."

Beth straightened, instantly defensive. "That's different. They wanted to be left out."

"Maybe they're sorry now?" suggested Hal.

"No, I don't think they are." Beth forced herself to stop before she said anything else. Hal didn't understand what her family was like and she wasn't about to enlighten him. Instead, she tried to offer him some assurance. "Please just believe me when I say that you and Margie will always be included in Risa's life."

"Thank you, Beth."

The relief in her father-in-law's face was evident and Beth felt guilty for making him worry in the first place. She bit her lip to hold back the emotions that surged inside her. "I'd better go," she mumbled. "I still have packing to do."

"Say good-bye to Risa for me."

"Why don't you come by and do that yourself?"

Hal shook his head and suddenly made a show of shuffling the papers on his desk. "No, I've got too much to do here today. You just tell her for me."

Beth knew that Hal was never too busy for Risa. It was just too hard for him to see her go. But she wasn't going to call him out. Let him keep his tough-guy image. "All right. I'll tell her."

At home Beth finished the last of her packing. She put out clean towels for Margie's cousin Sylvia, who had recently lost her house when her landlord sold it and was happy to sublet from her while she looked for a new apartment. It was a lucky coincidence for them both, although Beth had to agree to let her stay longer than the two weeks if necessary. She'd overheard a little of Margie and Sylvia's conversation and got the impression that they didn't think Sylvia would have to worry about moving out at all. Beth wanted to tell Margie not to count on it, but it would have disappointed her so she didn't.

She had dressed Risa in jeans and a T-shirt. Now she slipped a sweatshirt over her head. The sweatshirt was green with a silhouette of pine trees on the front. It said "Pine Away Resort" in bold black letters and had come in the mail the day before from Scott. He certainly loved Risa. Beth hoped he loved her, too, and didn't just want to stay married for Risa's sake.

He *said* that he loved her, but she knew that, in spite of what Hal thought, Scott took his responsibilities seriously. He would stay with her if he thought that was best for his daughter and not necessarily for their relationship's sake.

After all, they'd only gotten married in the first place because she was pregnant. He did say he wanted a second chance before she'd told him about Risa, but maybe he was only saying that because he thought she'd choose to get a divorce. He'd told her that's what he thought she would say.

Beth shook her head. She wished there

147

was some way she could know for sure. If it wasn't for her behavior, maybe he never would have left in the first place. But then again, maybe he would have.

The days since Scott had returned to the resort had given her too much time for thinking and most of it had been spent on doubts and worries. One evening, driven by her insecurities, Beth made a huge mistake. She'd called her mother. The phone rang four or five times before Beth heard her mother's voice.

"Hello."

"Mom, it's Beth."

Silence.

"I know it's been a long time. . . ."

"It has. So why are you calling now?" If her mother's voice had been any colder, Beth swore the receiver in her hand would be dripping with icicles.

"I've been thinking. . . ." Beth swallowed hard and gathered her courage. "Maybe I was wrong to shut you out of my life."

Another frigid silence. Then, "Are you in some kind of trouble?"

"What? Mom, no."

"Because if you are, you can forget about any help from me."

"I'm doing great."

"Then why did you call?"

"Because I thought you might want to hear about your granddaughter."

Her mother laughed. "Do you know what your sister Sophie is doing now?"

Her half sister, Sophie, had been the apple of her mother's eye since the day she was born. "No, tell me."

"She's at Marquette University with a full scholarship."

"That's great."

"Yes. She's studying hard and doing an excellent job of keeping up a high GPA. She's going to medical school, you know."

"No, I didn't know."

"And do you know why that is?"

"Why?" asked Beth, although she knew what the answer would be.

"Because she didn't get pregnant and throw everything away to marry a man who hadn't even finished school himself."

This was a disaster. "I guess I shouldn't have called."

But her mother didn't hear. She steamrolled on. "Of all people, Beth, one would think you would know better. You saw how your father and I ended up."

"That doesn't mean that it will be the same for Scott and me."

Her mother laughed. "You'll see Beth. You haven't been married that long. But one day it will happen."

"What will happen?"

"You'll both realize all you gave up for a few moments of pleasure. And then the resentment will begin."

"You resented me?"

"I resented your father and he resented me. It got so I couldn't even look at him without thinking of all that I'd given up. I could have had a career, or I could have at least married better."

"Scott isn't like that."

"Oh, you think so now. But one day he'll look at you and only think *what could have been* in his life. I know it."

"It doesn't have to be that way," whispered Beth, but she was thinking about how Scott had left for her sake and how his father hated him for it. If she hadn't gotten in the way, maybe Hal and Scott would have made their peace long ago. If Scott ever realized. . . .

"Do you have anything else to say to me?"

"No," Beth answered her mother. "I thought you might regret that we lost touch, but I guess I was wrong. Good-bye."

Her mother's words had haunted her ever since, eating at her heart like acid. She remembered acutely what it felt like to be unwanted by her own family. She wished she'd never called her mother, but it was too late now.

She considered calling her father, but after the dismal failure of her first phone call, Beth didn't have the courage. She wished her Grandma Jane was still alive. She'd have known exactly what to say to help Beth put things in perspective.

But she wasn't, and her mother's words haunted her. Today, she was going to be with Scott, Beth reminded herself. It wasn't the time to give in to insecurity and doubt. She'd ruin everything before they'd even reached the resort.

Beth pulled her thoughts back to the present as she smoothed the shirt down over Risa. "Your daddy will be so happy to see you."

Risa clapped her hands and smiled.

Scott pulled into the driveway while Beth was still piling their luggage by the door. He came in and swept her up into a huge hug, spinning her around. When he put her down, he kissed her and whispered in her ear, "I missed you, Beth. . . ." His voice was hoarse with emotion.

Then he turned to Risa. She was holding her arms out for him. He swung her up and around, too. And she giggled and laughed wildly.

Beth was glad to have a moment to collect herself. She hated that her heartbeat sped up the moment he'd walked in the door. His kiss left her feeling dizzy and confused.

Scott kissed Risa on the cheek. "Have you been a good girl for Mommy?"

Risa nodded and reached out to touch his cheek. "Daddy," she said clearly.

Beth gasped. "She's never said that before."

A new word was always a big accomplishment for Risa, and this word more so than usual. Scott looked immensely pleased and Beth understood. She remembered how excited she'd been the first time Risa called her "Mama."

He hugged Risa again. "It's good to hear you say that."

They looked so right together. Where did she fit in? Beth wondered. Panic suddenly assailed her.

"I . . . I want to make sure I've got everything," she said suddenly. "I'll be right back." Bolting up the stairs and into her bedroom, she closed the door behind her and sank to the floor.

Scott and Risa — she loved them both so much. She wanted them to be a family. She wanted it with all her heart. But her mother's words kept echoing in her ears — "But one day he'll look at you and only think *what could have been* in his life."

This situation had the potential to be the emotional equivalent of a train wreck. Beth leaned back against the door and took several deep breaths. You're overreacting, she told herself.

Soon Scott was at the door, knocking. "Are you ready, Beth?"

"Yes. I'll . . . I'll be right down."

"Okay. I'm going to put the bags in the car."

She was supposed to be making sure she hadn't forgotten anything, Beth remembered. Scanning the room, Beth's eyes rested on her grandmother's picture. One of Grandma Jane's favorite sayings was "Love never fails."

Grandma usually had a lot to say about love, especially about it conquering all. One year at Christmas she had given Beth a satin bookmark with that saying embroidered into it in tiny precise letters. Beth scrambled to her feet and went to the bookshelf. There it was, sticking out of her copy of Jane Austen's *Persuasion*.

She hoped remembering Grandma Jane's advice would help her blot out her mother's hurtful words. Beth took the book and went back downstairs, resolving that she wouldn't let this fear keep her from trying to make her marriage work.

Scott was waiting for her at the door, holding Risa. His smile made her heart flip over in her chest. She held up the book. "I wanted to read this again while I'm on vacation," she offered as an excuse.

"Haven't you read that one a million times already?"

"Well, this will make it a million and one."

She meant to sail confidently past him and out the door, but he caught her with his free hand and kissed her again. "I don't know how I lived without you for so long."

He'd been in the house ten minutes and already he'd turned her insides into a pile of mush. "I don't know, you seem to have survived."

"Let's just make sure I don't have to survive without you again. That's my intention." The words were light, but his face was serious.

She couldn't meet his eyes. "We'd better get going. We can't get there if we don't get started," Beth reminded him.

"You're right, let's go. I can't wait for you to see the resort."

Beth took one more quick look around the house to make sure everything was turned off, then she followed Scott and Risa out to his SUV.

The trip north was uneventful. Risa fell asleep before long, and Beth joined her soon after. She had wanted to spend the trip talking to Scott, but she'd stayed up late packing and getting the house ready for their absence. When she'd finally gone to bed the night before, she hadn't been able to sleep. She was too nervous.

So the smooth rocking of the car and the white noise sound of the wind soon had Beth sleeping as soundly as Risa.

A while later Beth shook her head to wake herself up. "Guess I needed a catnap. Where are we?"

"We've passed through Wausau and we're almost to Rhinelander. Do you want to stop to eat?"

She looked back at the still-sleeping Risa. "Maybe we should wake Risa up. If we let her sleep all the way to the resort, she may be awake all night."

For dinner, they stopped at a small family restaurant just off one of the exits. Beth's stomach was too full of butterflies to eat much, so she settled for a salad while Scott had a burger and fries. Risa was happy with chicken nuggets and a dish of applesauce.

They were back on the road again quickly.

It was around eight o'clock and growing dark when they reached the resort. Scott took them in on the private driveway that led to the employees' residences. "I don't want to share you tonight," he explained. "Tomorrow I'll introduce you to everyone and show you around. Tonight is just for the three of us."

Beth liked the sound of that so she didn't argue. Scott pulled up in front of a log-cabin style cottage and shut off the SUV. He pulled out some of the luggage while Beth took Risa from her car seat. She looked around in the dark trying to make out the buildings.

"This is Daddy's house," Beth told her as they climbed the steps to the porch. Scott was already unlocking the door. He opened it and motioned for Beth and Risa to go through ahead of him. They stepped into a small foyer. She could see the living room to the left and a stairway began on the right. Scott put the suitcases down next to the door. "Let me show you around," he said, "then I'll get the rest of your things."

The cottage was small. The foyer gave way to a great room. It had a kitchen, dining area and a sitting area with a fieldstone fireplace. The whole room had huge windows that overlooked the lake. A door on one side opened out to a deck. A perfect place to sit at night and count the stars, thought Beth. The rest of the first floor contained a utility room and a bathroom.

"Now for the second floor." Scott picked up Risa and carried her up the stairs. "This is your room, kiddo," he told her, putting her down. He opened the door and turned on the light.

Risa's face lit up. She rushed into the room and Scott motioned for Beth to go in.

Her mouth dropped open and no sound came out. Beth was absolutely speechless. The room was filled with the most girly stuff imaginable. There was a toddler bed with a pink canopy and matching comforter. There were teddy bears and dolls and a small vanity with a mirror.

"Scott, I can't believe this," she cried. "Did you pick all this out?"

"Well, not exactly. I'd never do this well. I asked Cindy, one of the restaurant managers, and her daughter, Shannon, to help me. I wanted it to be special for Risa."

Beth hugged him. She couldn't believe he'd thought of this. It must have cost a fortune, too.

He hugged her back until he felt Risa tug on his pants leg. Scott let go of Beth and scooped up his little girl. "What do you think of your room?" he asked.

Risa made the sign for thank you, then she hugged him tightly.

Tears came to Beth's eyes and she moved back out into the hall to give them a moment. Scott put Risa down and she hurried back to the toys.

"Where will I be staying?" she asked. They hadn't discussed this before. Would he still expect them to sleep in separate rooms or had he only planned for one?

"This way, my lady." Risa was making the acquaintance of all the stuffed animals and Beth decided she would be okay while he took her down the hall.

He opened the door to another bedroom. This one was larger than Risa's and simply furnished with a large, rustic-style bed, nightstands and twin dressers.

"I hope you don't mind, but I didn't do anything to fix it up. I thought you might like to do your own decorating."

Beth felt a stab of disappointment even though she knew what he said made sense. But she couldn't help wondering if he'd made the effort to make Risa's room special because she was the one he truly wanted here. "It's fine. Where are you going to be sleeping?"

"The sofa bed downstairs is comfortable," he said without hesitation. Had he anticipated sleeping down there?

"Is this your room? I hate to kick you out," protested Beth.

He gave her a lopsided grin. "I hope it won't be for too long."

Beth felt herself grow warm with embarrassment, and maybe something more. This frustrated her. She didn't want to feel like this with so many doubts about Scott still buzzing in her head.

"There's one more room you need to see."

"The bathroom? I think I can figure out where that is."

"Besides the bathroom."

Beth was puzzled, but she followed him back into the hall. Scott stopped in front of the last door. "This used to be my room when Henry was alive. After I moved into Henry's room I kept this room as sort of an office. But I don't really need it anymore, so. . . ."

Scott opened the door. It was sparsely furnished and had a large window that let in the moonlight. In the middle of the floor sat an upright piano.

Speechless again, she walked forward slowly and touched one key, listening to it ring out in the stillness.

159

"I noticed you didn't have a piano any-more."

Beth shook her head. "I had to sell it when Risa and I were first starting out. I couldn't make the rent one month."

"I want you to play again."

This was possibly the nicest thing anyone had ever done for her. Beth went forward cautiously and sat down at the keyboard. She was afraid to touch the keys. "It's been so long since I played."

"There's music in the bench. If it's not to your taste, we can get more."

Beth got up again and lifted the lid on the bench. On top of the stacks of sheet music was a book of songs from *Pirates of Penzance.*

"I'll go check on Risa," said Scott. He went out and shut the door behind him.

Beth took out the book of songs and laid it on the piano. Slowly she reached out and touched the keys of the piano. She did a few warm-up exercises she'd done so many times that her fingers remembered them even years after she'd last played. Then she began to pick out a simple tune, "Jesus loves me." It was one of the first songs she'd learned as a child. From there she worked up to a few slightly more difficult pieces she remembered. She'd just started to pick her way through "Climbing over a Rocky Mountain" from the *Pirates of Penzance* book when Scott came back with a pajama-clad Risa.

"Is it that late?" asked Beth, startled. "I'm sorry, I should have helped."

"No big deal," said Scott. "Do you like it?"

"I love it." She jumped up and hugged Scott. "I can't believe you thought of this."

"Mommy, bed?" Risa broke in.

"Yes, honey, it's time for bed." Beth hugged her and kissed her little girl good night.

"I'll tuck her in," said Scott. "You stay as long as you like."

Beth didn't stay too much longer. She didn't want the sounds from the piano to keep Risa awake. But she did sort through all the music Scott had put together. Many of the pieces she remembered playing for him. And *he'd* remembered. It couldn't be coincidence.

Beth closed the piano bench with a prayer on her lips. "Thank you, God, for this second chance. Don't let me mess it up again."

When Scott woke up the next morning, the sun was just starting to lighten the sky. He folded up the sofa bed and put away the comforter and pillows, started the coffee-maker and then took a shower. When he was dressed and ready for the day he returned to the kitchen, poured himself a cup of coffee and took it out on the deck. It looked like it would be a perfect early-June day.

He sat in one of the plastic deck chairs and sipped his coffee. It was good to know that Beth and Risa were here, but he also appreciated the chance to have a few quiet moments before the busy day began.

The sun was starting to rise above the trees when Beth came out onto the deck, her own mug of coffee in her hand.

"Hi," she said shyly, slipping into the chair next to him. Her long brown hair was still wet from the shower. She set her mug on the deck and began braiding it. "It's beautiful out here," she commented. "No wonder you love living here."

Scott reached out to touch her cheek. "It has its advantages."

She flushed when he touched her and he felt an answering stir within. Abruptly he dropped his hand and went back to concentrating on his coffee.

Beth finished braiding her hair and picked her mug up. "So, what's on the agenda today?"

"I'd like to introduce you to everyone, starting with Cindy and Ben. They run the restaurant here. During the off-season, the restaurant is only open for supper during the week and brunch and supper on weekends. Now that the summer season is starting it will be open for three meals, seven days a week."

"Is Cindy the one you asked to help with Risa's room?"

"Yes. Ben and Cindy have been here for years. Their daughter, Shannon, waits tables in the restaurant. Their sons, Sam and Shaun, should be coming home from college soon. They help out, too."

"Are you close to them?"

"Yeah, they're like family to me."

Beth nodded. "Who else works here year-round?"

"There's Veronica, or Ronnie, as she likes to be called. She runs the front desk and oversees housekeeping. Fred is in charge of boat rental in the summer and hanging around to drive me nuts the rest of the year."

"What?"

"Fred is retired. He only works here because he wants something to do and because he has a huge crush on Ronnie. So when he isn't working, he's usually here anyway. He's a font of endless advice." Scott rolled his eyes to show what he thought of Fred's wisdom.

Beth laughed. "He sounds like a character."

"I'd never have the heart to tell him he can't hang around, as much as he drives me crazy. His grandson is coming up to help with groundskeeping this summer. He's never been here before, so I hope that all works out."

Beth's stomach interrupted with a loud growl. She clapped her hand over it. "Sorry."

Scott grinned at her embarrassment. "That's what you get for only ordering a salad last night."

"What about breakfast?"

"I thought we'd go to the restaurant. We can cook here, but for our first day we should do something special."

Beth looked at her watch. "It's getting late. I'll get Risa going. We'll be ready in a jiffy."

"Do you want any help?"

"Nope. I've got it all under control."

Beth hurried back inside and Scott waited impatiently. He was anxious to show Beth and Risa around and introduce them to what he thought of as "the resort family." He hoped that once she got the whole picture, Beth would understand why he wanted to stay. And then he'd convince her that she wanted to stay, too.

CHAPTER 9

The three of them walked over to the restaurant, holding hands, with Risa in the middle. When the path got a little rough, Scott picked Risa up and moved closer to Beth, putting his free arm around her shoulder. His body was warm and solid, comforting in the chilly morning air. She slipped an arm around his waist, happy for the moment just to appreciate being with Scott.

They came out of the woods on a small rise. The resort was laid out before them. All of the buildings were built in the log-cabin style popular in the north woods. The lodge was large and imposing, a two-story building with a wraparound porch and lots of floor-to-ceiling windows. Behind it, the lake shimmered in the morning light. The surrounding pines really did give the water the emerald color the lake was named for. On one side of the lodge, a row of smaller cabins was strung out along the lakeshore. Though it was surrounded by woods, there was neatly mowed lawn around the lodge, cabins, and children's playground.

"It's beautiful, Scott," said Beth.

"Thank you. I think so."

When Risa saw the playground she pointed and tried to squirm out of Scott's hold.

"No, sweetie," Beth told her. "Breakfast first."

The little girl let out a pitiful wail and tears slid down her cheeks.

Scott caved. "Maybe just a few minutes."

"She needs breakfast. You can't give in to her on every little whim, Scott." Beth took Risa from him. "Do you want a pancake, honey? We can play later. Let's eat now."

"It's not a big deal," Scott protested.

"It will be when you have a hungry, cranky toddler on your hands."

"A few minutes won't hurt."

This was one aspect of co-parenting that she hadn't encountered before. Beth had liked the idea of having someone to help her make decisions. But she hadn't thought about what would happen if they disagreed.

"You're right," she said, as calmly as possible. "But if you let her go on the playground, I can guarantee that you won't get her off without a major battle. A few tears are nothing compared to that."

He didn't look like he was buying it, so Beth added, "Please, Scott, trust my experience on this one."

After a moment, he nodded. "All right." To Risa he made the sign for eat. "Let's go get some breakfast, kiddo."

Risa's sobs slowed and tapered off all together before they'd gone much farther.

As they entered the lodge, Beth noted that the rustic theme continued inside. Gleaming wood was everywhere. They passed through the lobby and stopped at the entrance to the restaurant. A short, pleasantly plump woman with her black hair in a tidy bun greeted them.

"Hi, Scott. This must be Beth and Risa. We're so pleased you're here," said the woman, taking Beth's hand.

"Thank you. I'm glad to be here." Beth attempted a smile. She remembered what Scott had said about these people being like family to him and wanted to make a good impression.

"Beth, this is Cindy," said Scott. "Remember I told you she and her husband, Ben, run the restaurant."

Recognition of the name sparked a true smile from Beth. "You chose the things for

Risa's room, didn't you? She loves it."

"Shannon and I had fun picking it out." Cindy held out her arms and Risa went from Scott's hold to hers.

Cindy hugged her. "Risa, I'm so glad you're staying with us." A teardrop had clung to her cheek and Cindy noticed. "Have you been crying?"

Risa nodded and Scott explained.

"That's okay," Cindy assured Risa. "There will be plenty of time for playing later. Are you hungry?"

Risa nodded again and made the sign for "eat." Scott translated for Cindy.

"Well, I guess we'd better stop standing around talking then. We reserved a table." Cindy led them to the back of the restaurant.

"Cindy, you didn't have to . . . ," began Scott but she waved his concerns away.

"It's Beth and Risa's first day. We thought a family breakfast was in order."

At a long table toward the back of the restaurant sat three teenagers, an elderly lady with blue-tinted hair and an elderly man in a fishing vest.

Cindy set Risa in a booster seat and said, "I'll go get Ben."

Scott smiled at the assembled "family." "Everyone, I'd like you to meet my wife,

Beth, and my daughter, Risa. Ladies, this is Fred," he said, starting with the man in fishing gear. He continued with the older lady. "This is Ronnie, and these three are Ben and Cindy's children: Shannon, and the twins, Shaun and Sam."

Beth smiled shyly at them. "I'm pleased to meet you."

Similar greetings chorused back at her. Scott held her chair out and Beth sat down next to Risa. Scott took the seat beside her. As he was sitting, Cindy came back with her husband in tow. Ben was a tall, burly man. Cindy's head barely came up to his chest. He took Beth's hand in one giant, bear-like paw and shook it heartily. "Glad to have you with us, Beth. Good to know someone out there would have this guy. Maybe there's hope for my sons yet."

Shannon rolled her eyes. "I doubt it." She had her father's auburn hair but none of his bulk.

"When did you two get in?" asked Scott of the twins.

The one he'd introduced as Shaun answered. "Last night. We saw lights on at your place, but we figured you were busy."

"We could have used you two last week," said Ben, "when Scott and I were cleaning up the mess from that storm."

"How bad was it?" asked Sam.

Scott replied, "One of the cottages needed a fair amount of work. The rest was minimal."

While they continued to discuss the storm and its damage, Beth studied the menu Cindy had given her. No one else seemed to need one.

She was brought back into the conversation when she heard Ben say, "And as if taking care of all that mess weren't enough, Scott insisted we go out and buy a piano."

"A piano?" asked one of the twins. Beth wasn't sure which one was which. They had to be identical. Both were tall and slim with thick manes of dark hair. "What do you need a piano for? Are you going to hire someone to play in the restaurant? A little dinner music."

"No," the other twin argued. "He's going to take lessons and become a concert pianist as a second career."

"Ha-ha," Scott said. "It's for Beth."

"The piano is beautiful. I love it," Beth hurried to say.

He put an arm around her shoulder. "It was good to hear you play again last night."

"She'd better like it," grumbled Ben, "after we went through all the work of getting it upstairs."

"Don't mind him," Cindy said with a reproachful look at her husband. "He's always a bear before he gets his breakfast."

"I don't mind," Beth told her. To Ben she said, "Thank you for helping Scott."

While complaining seemed to come naturally to the big man, accepting compliments was more difficult. She just barely caught his mumbled reply. "I guess it wasn't that much trouble."

"Will you play for us sometime?" asked Cindy.

"I haven't played in a long time," she admitted. "I need some practice first."

An argument broke out between the twins and Shannon. Cindy defused it. Fred announced his intention of having the fisherman's breakfast and Ronnie scolded him for eating so much fried food. Beth went back to her menu, letting the banter from everyone else wash over her. It was obvious that they all knew each other well and cared about each other. They *were* like a family.

A waitress, painfully new at her job, took their order. Cindy was patient with her, repeating everyone's choices to make sure the girl got it all down and giving her an encouraging smile before she headed back to the kitchen.

"It's that time of year," she explained.

"We're training all the summer help. Sam and Shaun, do you remember how things work or will we have to break you in all over again?"

"No," Shaun assured his mother. "Sam and I are ready to report for duty this morning."

"Good," said Ben. "We can start you out washing dishes."

The brothers groaned and slumped in their chairs.

"When's your grandson coming, Fred?" asked Scott.

"He should be here in a couple of days."

Their food arrived and conversation was abandoned momentarily in favor of eating the fluffy scrambled eggs, crisp bacon, pancakes and other breakfast fare. The food was plentiful and delicious. Beth wondered if she'd need bigger clothes by the time she returned to Green Bay. If she returned, she reminded herself.

After breakfast Shannon offered to take Risa to the playground so Scott could continue showing Beth around. "Thank you, Shannon," said Beth. "That's very nice of you."

"I love kids," Shannon answered. "I want to be a teacher someday."

"You can have Risa anytime you want to

173

practice," Scott assured her.

"What about us?" demanded Shaun, who Beth began to see was the more outgoing twin. "We can babysit."

"Right now you two have dishes to do," Cindy reminded them.

With double groans the boys got up and began clearing the table. "You're really going to make them work on their first day home?" asked Beth.

"If you saw the mountain of laundry they brought home for me to do, you'd put them to work, too." Cindy laughed. "It's only fair."

Beth smiled. "I guess when you put it that way. . . ."

Fred and Ben declared they needed to get to work, too. As they were walking away from the table, Fred was giving Ben suggestions on some changes for the summer menu. Scott looked at Beth as if to say, "See, I told you."

"Scott," asked Ronnie, "are you going to monopolize Beth all day?"

"It's her first day here. I wanted to show her around."

"Yes, but Cindy and I would like to have lunch with her, just us girls."

"Oh, thank you. That sounds like fun," said Beth.

"All right," Scott conceded. "I want to spend the morning with her, but you can have her for lunch."

The reluctance in his voice caused Cindy to laugh. "For heaven's sake, Scott, Beth can't spend every minute of the day with you. You'll have plenty of time to enjoy her company."

Scott stood and taking her hand, pulled Beth away from the table with him. "Let's go before Risa gets tired of the playground and wants her mommy. Then I won't get any time alone with you."

Beth smiled at his comment and called a "See you later," over her shoulder to the women.

"I can't believe how gorgeous everything is here," Beth told him as they strolled past the cottages. "You must have done a great job fixing things up."

Scott shrugged, attempting to hide the pride he felt. "I've always liked working with my hands. I kind of miss it now that I'm the manager."

"Your dad will be so proud of you when he sees all this."

"Maybe. I didn't get a chance to show my skills working at the dealership. Do you think he will even come here?"

She slipped her arm around his waist. "Of course he will. He loves you."

"Does he? It's hard to tell."

"Well, he'll have to come here if he wants to be at Risa's birthday party, won't he?" Beth pointed out.

"I guess so." Scott looked around him, trying to see the resort through his father's critical eyes. Would his dad be impressed? Could he possibly do something right? "I always hire lifeguards and all boaters are required to wear floatation vests. He should approve of that."

"What?" Beth was confused by the seemingly abrupt change of subject.

"Because Dave died in a water-related accident."

"Oh."

Scott felt his spirits taking a nosedive as they always did when he thought about his father and his brother. This wasn't how he wanted to spend his first day with Beth.

"Let's walk along the lake," he suggested. "There's a nice path there."

Scott took Beth's hand and led her to a blacktopped path that meandered along the lake. She took a deep breath. "The pines smell heavenly."

"Are you ready to pack up your stuff and move up here permanently?"

She looked surprised. "I haven't even been here for a whole day yet."

"I know. I guess I was just hoping the whole place would just blow you away and you'd never want to leave."

"That's how you feel about the resort, isn't it?"

"Yeah, I guess it is. But I also want to live with you and Risa."

"I wish I could say yes, Scott, but this is all moving so fast. A month ago I had no idea where you were. I had no reason to think I'd ever see you again, or if you were even alive."

"I'm sorry, Beth. You're right. You shouldn't rush into anything." His heart felt like it was being squeezed by a giant fist. He was sure about wanting her here. He wanted to press her to renew their commitment, but she had to be sure of it, too.

He was confused. He thought she'd seemed ready to recommit to their marriage that last night they'd spent together at her place. Everything had been going so well. And that last night she'd even wanted to . . . but maybe she'd just been afraid that he wouldn't keep his promise and return. She seemed more distant than she had before.

They came upon a bench strategically placed so walkers could rest and look out over the lake. "Do you want to sit a while?" asked Scott.

Beth sat down. "I'm not really tired, but I don't mind soaking up some of the scenery. We shouldn't leave Risa with Shannon too long, though."

Scott sat down next to her and put his arm around her shoulders. A wisp of hair had escaped from her braid and he tucked it behind her ear.

A smile flitted across her face. "I thought we were looking at the scenery."

He kissed her neck. "I am."

Beth turned to look at him. "Somehow I don't think we're looking at the same scenery."

Maybe this wouldn't work out, but he'd be a fool not to give it his best shot. He kissed her lips. "I just know I like what I see." He kissed her again, longer this time.

The sound of voices jolted them back to reality.

"Look at that display, Sam, and in a public place, too."

"I thought grownups were supposed to set a good example."

Scott looked up at the twins approaching on the path. "And I thought you two were supposed to be doing dishes."

Shaun shrugged. "We're fast workers."

"And besides, we were driving Mom crazy," added Sam. "She said you should find something for us to do. Preferably separate jobs. I don't know why she said that, though."

Scott thought for a moment, and then he said, "Sam, can you go help Fred take an inventory of the boating equipment and see if anything needs to be repaired or replaced. Shaun, you go see if Ronnie needs help stocking shelves in the canteen."

Both boys groaned. "I told you we should have stayed at school for a few more days," Shaun said.

"If you don't like those jobs, I have others. I believe there's some landscaping work that needs to be done."

"No, no," insisted Sam. "We're fine."

"Right," agreed Shaun. "No need to look any further."

"I didn't think so."

Shaun let out a theatrical sigh. "There's no rest for the wicked, Sam. We'd better get going."

But Sam paused for a moment and said to Beth, who was still trying to regain her composure after their teasing, "I'm sorry if we embarrassed you, Beth. We always kid around with Scott. But we're glad you're here."

Surprised at his sensitivity, Beth could only stammer her thanks. Then the boys took off at a jog, back toward the lodge.

"Don't mind them," said Scott. "They didn't mean any harm."

"I'm sure they're just normal teenage boys. It was nice of the one to apologize."

"That's Sam. He's the quiet one. It won't be long before you can tell them apart."

"You really do operate like a family here. Scott, you sounded just like a big brother. And breakfast this morning was great."

"And so was dessert."

"Dessert? You don't have dessert with breakfast."

Scott pulled her back into his arms. "Really? I did, and I think I'd like seconds."

"Maybe we shouldn't. . . ."

He stopped her protests with a kiss, but this time he knew better than to linger. He wasn't a teenager anymore but being with Beth tested his self-control. Still, making out on park benches wasn't appropriate. "Just enough to hold me until later," he teased, enjoying the look on Beth's face.

Scott got to his feet and Beth followed. "Come on, let's finish our walk."

Beth was sorry to end her time with Scott, but she did want to have lunch with Cindy and Ronnie. They collected Risa from Shannon and walked to the lodge where both women waited for her, purses in their laps. "Aren't we eating here?" she asked.

"No way. Scott would just hang around and we wouldn't be able to talk about him," insisted Ronnie. "We'll go to Chloe Belle's Café."

"So you *can* talk about me?" asked Scott with mock indignation.

"We wanted to show Beth a little of the town," explained Cindy. Then she grinned. "And talk about you."

Scott manufactured a scowl for Cindy. "Ha, ha, very funny."

"I'll just run up to the cottage and grab my purse," said Beth. "Am I dressed all right?"

"You look fine," Ronnie assured Beth. "And you won't need your purse. It's our treat today."

"Oh. Thank you. What about Risa? She got a bit grubby this morning. I should change her."

"Risa's not going," said Scott. "She can eat with me. Then she can sit in my office and color while I do paperwork."

"If you think you can handle her and work, all right. But make sure she doesn't eat the crayons."

Scott swung Risa up in the air. "You wouldn't do that, would you, kiddo?" Her response was a pleased giggle.

"We're not getting any younger here," Ronnie pointed out. "I'd like to get going before all the good tables are taken."

Scott and Risa kissed Beth. "Have a good time," he told her.

The women headed out into the small town nearest to the resort. The sign at the outskirts read,

Spruce Point, Population 464

"This really is a small town," exclaimed Beth.

"Just the right size," Ronnie said firmly.

Chloe Belle's Café was on Main Street, along with a gas station, a pharmacy, a bank, a grocery store, and a hardware store. Cindy informed her that this was pretty much it as far as businesses were concerned.

The restaurant was small, but busy. The women sat down at a circular table rather than one of the vinyl-covered, bright-orange booths. They were lucky to get any table at all. The restaurant was filled with people and the noise from their chatter. Large windows let in the sunshine, lending a bit of cheer to the faded curtains and scuffed linoleum floor. The walls were decorated with different types of saw blades, painted with country landscapes.

"Chloe's husband does those," Ronnie told Beth. "He's very talented."

"At least they're very popular with the tourists," Cindy added. "A little bit of rustic folk art to remind them of their vacation."

A waitress came over with menus and glasses of water. She recited the soups of the day and the pies that were available, and left. They were ready to order when she came back a few minutes later.

Once orders had been taken, Beth felt a wave of shyness roll over her. She didn't know what to say to these women.

"I don't believe in beating around the bush," declared Ronnie, patting her blue-tinted curls. "We're here to check you out and to give you a chance to do the same with us."

Cindy frowned. "Full of tact as usual, Ronnie. I'm not sure Beth picked up on your subtlety."

"It's okay." Beth fiddled with her silverware. "I guess it's better to just be up-front about it. My situation with Scott is . . . unusual. I can tell you care about him a lot and if I were in your shoes, I'd want to check me out, too."

Ronnie beamed at her. "Well said. I can already tell she's a good one, Cindy."

Cindy threw up her hands. "I guess it's a day for plain speaking. I may as well join in."

Beth waited expectantly as Cindy gathered her words. "Scott told us a little about you, but he didn't mention how the two of you happened to get married so young or why you split up. I admit I'm dying of curiosity. But if you don't want to tell us, that's okay, too."

Beth took a deep breath and nodded. She didn't usually blurt out her personal problems to relative strangers — or even to those she was close to, but she decided to make an exception. These women were family to Scott and she didn't want to start out on the wrong foot. There were some things she could share and maybe in return they could give her some advice.

"We met in college, fell in love and . . . I got pregnant."

Beth was not surprised when the women exchanged looks that clearly said "I told you so."

"Of course Scott married me. He thought it was the right thing to do — we both did — and you must know Scott always does what he thinks is honorable."

Cindy nodded. "Yes, an impressive quality in one so young."

"It was an awful time. Our parents were furious. Scott dropped out of school and went to work for his dad, but he hated it. My parents practically disowned me and refused to pay for my tuition anymore so I had to quit school, too."

Beth paused. She hadn't ever told anyone the whole story like this and it was unexpectedly painful after all this time. "Then I lost the baby."

Cindy's eyes filled with sympathy and Ronnie took Beth's hand.

She used her other hand to wipe away a tear. "It was too much for me. I felt like I'd ruined both of our lives. My parents wouldn't talk to me. My in-laws didn't like me. Scott was stuck with a job he hated and. . . ."

"And a wife he didn't want? Is that what you thought?" asked Cindy.

Beth nodded. "And now we wouldn't even have the baby," she said, when she could swallow the lump in her throat.

"Wait a minute," said Ronnie. "If you lost the baby, where did Risa come from? It's not hard to tell she's Scott's daughter."

"I was pregnant again when Scott left, but he didn't know. I found out just that day and when I went home to tell him. . . ."

"He was gone?" For someone who didn't know the story, Cindy was sure good at filling in the blanks.

"But I don't blame him for leaving," Beth added hastily. "I was impossible to live with then. And he says he did it because he thought if we weren't married anymore my parents would pay for me to go back to school."

"Do you believe him?" asked Ronnie.

Beth nodded. "It's the kind of thing Scott would do."

Cindy agreed. "It does sound like him."

"Then when he showed up again a few weeks ago, I was shocked. I couldn't believe he wanted to give our marriage a second chance. I know most women would be furious, but. . . ."

"But you still love him?" Cindy finished for her again.

Beth nodded.

"That's great," exclaimed Ronnie. "So what's the problem?"

Cindy studied Beth. "She doesn't know if Scott really loves her, or if he's just being noble again."

"What?" asked Ronnie.

Cindy explained. "Does he want to stay married because he inherited the resort and he feels it's his duty to share it with her or. . . ."

"Or is it for Risa?" This time Beth finished for Cindy. "You probably know Scott better than I do, after our being apart for so long. What do you think?"

Ronnie shrugged. "The man is willing to take responsibility for his wife and child. He's obviously trying hard to make you happy. I'd say who cares what's behind it."

"Ronnie." Cindy shook her head. "You can't fool me. I know you're a romantic at heart. You'd never settle for a loveless marriage."

"Maybe, but there's something to be said for security, too," Ronnie argued.

"This isn't helping," Beth interrupted. "How can I tell if Scott loves me or not? Or if our marriage will work or not!"

"Well it's obvious that Scott loves you," said Cindy. "But there are no guarantees on any marriage working out. Ben and I have been married over twenty years and we still go through rough patches. It's still possible that one of those rough patches may turn into an irresolvable problem."

"Great." Beth moaned and laid her head on her arms.

"You're dwelling on this too much," Ronnie told her. "Just relax and see what happens."

Unbidden, memories of her parents' divorce came to mind. To her, their relationship had ended in a jumble of arguments and slammed doors. After the divorce, Mom moved to one house and Dad to another. She was constantly shuttled between, never feeling she had a home at either place. Her parents' bitterness toward each other had remained long after they split up, so that each time she had to decide where to spend a holiday or who to ask to a school event she would inevitably hurt the feelings of one of them. It was a terrible position to put a child in.

Forcing a smile, Beth agreed with Ronnie in order to end the conversation. She told herself she never should have confided in them. Ronnie and Cindy obviously didn't understand. They probably came from picture-perfect families themselves.

The conversation turned to small talk and Beth intentionally kept her answers light. Cindy and Ronnie asked about her life in Green Bay, so she told them about her job and related a few stories about some of the more eccentric customers she'd ended up dealing with.

All three women had ordered the special, a BLT with fries and a free dessert. They dug into their lunches enthusiastically. Even Beth found she was hungry, which she hadn't thought possible after the huge breakfast she'd eaten at the resort. She must have worked up an appetite again walking around with Scott that morning.

Finally Beth pushed her plate away. "I'm stuffed. I can't finish this, even though it's delicious."

"It's the mark of a small-town restaurant," Ronnie said. "They always have big portions and small prices."

"Maybe we should be getting back. Risa is probably driving Scott nuts by now. Thank you for lunch. I hope I passed inspection."

"Of course you did, honey," Cindy assured her. "Scott has been walking on air since he got back from vacation. You've made him so happy."

"And we're all for keeping the boss happy," Ronnie finished with a wink.

"We'd want Scott to be happy even if he weren't the boss," said Cindy. "He's a great guy and we're glad Henry left him the resort. Ben and I have been here for years and we've put up with some horrible managers."

"We did wonder about Scott a bit," confided Ronnie, "because it wasn't for lack of opportunity that he wasn't dating. There were plenty of guests as well as local girls that would have liked to stake a claim with him. But when we found out about you, it all made sense."

"Really? He never dated?" Beth wished she could hide the relief she felt at this disclosure, but these women were too astute to miss it. "Not that I would have blamed him . . . but it's good to know that he didn't. I mean, we were still married."

Ronnie laughed. "You have nothing to worry about. After seeing you two together this morning, I can assure you, that boy only has eyes for you."

Beth lowered her gaze to hide the pleasure that statement brought her. "Sometimes I still think this is a dream and I'll wake up and realize I have no idea where he is."

Leaning over, Cindy took Beth's hand and gave it a squeeze. "Oh, honey, this is no dream. Scott is one-hundred-percent real."

"Good," Beth said, returning the squeeze. "Because I think I'm going to like it here."

Maybe there was hope for her and Scott after all.

CHAPTER 10

Scott took Risa home and made lunch for her and himself. Afterwards, they worked on stringing some colorful wooden beads on a string. He didn't want Beth to worry Risa was falling behind while she visited.

It was obviously not Risa's favorite activity. She kept trying to hide the beads behind her back. Scott had to laugh at her attempt to get out of the task, but he let her quit after a few minutes. He remembered what her therapist had said about not letting her get too frustrated. Then he gathered up a few toys, crayons and coloring books and they headed to the lodge.

Scott had to stop and let several employees meet Risa. They all wanted to hold her and talk to her and discuss how cute she was. It had never taken him so long to walk from the front door to his office, but this was the first chance he'd had to show his daughter off and he was enjoying every minute of it.

Once they finally made it into his office, Scott got Risa settled. The room was large enough to accommodate some comfortable chairs and a coffee table. He put Risa down by the coffee table and set out the crayons and coloring books. Then he went to his desk and pulled out some paperwork.

He'd barely gotten started when there was a knock on his door.

"Come in," Scott called.

Jean, one of the waitresses from the restaurant, stepped in. This was not one of the new recruits, but a sweet middle-aged lady who worked for them all year round. She carried a plate of cookies and a glass of milk.

"I thought your daughter might like a snack," Jean said.

"Well, we just had lunch," Scott replied, "but she might be hungry later."

"I'll leave this here then."

"All right. Thank you."

Jean set the plate and glass on his desk and then bent down to talk to Risa, who had toddled over to see their visitor. After a few minutes of baby talk, Jean went back to the restaurant.

Scott led Risa back to the coffee table and brought out one of the toys. Maybe she'd find that more interesting than the coloring book. Then it was back to his desk and the paperwork.

It didn't take long for Risa to become bored. She wandered over to the window and peered out. Soon she was giggling and Scott looked up to see what was so funny.

Sam and Shaun, were standing outside, making faces at Risa. She laughed and bounced with excitement. With a sigh, Scott got up and opened the window.

"What are you two supposed to be doing?" he asked.

"One of the housekeeping crew didn't show up so we volunteered to clean cottages," Shaun explained.

"Oh really? Isn't it sort of hard to clean them from here?"

"Well," amended Shaun, "we were going to clean them right after our break."

"And when does this break end?"

"I think it just did," replied Sam. "Sorry for interrupting, but we saw Risa there by the window. . . ."

"Yeah, I know," grumbled Scott. "And she's just too cute to resist."

Shaun shrugged. "Little kids are fun."

Sam, always the more responsible of the pair, pulled on his brother's arm. "Let's get started on that cleaning," he said.

After watching to make sure the twins

actually headed down the path toward the cottages, Scott shut the window and turned back to Risa. She lifted her arms, begging to be picked up.

How could he be mad at the twins, Scott thought as he lifted the little girl into his arms. I can't resist her either.

Risa sat with him at his desk for a few minutes, then got bored and climbed down. Scott, finally making some headway, assumed that she'd gone back to her toys and colors. But when he looked up a minute or so later, she was gone.

Scott vaulted out of his chair and did a circuit of the office. He noticed the door was open. Jean must not have shut it all the way when she left. He didn't usually shut his office door, so it might not have occurred to her to do it.

He sprinted out into the hallway and looked around. The sound of voices and laughter drew him toward the gift shop where he saw a group of his employees had gathered. By the oohs and aahs he was hearing, he guessed that Risa was in the center of that group.

The employees parted to let him into their circle. Just as he suspected, Risa was the cause of the commotion. She was sitting on the floor, several "Pine Away Inn" hats around her. She had a bucket-style hat on her head. It was so big it covered her eyes. Scott knelt down next to her and pushed the hat back on her head.

Risa was delighted to see him. "Daddy," she cried and threw her arms around his neck. There was a chorus of "aaaawwww" from the employees. How could he be angry at them for being drawn to his daughter? How could *they* not be? She turned his heart to mush just by smiling at him.

But they didn't need to know that. Scott rose, Risa in his arms and a stern look on his face. "I'm not paying you to stand around, am I? Let's get back to work."

The employees scattered and he took Risa back to the office, making sure the door was closed firmly this time. He gave in and let her have the cookie from Jean. It kept her attention longer than the coloring books and he finally had a few moments for his paperwork.

When Beth came back from her lunch date, she checked in with Scott. Buried under an avalanche of paperwork, he was a little relieved when she told him she would put Risa down for her nap and finish unpacking.

Risa was usually a bit uncooperative about

napping, but today she fell into her new bed and right into dreamland. The last couple of days had been unusually busy for her. No wonder she was tired out.

Beth meant to go to the bedroom and finish unpacking, but the piano in the room at the end of the hall called to her. She told herself she'd just stay a few minutes. The sound of the music coupled with the gorgeous view from the window and the fresh, pine-scented breeze wafting in had entranced her. Beth wasn't really aware of time passing until Risa toddled in with rumpled hair and sleepy eyes.

"Hey, sweetie," called Beth. "Did you have a good nap?"

She yawned and climbed up onto Beth's lap. "This is a piano. We used to have one a long time ago."

Risa leaned back against her mother and contemplated the instrument. She reached out a hand to touch and smiled at the noise it made. She leaned forward and was soon touching all the keys, making all the noise she could. Laughing, Beth pulled her daughter's hands back. "That's not exactly the way it should sound. Here, do this." Beth took one finger and touched the middle C, pressing down until it sounded. Risa looked at her mother, then down at the keys. She placed her right hand next to her mother's and tried to hit one key, though it came out as two.

Beth smiled at her daughter's attempt and squeezed Risa. The girl was such a joy to her.

She set Risa on her feet. "Come and help Mommy unpack."

Beth was just putting the last of Risa's clothes into her new dresser when she heard the door close and called out, "Scott, is that you?"

A few seconds later he stuck his head in the doorway of Risa's room. "Yes, it's me. Are you getting things done?"

She closed the bottom dresser drawer and stood up. "Yes, I'm just finishing. I had good intentions but I admit I could have gotten more done if I'd spent less time playing the piano. Thank you again."

She went into his arms for a hug and a kiss. "You're welcome," he answered.

"Well, I know how much pianos cost. You didn't have to spend all that money on me, you know."

"I know. But you love the piano. It bothered me that you didn't have one." He turned to greet Risa.

For supper, they made hamburgers on the

grill with salad and chips on the side.

"I got a phone call today," said Scott after they'd said grace and began passing serving dishes around. "The Early Childhood teacher from the Spruce Point School called me back. She said she would have returned my call sooner, but she was busy with the school year ending and all."

"You called the Early Childhood teacher about Risa?" Beth was surprised and not necessarily happy about this news.

"Yeah, almost as soon as I got back. I want to find out if Risa can get the services she needs here. That's going to be a big factor in deciding where we'll live."

He was right. They needed to know that. But Beth was still dreading Risa's leaving the Birth to Three program and she wasn't sure if she was ready to hear this yet.

"She can meet with us next week at the school. How does Wednesday sound?"

"Oh," said Beth, trying to dredge up some enthusiasm. "That's good, I guess."

"Was I wrong to do that?" asked Scott. "I thought you'd be happy."

"Of course, it's fine that you called. It's just . . . it's just that I'm worried about this transition from the Birth to Three program. Now the therapists come to us. After she turns three she'll be put into the school system. I can't imagine my baby going to school, with all those older kids. What if she's scared? What if she gets teased? It's . . . it's overwhelming." Her appetite deserted her and she pushed her plate away.

"Don't worry. She'll do fine." Scott squeezed Beth's hand. "Everything was new when she started the program, wasn't it?"

"Yes, but that's precisely why I came to count on those people. I know it sounds childish, but I don't want new teachers and new therapists. I like the ones we have."

"That's not an option though, no matter what happens."

"I know. I'm really trying not to let it bother me, but. . . ." She shook her head, not trusting herself to say more.

Scott squeezed her hand again. "We'll go see this teacher, Mrs. Gilly, next week. You'll feel better when you get to know her and you see the school Risa will be attending."

"Maybe." She looked at Risa, who was playing with her food more than she was eating it. "It's just that she's growing up so fast."

"I'm told children do that," he said with a smile.

"It's good that you set up the meeting. I would have put it off just because I don't want to think about it," Beth admitted.

Scott let the subject drop. They finished supper and Beth insisted on doing the dishes. "I didn't work today. You did."

"I'm not the one on vacation," Scott countered.

"Then why don't you go read to Risa. That counts as a chore, since it's good for her."

"That's not a chore," Scott argued.

"Believe me, when you've read the same book twenty times and she keeps asking for it again and again, you'll think it's a chore."

Scott gave up and took Risa to find a book. Beth was thankful for a few minutes alone. The idea of Risa starting school was scarier than she wanted to admit. She hated the idea of dropping her off and leaving her every day — or worse, of putting Risa on the school bus. Of course they didn't have to send Risa to school. But then what would they do for her therapies? Private therapists were very expensive and there was no way Risa could keep up her level of progress without some extra help. Beth sighed. It really seemed like she had no choice.

When they got home to Green Bay, she'd have to contact the school there, too. If she went home. Beth looked out the window. Through the trees she caught a sparkle from the lake. The sun was sinking in the west and all was peaceful. She could get used to living here. She could get used to living with Scott. But could she really give up everything and move here? She'd be leaving behind her home, her job, her friends, everything.

But by now she was convinced that Scott would never leave the resort. It was obvious that he loved everything about it. How could she even ask him to leave?

On Sunday, Scott suggested that they all go to church together. And he did mean "all." It turned out that Cindy and Ben and family went to the same church as Scott, as well as Ronnie and Fred.

Beth loved the small white church straddling the line where town ended and country began. On one side you could see houses and sidewalks. On the other side, the fields and pastures began. It was nice to have a few people she knew there as well. Shannon took Risa up for the children's sermon and Cindy introduced her to several young moms after the short service.

In the afternoon Scott took them to Rhinelander for lunch and a little sightseeing. Beth noticed that images of the famous Hodag, a mythical monster said to live in the area, were everywhere. It was a fun, carefree afternoon.

The next week started out much the same way. Scott had to work during the day but Beth had fun playing with Risa, getting reacquainted with the piano and getting to know the resort employees.

On Wednesday after lunch, Beth, Risa, and Scott went into town to meet with Mrs. Gilly. They pulled up outside a large, one-story brick building that was the combined elementary, middle school and high school for the town.

Beth tried not to worry. She knew Risa was going to have to move into a new program, no matter where they lived. It was just that she felt as if her support system were being taken away, like she'd be walking the tightrope of parenting without a safety net. She reminded herself that she had Scott now but somehow a group of experts seemed more reliable.

Scott put his arm around her as they walked into the building. "It'll be all right, Beth," he assured her.

"Am I that transparent?" she asked.

"Completely, but I'm sure they've seen nervous parents before."

Beth sighed and allowed him to pull her along the hall to the office. Risa held onto his other hand. She was certainly becoming a daddy's girl.

They checked in at the office and were given directions on how to find Mrs. Gilly's room. Their steps echoed in the empty halls. The Early Childhood, pre-kindergarten and kindergarten rooms were housed in their own "pod." The walls were painted white, and the cubbies that lined them were painted in bright primary colors. A border of colored handprints had been painted along the top of the walls.

"It looks cheerful," said Beth cautiously. She wanted this to work, but she was afraid to hope *too* much.

Scott found the door with Mrs. Gilly's name on it and knocked. The door was opened by a young woman whose face looked as bright and cheerful as the hallway. Beth couldn't help returning her smile.

"Hello. You must be Scott and Beth. I'm Linda Gilly." The teacher shook hands with both of them. "And who is this?" she asked kneeling down in front of Risa.

She imitated the adults and held out her hand. Mrs. Gilly shook it. "You must be Risa. I'm so glad to meet you."

Beth noted that the woman's warmth and enthusiasm seemed genuine.

"Would you like to come in and see my room?" Mrs. Gilly asked. Risa nodded her head. The teacher rose and took Risa's hand, leading her into the room.

The walls were white here, too, and the theme of primary-colored accents carried over as well. The tables and chairs were painted in bright blue, red and yellow. There was a carpeted area with a calendar, books, and a felt board. The carpet itself was blue with shapes of green, yellow, red, orange and purple on it. The room had a couple of sinks, its own bathroom and lots of toys arranged into "centers."

Risa quickly busied herself in the house center, with dress-up clothes, plastic dishes and dolls.

"I think Risa will find enough to keep her occupied for a little while," Mrs. Gilly said. "Let's sit down and talk. I'm sorry about the small chairs and table, but it's all I've got."

"That's okay," said Beth, sinking into the child-sized chair. Scott didn't complain, but he looked a bit funny with his knees poking up above the table. She looked away before she started to laugh.

Mrs. Gilly began by outlining their program. She brought out calendars from the last year that showed the different concepts they worked on each week. She gave them an idea of what the daily schedule was like, how therapy fit in and what sort of field trips the children went on. Then they covered meals that were available and transportation.

"Oh, I'd bring Risa in," Beth assured the teacher. "I think she's too young to ride the bus."

"That's fine," Mrs. Gilly agreed. "But if you change your mind, just let me know. The bus Risa would ride is only for young children. She wouldn't be thrown on a bus with older elementary students or teenagers. And there is an aide on her bus to help with safety harnesses and to discourage unwanted behavior."

Beth had a lot of questions and Mrs. Gilly answered them all patiently.

"If we want to enroll Risa, what's our next step?" Beth finally asked.

"We'd need to have her records transferred from the Birth to Three program," she explained. "Then the therapists and I would need to see Risa so we could do our own evaluations of her skills. Finally, we'd have a meeting of all the people involved and decide on a plan with specific goals for Risa's education."

By the time the meeting was over, Beth was feeling a little better about the transition out of the Birth to Three program.

Scott and Beth signed a form that would allow Mrs. Gilly to get Risa's records from Green Bay. This was only the first step in the process, Beth told herself. She wasn't committing Risa to attend school here.

It took some persuasion to get Risa away from the toys and out of the room, but that was good, too. It was nice to know she liked the place.

Once they were back in the SUV, Beth heaved a sigh of relief.

"See, that wasn't so bad, was it?" asked Scott.

"No," she admitted. "Actually, I feel a lot better. Even if we end up enrolling her in school in Green Bay, at least I know the process now."

"I thought you seemed pretty sold on this program."

"I am . . . but what if things don't work out between us?"

There was an edge of frustration in Scott's voice as he answered her. "Beth, I think it's time we started thinking positive here."

"I'm sorry, Scott, but I keep thinking, if I move up here and we . . . we decide to split up, then I'm stuck with no friends, no job, and no place to live."

"If I moved to Green Bay with you, the same thing could happen to me."

"But Green Bay is a much bigger city. There would be lots of options for you there. And you grew up there, you have family there. I'd have no one here."

They were silent the rest of the way home. The look on Scott's face told Beth he wasn't happy with her, but she told herself that she had to be practical. As much as she wanted things to work out between them, they might not. She had to be prepared for the worst.

CHAPTER 11

When they got home, Scott immediately went to his office at the lodge. They spoke only when they needed to that evening. It was tense and unpleasant. By the time Beth had Risa tucked into bed, she wanted to lock herself in her own bedroom and not come out again until morning.

Only it wasn't her bedroom. It was Scott's. And this was Scott's house. And she wanted to share it with Scott. She wanted to be a part of his life here. But truthfully, she was scared.

Beth retreated to the piano instead. She was improving, just in the few days she'd been practicing. It was like her fingers were waking up again, remembering how to touch the keys to produce the music she loved.

She played softly, so as not to wake up Risa. But she played for a long time, until her fingers began to feel stiff. When she finally decided she had to quit or risk her hands being too sore to play the next day, Beth rose and turned to put her music away in the bench.

Scott was standing in the doorway. How long had he been there?

"Hi," he said.

"I didn't know you were there."

"I didn't want to bother you. I just wanted to listen." He took a few steps into the room.

Beth put the music back in the bench and shut the lid. "It's late. I should. . . ."

"What's wrong, Beth?"

She couldn't meet his eyes. "What do you mean?"

"Before I left you in Green Bay you seemed so sure you wanted to make this marriage work. Now it feels like you're holding me at arm's length. Is it just that you don't like it here, or have you changed your mind about me?"

She shook her head. "I don't know how to say what I feel."

"Just try, please. I have to know." His voice sounded sincere.

She closed her eyes and tried to find the words. He was standing just a few steps away from her but she felt like the Grand Canyon stretched between them. She kept hearing her mother's words echoing in her head. "But one day he'll look at you and only think *what could have been* in his life."

She wanted to tell him about it, but she couldn't admit that her own mother would say such hurtful things to her.

When she finally spoke, it was in a low and controlled voice. "I keep thinking of my parents. They really tried to make things work, but they couldn't. Then when they divorced, I was left out in the cold. All I could ever be to them was a reminder of a mistake. I don't want that to happen to Risa."

"That will never happen to her. I will always love her and I know you will, too."

"Is that why you want us to stay together? For Risa? Is it just her you want? Are you trying to make this marriage work because you think you have to take *me* to get Risa?" It physically hurt her to say the words, but no matter what, she had to know.

Scott crossed the space between them and took her in his arms. "Beth, we were apart three years. And I'm sorry I left. But I never dated another woman. I never wanted anyone but you. You can ask anyone about it if you want. I had no idea Risa existed and I still wanted you. Don't you believe that?"

She wanted to believe him, but her mother's words still rang in her ears. "I'm not just a reminder of a mistake for you, too, am I?"

"What do you mean?"

"When you look at me, don't you think about how you could have finished college if I hadn't come along? Don't you think that your dad would be happier with you, if I hadn't messed up your life?"

Scott's arms tightened around her. "My life isn't messed up. I like my life. The only thing I need to make it complete is for you and Risa to stay here with me always. How can I make you believe that?"

She shook her head. "I don't know."

The gentle tone he'd started the conversation with had gradually disappeared and now his voice was harsh and rough. "I came looking for you, I practically begged you for a second chance. I brought you here. I'm offering you and Risa a home. What do you want from me?"

Beth backed away from him. "I didn't ask you to come looking for me. I didn't ask you to do any of this."

"Well I did. What else do I have to do? Sell the resort and move back to Green Bay? Would that make you happy?"

She shook her head.

Scott backed up and ran his fingers

through his hair in frustration. "I don't know what to do, Beth. I think we make a great family. I think we have a great place here and now that I know Risa will get the help she needs, I don't see any reason for you two not to stay. You wouldn't even have to work. You could have a lot more time with Risa. What more do you need? How can I help you to trust me?"

"I don't know," she whispered, shaking her head.

Scott turned away from her. "I'm going for a walk," he said. "I need to think."

Beth sank back down on the piano bench as he strode angrily from the room. She was doing it again. She was ruining everything just like before. She just couldn't stop herself.

Scott was dreaming. In his dream he and Beth were alone and there was no anger, no resentment between them. She smiled at him and he took her into his arms and kissed her. The kiss was slow and sweet and it made his blood boil. He wanted more of her, needed more of her. Pulling her closer to him, Scott pressed a trail of kisses along her throat. His hand came up and undid the first button on her blouse. She didn't stop him, so he moved to the second. . . .

And then Fred's voice came booming into his dream. "Well, who do we have here? Goldilocks?"

Scott's eyes fluttered open and he winced at the bright sunlight streaming in through the windows. He looked around, squinting, and then realized he was in Fred's office at the boat-rental dock. He'd fallen asleep on the lumpy tattered couch.

"Morning, Fred," mumbled Scott, sitting up and rubbing his face. His stiff muscles all protested when he moved.

"Did your pretty wife throw you out already?"

He supposed there was no way to cover up that they'd had a fight. "No, I sort of threw myself out. I went for a walk. Ended up here."

Fred nodded. "They say the road to true love never runs smoothly."

"This must be the truest love ever then," he grumbled, then winced at the sound of the old man's cackling laugh.

Scott sighed and stretched. "I guess I'd better go home and shower. What time is it?"

"Almost nine o'clock. I'm getting ready to open up here."

Scott leaped off the couch. "Almost nine? I thought you opened earlier than that?"

"I didn't have any reservations this morning so I stopped to have breakfast at the lodge. Ronnie was there and. . . ."

"Spare me the details. I'd better get going. Beth must be worried about me."

Scott sprinted all the way back to the cottage, his bad knee protesting. When he opened the door he saw that Beth wasn't alone. Cindy was with her and both women met him with furious glares when he came in.

"Where were you?" they cried out in stereo.

"I fell asleep on the couch in Fred's shop. Sorry."

"I thought you'd fallen in the lake and drowned or something," cried Beth. "We were about to put together a search party."

"Really, Scott, this isn't like you," added Cindy.

Scott closed his eyes and counted to ten.

"I'm sorry. I didn't mean to upset you. Cindy, could you give us a little privacy, please?"

Cindy nodded and quietly left. "I'll be at the restaurant if you need me. Don't worry about Shannon. She can take care of Risa for as long as you need her to," she said to Beth on her way out.

Scott heard the front door close and he

and Beth were alone, staring at each other.

"Are you okay?" he finally asked.

"Yes, I'm fine."

She didn't look fine. She looked like she'd been crying. He wondered if she'd slept at all last night. Guilt stabbed at him. "I didn't mean to scare you."

"I'm just glad you're okay."

She was standing there with her arms wrapped around herself, her face pale and tense. There must be more she wanted to say to him. Why wasn't she saying anything? Her silence bothered him more than if she'd gotten furious and shouted at him.

"Do you want to talk about it?" he offered.

"You said you didn't intend to stay out all night. I believe you. There's nothing to talk about."

"What about the argument we had before I left. We never resolved that." He moved closer to her and she backed away, keeping the distance between them.

"I don't think I'm up to that right now."

He gave in then. It was obvious that Beth wasn't going to talk to him about anything. "I'm going to take a shower and get to work. You look like you should go to bed." Maybe she'd be more reasonable after a few hours' sleep.

She didn't say anything to him. Just glared

and then melted from the room as quietly as a shadow.

Scott couldn't remember being so frustrated since . . . since right before he'd left her three years ago. How did she manage to tie him up in knots like this?

If trust was the issue, he'd just taken a giant step back from solving it. How could he have made such a stupid mistake? Maybe his father was right about him after all.

Scott headed for the shower. No sense standing there stewing over things when he had problems he *could* solve waiting for him at the lodge.

He checked on Beth before he left. She appeared to be sleeping. He wasn't sure if she really was or not. He kissed her cheek and whispered, "Sorry." If she heard him, she didn't respond at all.

By midmorning it was apparent that he wasn't going to get anything done. He just couldn't concentrate. What if Beth was ready to give up on him now?

When a knock sounded on his door, Scott almost welcomed the interruption. "Come in," he called out.

Fred ambled in, followed by a surly-looking teen in a black T-shirt and jeans. "I just wanted to introduce you to my grandson, Troy."

Scott stood up and offered his hand to the teen. "Hi, Troy. Nice to have you with us this summer."

Troy shook his hand reluctantly and mumbled, "Yeah, thanks."

"Has your grandfather shown you around yet?"

"Not really," Fred answered. "I thought you might want to do that, Scott."

Of course Fred would think that Scott wanted to spend the morning showing a teenage employee, with attitude to spare, around the resort. But then again, why not? He'd rather get out than sit cooped up in his office all day thinking.

"Sure. Come on Troy, I'll give you the grand tour." Scott got up and led the way out. Troy and Fred followed.

He wondered why Fred had asked him to show Troy the resort, since the old coot insisted on tagging along and did more of the talking than Scott did. But he decided it was useless to complain and used the time to evaluate Troy instead.

He was insecure, Scott decided, which wasn't unusual in a teen. The insecurity was making him defensive, and thus the attitude. But there was something more going on as well. He'd have to keep an eye on Troy until he figured it out.

The teen remained unimpressed by the beauty that surrounded him as well as by the people who extended a welcome to him. At least he did until they ran into Shannon and Risa. Shannon was pushing Risa on the swings when the three men came through that part of the grounds.

When Risa saw her daddy she held out her arms to him. Shannon stopped the swing, scooped up Risa and brought her over.

Scott did the introductions. "Shannon, this is Fred's grandson, Troy. Troy, Shannon's parents manage the restaurant and Shannon waitresses there. Only this summer, my daughter, Risa here, is monopolizing all of her time."

Shannon smiled. "I don't mind, Scott. I love playing with Risa. It's nice to meet you, Troy."

Troy stared at Risa. "Is she . . . does she have Down syndrome?" he asked.

"Yes, as a matter of fact, she does," Scott answered. This was the first time anyone had asked him that. He wondered what Troy's reaction would be.

"One of my cousins has Down syndrome," Troy said, surprising Scott. He reached out a hand, hesitated, and then patted Risa's back. She rewarded him with a smile. Troy smiled back, the first time all morning. "I'm going to miss him this summer," he admitted, somewhat reluctantly.

"Maybe he could visit sometime," suggested Shannon. "I bet he'd like it here. I think you will, too. There's always a lot to do when you aren't working."

"Like what?"

"Swimming, for one. Then there's boating, fishing, hiking. . . ."

"That's a lot of outdoors stuff," Troy said.

"Yeah, but it's still fun."

"More fun than sitting in front of the TV playing video games," mumbled Fred. His grandson shot him a look but said nothing.

"Have you seen the lodge yet?" asked Shannon.

"That's where we were heading now," Scott told her. "It's almost lunchtime. I thought we'd treat Troy to lunch on his first day."

"That's a great idea. Want me to take Risa so you can go get Beth?"

Scott nodded. "Sure. Why don't you head over to the restaurant?" Risa held out her arms to Shannon and Scott gratefully handed her over. He wasn't sure if Beth would eat lunch with them, but it was a good time to check on her and see how she was doing.

The teenagers and Risa started walking toward the lodge. Scott looked at Fred pointedly. "Aren't you going with them?"

Fred shrugged. "They won't want an old fogy like me around. I thought maybe I'd come with you."

"That may not be the best idea."

"Oh, I get it. You're still in the doghouse, aren't you?" Fred let out a wheezy laugh. "Okay, you don't need an audience when you try to make up with Beth. But while we have a minute alone together, I want to thank you, Scott."

"For what?"

"For hiring Troy, sight unseen. He really needs this job. His dad left him and my daughter this last year. Money's been tight for them. Plus he has a little bit of a chip on his shoulder since his dad left."

Scott raised his eyebrows. "Really? I couldn't tell."

"He'll straighten out. It will do him good to get away from his hometown, where his family has been the subject of gossip. He can make a new start here."

Remembering his own new start that had happened at the resort, Scott said, "I'm glad I could help, Fred. I'm sure Troy will be okay."

"Well, I guess you'd better get to making up, so we can eat. Now if it were me. . . ."

He held up a hand. "Thanks, Fred, but when it comes to matters of the heart, I'd rather not know what you're thinking."

The old man shrugged. "Have it your way. I'll go see if Ronnie can join us for lunch." He sauntered away, down the path toward the lodge.

Scott shook his head and sprinted up the trail that led to his cottage.

CHAPTER 12

Beth was sitting at the kitchen table when Scott crossed the deck and came in. He closed the sliding door behind him, but didn't come any further into the room. He had to find out where he stood with Beth first. "I thought you'd still be sleeping," he said.

She shook her head. "I couldn't sleep. I gave up and came down here to go over Risa's therapy schedule. I have to make sure we keep up with everything while she isn't seeing her therapists."

"Beth, you worry too much."

"I know." She kept her gaze low, avoiding his eyes. "I don't want to talk about Risa now."

Scott took a cautious step into the room. "What do you want to talk about?"

"Let's talk about us."

"All right." He tensed, anticipating a fight. Slowly, she lifted her eyes to his. "I'm sorry for the way I acted, Scott."

"What?" That was the last thing he expected her to say.

Beth dropped her gaze again, to her clenched hands, resting on the table. "I'm sorry I doubted your motivations for wanting us to stay married. I do worry too much. Sometimes I just can't help it."

Scott was speechless. He had gotten angry, stormed out and didn't come home all night and she was apologizing?

As the silence extended, Beth began to fidget. "You aren't . . . you aren't going to ask me to leave, are you?"

"What?" he repeated, confused.

"I mean, I know it would only be fair for you to have some more time with Risa, but do you want me to leave?"

"No!" he exclaimed, crossing the room to the table. "No, I don't want you to leave, Beth."

She peered up at him. "Really?"

Scott reached out and drew Beth to her feet. How could she even think he would give up just like that? "It was just one argument. I'm hardly going to throw in the towel over that!"

"Because . . . because if you let me stay, I promise . . . I promise not to keep you at arm's length anymore. I won't hold anything back from our marriage or let any worries overcome me again."

Scott pulled her close and cradled her head against his shoulder. "It wasn't just you, Beth. It was wrong of me to push you for a decision. You haven't been here that long."

She let out a shuddering sigh and tightened her arms around his waist. He kissed the top of her head and she lifted her face to him. He kissed her lips and she responded with fierce passion, pressing against him. His body responded instantly, wanting more. But in his head, alarms were going off.

Scott gentled the kiss. He caressed her cheek with his thumb and slowly, regretfully, drew away. He needed to think about this.

Did she really mean it about not holding back anymore? Anything? It occurred to him that his nights on the couch could be over. The last time she'd responded like this had been their final night in Green Bay. She'd been afraid because he was leaving. Today she'd been afraid that he was going to send her away.

"They're waiting for us at the restaurant, Beth."

"Who is?"

"Fred's grandson got in this morning. Everyone's getting together for lunch to welcome him."

"Oh," she pulled away. Scott let her go but held on to her hand.

"I don't know about you," he said, "but I'm starving. Let's go." He dropped one more kiss on her mouth, to reassure her, and then they set out for the lodge.

Scott held the door open for Beth as they stepped inside. Fred was still standing at the front desk, talking to Ronnie.

"Are you joining us for lunch, Ronnie?" asked Beth.

"Oh, I guess so," she said, "as long as I don't have to sit next to this old goat."

"Are you trying to get Ronnie to go out with you again, Fred?" Scott teased.

"I'm wearing her down," he insisted. "She's almost ready to crack. I can tell."

Ronnie glared at him. "You senile old fool, the only thing that's cracked around here is your head, if you think I'd go out with you."

"All right, kids," said Scott, trying to keep a straight face, "let's give it a rest until lunch is over, okay?"

"He started it," sniffed Ronnie. She told the other woman who was working the desk that she was taking her lunch break and added, "I'll be in the restaurant if you need me."

Shannon and Troy had staked out a table for the resort family. Troy was bouncing Risa on his lap. "He doesn't look so tough now," observed Scott. To Beth he added, "You should have seen Troy this morning. He had attitude to spare."

"I told you he was a good kid," remarked Fred.

Ben and Cindy got to the table soon after Fred, Ronnie, Scott and Beth. Fred introduced Troy to them.

"Where are the twins?" asked Beth.

"They went into town," answered Cindy. "They'll probably eat at Chloe Belle's."

When Risa saw Beth, she squirmed away from Troy and toddled to her mother.

Beth's face lit up almost as much as Risa's. "Hi, pumpkin," she cooed. "I haven't seen you all morning. Were you good for Shannon?"

"Yes, Beth. She was great."

"Thank you for taking care of her."

"It's no problem," Shannon replied. "I like spending time with Risa. She's a good kid."

"So, Troy, where are you from?" asked Ben.

"Hudson," he answered, a surly curl returning to his lip. "You know, over by the

Twin Cities."

Ben nodded. "That's a nice area. Right along the St. Croix."

"I hope you'll enjoy working here," Cindy said.

"If living with your grandfather doesn't drive you crazy," added Ronnie.

"Grandpa Fred and I get along all right." Troy seemed uncomfortable with the attention aimed at him.

Shannon spoke up shyly. "It must be cool living so close to a big city. I love it here in the country but it would be nice not to have to drive for two hours to get to a decent mall."

"Have you ever been to the Mall of America?" asked Troy.

Shannon shook her head.

Troy began describing the mall — how big it was, the amusement park in the center, Legoland, the aquarium, the restaurants and movie theaters.

"I'd love to go sometime," said Shannon. "Do you go often?"

"Yeah," said Troy, and then his expression changed. He leaned forward and let his shaggy brown hair fall over his eyes. "At least, I used to."

After lunch Scott offered to walk Beth and Risa to the cottage before returning to work.

Beth remarked as they walked up the path, "Having a restaurant in your backyard is great, but I may weigh three hundred pounds before my vacation is over."

Scott laughed. "Then I'll just have to put you to work; let you burn some of those calories off."

"Really?"

"No, not really. I don't expect you to wait tables or anything."

"But what if I wanted to work, Scott? Would you have anything for me to do?"

Scott tried to hide his surprise. "You want to have a job?"

"Maybe not yet. But if . . . if Risa and I stayed permanently, I guess I'd like to help out with something."

She was thinking long range! Maybe they were getting things back on track now. "I'd have to think about it," Scott said. "But just being Risa's mom is enough if that's what you want to do."

"Mostly, yes. But I want to be a part of the resort, too. If we stay."

She couldn't let go of that "if" yet. Still, it was progress.

After a morning spent in the fresh air, Risa was already drowsy when Scott carried her up to bed for her nap. The phone rang as he tucked her in. Coming back down the stairs, Scott followed the sound of Beth's voice into the kitchen.

"Yes, Hal, it really is beautiful up here. You should visit. . . . No, I don't know when I'm coming back yet. . . . I know I've been gone for a week, but you said. . . ."

She turned her back to Scott, but he could still hear her murmur into the cell phone, "No, we haven't decided. . . . I'm sorry, Hal, but it's a big decision. I'll let you know soon. Hey, what weekend would be good for you to come up for Risa's birthday? No, I'm not necessarily planning to stay through July. We'll have to see."

Beth quickly wrapped up the conversation at that point and hung up the phone.

"He wants you to go back," said Scott. It was a statement, not a question.

Beth nodded. "But I'm not ready yet," she added hastily.

"Is it that hard for him to work without you?" He was surprised at the bitterness he heard in his own voice and at the wave of anger he felt over his father wanting Beth, but not him. He thought his heart was hardened to that source of rejection.

"He just wants me to make a final decision. That's all, Scott."

"Well, that makes two of us." He wished he could take back his hasty words when he saw Beth cringe. He had to get himself under control. His relationship with his father was not her fault.

"What did he say about Risa's birthday party?" asked Scott, hoping to steer the conversation to a more neutral topic.

"He has to talk to your mom," Beth replied.

"What about your parents?"

He saw her shoulders stiffen. "What about them?"

"Do you want to invite them?"

"Why would I want to do that?" Beth frowned.

He shrugged. "I thought it might be a good way to invite them back into your life?"

She turned away from him and suddenly became very busy wiping crumbs from the counter and tidying up. "No. They don't even know Risa exists. There's no point to inviting them."

"You never told them about Risa?"

"Let's not get into this now."

"Why not?" It was obvious that this was a sensitive topic, but Scott was intrigued. He wanted to understand what had happened with Beth and her parents.

"My parents didn't *want* me after they found out I got pregnant and married. Why would they want anything to do with my daughter?"

"So the last time you talked to them was really when we told them we got married."

Her busy hands suddenly stilled. "No. . . . Well, yes, pretty much."

"What does that mean? When did you last talk to them?"

"Why do you care?" Beth asked, turning back to him, her body quivering with tension. "It has nothing to do with us."

Scott decided to let it go. He didn't want to start another argument. Not today, at least. He changed the subject instead.

"Why don't you talk to Cindy? She could help you plan the party," Scott suggested.

"If you don't mind," Beth agreed, relaxing visibly now that he'd dropped the subject of her parents.

"I don't mind. Tell me what you come up with. I guess I should get back to work."

"Okay. I'll see you later." Beth turned from him and started to scrub the perfectly clean kitchen sink. No offer of a kiss or hug. Oh yeah, they were getting things back on track all right.

After Scott left, Beth called Cindy. They agreed to meet at four, when Cindy got off work for the day. In the meantime, Beth did a little cleaning — she knew Scott would protest that she was on vacation, but she had to do something to help out. Then she practiced on the piano until Risa woke up from her nap. But the activity couldn't keep her from remembering Scott's reaction to Hal's phone call. Did he resent her already?

Cindy came over as promised and Beth was relieved to have someone to distract her from her thoughts. She had coffee ready, and the two women sat down at the kitchen table with paper and pen. They jotted down ideas and made lists of things needed and people to invite.

Finally, Cindy leaned back in her chair. "There, that's it. I think that's all we can do for now."

Beth put down her pen. "I think you're right. Do you want another cup of coffee?"

"Sure. Can I ask — did you and Scott settle things?"

"Yes, we made up." And then started a new fight. Maybe she shouldn't have snapped at him about inviting her parents. He didn't know about the phone call to her mother.

"Everything is going all right between you two?"

Beth shrugged. "Yeah, we're doing okay," she replied, but doubted Cindy would be convinced. In the short time Beth had known her she'd discovered that Cindy was pretty adept at reading people and even she could hear the lack of enthusiasm in her own voice. Although Beth really wanted to be friends with Cindy, she hesitated to say too much to her after that first day when she'd revealed her doubts about Scott. After all, Cindy had been Scott's friend first. What if she reported what Beth said to Scott?

"Hmm. You don't sound too sure of that," said Cindy, as she held her mug out for Beth to refill.

"Oh, I guess it was too much to expect that we'd be able to pick up where we left off."

"It sounds like you didn't leave off in a very good place anyway."

Beth shrugged. "It will get better."

"Do you want to talk about it, honey?"

She shook her head.

"You can't keep everything bottled up inside you," argued Cindy. "I tell Ben that all the time."

"No, really," Beth insisted, "there's nothing to talk about right now."

Cindy wasn't fooled. "Well, if you change your mind, you know where to find me."

Beth forced a smile to her face. "Thank you. I'll keep that in mind."

It was late when Scott got home that evening. He climbed the stairs of the deck wearily and walked inside to the kitchen.

"There's Daddy," said Beth as Risa ran to greet him, arms stretched out for a hug. He scooped her up and kissed her cheek.

"How was your day?" Beth asked.

He studied her carefully, hoping to find a clue to her mood. "It was long. I spent all afternoon putting out 'fires.' Sorry I'm late."

"Is everything okay?"

Scott nodded.

"Well then, I don't mind that you're late. Supper is almost ready."

Apparently they were going to ignore the flare-up from this afternoon and pretend everything was fine between them. That was okay with him. He was too tired to prod old wounds. "Thanks for making supper, Beth. I'm afraid you aren't getting much of a vacation."

"I enjoy puttering around the house. I like playing the piano. Most of all I love having time to spend with Risa — and with you. I think it's been a great vacation."

As Beth talked she transferred things to the table — a bowl of salad, some rolls, and a pitcher of lemonade. Then she grabbed a serving platter and an oven mitt. "I'll be right back. I have to get the chicken off the grill."

"Risa and I will wash up then."

The little family gathered around the table and said grace. Then they began to pass the dishes around. "It sure is nice to have supper ready when I come home," Scott commented. "I could get used to this."

"Tell me the truth," said Beth. "Do you usually eat at the restaurant?"

Scott nodded. "Most nights. I hate cooking when it's just me."

"You're in luck then. Today I decided to extend my vacation until Risa's party is over."

"And then what?"

"And then, we'll see."

Scott's first instinct was to push her for more, but he squashed it. It was progress, he reminded himself. Arguing with her might just send her running back to Green Bay sooner instead of committing to make her home with him here. The party was weeks away. Surely by then he could convince her that she and Risa belonged here with him.

They finished supper and Scott insisted on doing dishes this time. He was tired but he didn't want her to feel she was doing everything around the house. Afterward, he found Beth and Risa settled on the floor in the family room. A playful smile lit Beth's face.

"We have a surprise for you," she said.

He raised his eyebrows. "For me?"

Beth nodded. "Give Daddy his surprise, honey," she urged Risa.

Risa held a large white book. She stood and held it out to Scott. Scott looked at the cover. It was Risa's baby book.

"I didn't think to pack it," said Beth. "After we got here, it occurred to me you might like to see it so I called and asked your mom to mail it."

Scott nodded, unable to speak around the lump in his throat. He sat on the couch. Risa scrambled up beside him and Beth sat on the other side. Together they looked through the book. Risa pointed at the pictures of herself and made the sign for baby.

Scott read the statistics and journaling written in Beth's hand. She added some background and stories to the facts recorded there. They were almost through the book a second time when they were interrupted by the sound of the phone ringing.

Scott got up and answered the phone. "Hi,

Mom. How are you? . . . Yes, it came today. I really appreciate it."

Scott talked to his mom for a few minutes and then he handed the receiver over to Risa. "It's Grandma," he told her.

Risa's eyes got big when she heard her grandmother's voice on the phone. Scott and Beth laughed when Risa tried to sign to Margie. Beth picked up the extension and described what Risa was saying. Between Risa's garbled words and Beth's sign interpretation the two managed to have a conversation.

Risa said, "Daddy."

"Are you visiting your daddy?" Margie asked, obviously delighted to hear Risa's voice.

She made the sign for water. "Water," repeated Beth. "We're right by the lake. Is that what you mean, honey?"

Risa nodded.

"It hasn't been warm enough for swimming yet, but it should be soon," said Beth.

Risa said something that sounded like "Sa-Na."

It took Beth a moment to figure that one out. "I think she said 'Shannon.' Shannon lives next door to us and her parents run the restaurant. She's watched Risa a few times for us. They really hit it off."

"That's good to know," said Margie. "I'm glad you have some help there, Beth."

Then Hal asked to talk to his granddaughter and after Margie told Risa she loved her, she handed the phone to him and the process repeated itself. When Risa had finished talking, Scott took the phone from her.

"Hi, Dad."

There was a moment of silence on the other end before Hal replied. "Hi, Scott. How is everything going?"

"It's going fine. We're getting our summer staff trained in now."

Another pause. "Training new people is always a challenge."

"Yes," Scott agreed. "But we do it every summer so we have a system down."

"That's good. Get a lot of teens to work there?"

"Teens and college students, yes."

Hal switched subjects. "Beth told me today that you bought her a piano."

"Um, yeah, I did."

"That was nice of you."

Scott was so surprised by his father's approval that he almost didn't reply. "Thanks," he managed.

"Here's your mother. She wants to talk about the party."

"Beth, that's your department."

Scott hardly heard a word that was said between his mother and his wife. His dad had actually paid him a compliment. He couldn't remember the last time that happened. Before his knee injury, perhaps.

He grinned, feeling giddy at this accomplishment. But his smile quickly faded and a knot of anger formed in his stomach. Why should he be so eager to accept this scrap of approval, Scott asked himself. It was pathetic and he wished he didn't care.

"I'm going to put Risa to bed," whispered Scott as Beth described to his mother the birthday cake she and Cindy had planned. "Night, Mom; Night, Dad," he said into the phone and hung up his extension.

Risa's eyes were drooping and it seemed that even the excitement of a phone call from her grandparents wouldn't keep her up much longer. Scott carried her up the stairs and helped her with her bedtime preparations, glad for an excuse to leave the room for a while so he could sort this out.

Once Risa was all tucked in under her pink fairy princess comforter, Scott lingered. She slipped off to sleep while he watched her. Beth came upstairs later and found Scott sitting in the rocking chair, watching Risa sleep.

"Hey," she called softly to him. "What are you doing? Are you going to spend the night in that chair?"

He smiled. "No. Risa just looks so sweet when she's sleeping. I've missed seeing her sleeping too many times." Beth crossed the room to stand beside the rocking chair.

"Yes, she does look sweet."

"Did you hear what my dad said to me?" Scott asked softly.

"What?"

"He said it was nice of me to buy the piano for you."

"Nice!" Beth protested and then lowered her voice so she didn't wake Risa. "It was more than nice!"

With a last look at Risa, Scott stood and took Beth's hand. He led her out of the room. "I don't think I'll get any higher praise than that from my father."

"You two actually had a conversation tonight. That's good, isn't it?"

Scott shrugged. "Will I ever be like that?"

"Like what?"

"So critical. Will I treat Risa that way?"

Beth placed a hand on his shoulder. "No, Scott. I don't think you ever will. One thing about missing almost three years of her life — you'll never take another second of it for granted."

"But Risa will be . . . different. Will I pressure her to keep up with other kids her age? Will I be disappointed when they pass her up?"

"You know, I don't think you will. I wondered about that too, when she was a baby. And sometimes it's hard to see other children the same age, who are way ahead of her."

"What do you do?"

"When Risa was just an infant, an older lady at church told me about her grandson who had cerebral palsy. She said that when other people looked at him, they could find lots of imperfections. But to her, he was perfect. It reminded her of the way God sees us and loves us in spite of our own, often glaring, imperfections."

"I like that."

"Yes. It helped me a lot."

"Let's go back downstairs," Scott suggested.

They returned to the cozy family area. Scott picked up the baby book again. "Thank you for sharing this with me, Beth."

"You're welcome. Now, enough about Risa. What about us?"

"What about us?"

"Risa's sleeping, we're alone. What do *you* think?"

Scott thought this was a perfect time for a kiss. He laid the book aside and followed that thought. One kiss led to another and another, each becoming more passionate than the last. It would be easy to keep going, but something was bothering him. With great reluctance, he pulled away.

"It's been a long day, Beth. I think I should get some sleep."

She hooked an arm around his neck, bringing him back to her. "Aren't you tired of the couch?"

"I'm fine down here," he assured her, easing away to put more distance between them.

"You don't have to stay down here."

Scott cupped her chin in his hand and looked her in the eye. "What exactly are you offering, Beth?"

Even in the dim light, he knew her cheeks were red. She would never cut it as a seductress, he thought with affection.

She pulled away and turned her head from him. "I think you know, Scott."

"Why, Beth? Why now?"

"Because . . . because I said I wouldn't hold anything back anymore." Now she was the one trying to put some distance between them.

Scott caught her hands before she slipped

242

away altogether. "You said that because you thought I was going to ask you to leave."

"Yes. I realized I wasn't being fair and. . . ." She looked confused and hurt.

"You're afraid. You try to stay aloof because you're afraid of getting hurt. Then when it looks like things are going bad, you do a one-eighty turn because you're afraid we'll break up."

"That's . . . that's not true." The tremor in her voice revealed her own doubt. "Don't you love me, Scott?"

"Believe me, if I loved you any less we'd be upstairs by now."

"I don't understand."

"Beth, your body is not the payment for my fidelity. You shouldn't do this because you're scared of losing me."

She scooted away from him again and crossed her arms over her chest. "Fine. You aren't interested. I get the picture."

"Oh, I'm definitely interested. But I'd also like to think that I'm older and wiser than I was before. This time, I know I'm playing for keeps. I don't want to make love to you until the time is right."

"When will that be?"

"When we're ready to finalize our commitment to each other. When there's no doubt between us."

"And that's not now?"

"Can you honestly say that you have no doubts?"

He could see in her face that she wanted to say yes. But she remained quiet.

"It's all right, Beth. The couch is fine for me."

"We could sleep — just sleep — together in your bed."

Definitely not a good plan, he thought. "I don't think so. I'm trying to be strong here, but I'm not a saint. I know I couldn't resist that temptation."

She nodded. "The couch it is then."

"I guess."

"I could switch with you for the night," she offered.

"Thanks, but no. I'm good."

She hesitated, seeming uncertain what to do next. "I'm going to bed then."

"All right."

She gave him a weak smile and walked to the stairs. He stood still and watched until she rounded the corner, out of sight.

Then Scott let out a long sigh. He knew he wouldn't be sleeping for a while yet. He'd be taking a shower — a long, cold one — first.

Beth lay awake for a long time that night,

thinking about what Scott had said. At first she just felt humiliated that he had turned her down. Then she began to focus on his reasons. Could he be right?

She considered her worries. Is Scott trying to make our marriage work because of Risa? I'm pretty sure that's not it. But maybe not one-hundred-percent sure.

The biggest worry was that he was staying with her out of a sense of responsibility. One thing about us, even though we were young when we got married, we took our wedding vows seriously. Now that Scott had inherited the resort, he may have thought it was his duty to share it with her.

Yes, that's probably the answer. He wants to share his inheritance with his wife; he wants to share Risa with me. He wants to live up to Hal's expectations.

That's what Beth truly believed was behind Scott's effort to renew their marriage. The question was why that wasn't enough? Many people stayed married for worse reasons than that. Why couldn't she be happy with it?

"Because deep inside, I want him to love me for myself," Beth whispered into the blankets. "The way I love him."

CHAPTER 13

After a few weeks at the resort, Beth felt she had settled in. She'd slipped into a routine with time for working and playing with Risa, keeping house and having coffee with Cindy. On weekends with Scott along, they went on picnics, explored the farmer's market and swam on the resort's beach. She loved Scott's little cottage in the woods and she was coming to feel like she was making friends with the "resort family." It was so much different than working in the fast-paced, male-dominated car dealership.

As much as she was enjoying her time here, a little voice, surprisingly similar to her mother's, kept whispering that it was too good to last.

On Friday afternoon Shannon came over. Beth was surprised, but happy to see her. "Aren't they keeping you busy enough at the restaurant?" she teased. "You have to come here and look for something to do?"

"No. I just wanted to visit."

Beth made some tea for them and put cookies on a plate. Risa climbed up on Shannon's lap and reached for one.

"So how are things going at work?" asked Beth.

"Pretty good. One of the girls in my class, Rhonda, is working here for the summer. She dropped a whole tray of glasses yesterday. She was so upset, she was crying and everything. I told her everyone makes mistakes and I couldn't even count all the glasses I've broken by now."

"That was nice of you," Beth said, stirring a bit of honey into her tea. "Have you heard how Fred's grandson is doing?"

Shannon's arms tightened around Risa. "I think Troy's having a little trouble adjusting. He's supposed to be mowing the lawn and stuff. He gets so frustrated when he doesn't know how to do something. Sam and Shaun don't like him."

"What about you, Shannon?"

"I like Troy. I . . . I like him a lot," she said with a blush beginning in her cheeks.

"A lot?"

"Yeah. He asked me to go out with him tonight."

Beth stirred her tea. "What did you tell him?"

Her blush deepened. "I told him yes. We're going to drive into Rhinelander and see a movie."

"That sounds like fun."

"Yeah," said Shannon softly.

"What's the problem?"

"I've just never . . . I've never been on a date before. I'm seventeen and I've never dated. I don't know how to act or anything, Beth. Will Troy think I'm a total geek?"

Beth bit the inside of her cheek to keep from laughing. "Of course not, Shannon. And you don't have to act any differently than you normally do around Troy. If he didn't like you he wouldn't have asked you out. Just think of all the pretty waitresses he had to choose from."

"Yeah," she smiled this time. "And none of them have brothers who hate him already."

"I'm sure Shaun and Sam don't *hate* him. They haven't gotten a chance to know him yet."

Shannon tucked a strand of red hair behind her ear. "I guess I'm nervous because Rhinelander is so far away. What if things don't work out and I want to go home? It's a long way back to the resort."

"You don't think he'll leave you stranded, do you?"

"No, I wouldn't go if I were worried about that. I mean, it's just a long ride with someone who's mad at you."

"What does your mother say?"

"She doesn't really like the idea of us going so far, but there's nothing to do in town, at least during the summer. During the school year there's always a game or something. But now there's nothing."

Beth thought for a minute. "What if I lend you my cell phone? Then if you had any problems, car problems or arguments with your date or whatever, you can call."

Shannon's face brightened. "Beth, that would be perfect! Would you do that?"

She laughed. "Of course I would. I wouldn't have offered if I didn't mean it. Let me just go get it."

When Beth handed the phone to Shannon, she took it, saying, "Thank you, thank you, Beth. I owe you one."

"You're welcome." She showed Shannon how to work it. "You don't owe me anything, but. . . ."

"What do you need?"

"Would you watch Risa for a little while? I need to run into town for some groceries and I'm getting used to not having to take her. You're spoiling me."

"No problem." Shannon stood, sliding

Risa to her hip. "Come on, Risa. You can help me pick out an outfit for tonight."

Beth made her promise to give a report the next day. Shannon thanked her again and left. She remained at the table a while, sipping her tea and thinking about the past. She hadn't had many boyfriends before Scott and none that she'd gone out with more than a few times.

She had known Scott was different right from the start. She felt safe with him and, more importantly, he made her feel cherished. But since he'd left her, she didn't feel that anymore. He treated her the same, but somehow the idea that Scott could just disappear from her life hovered at the back of her mind. That certainly didn't make her feel secure.

But she promised herself that she wasn't going to think negatively anymore. Instead of sitting and brooding, Beth got up and made a list. Grabbing her purse, she walked over to Scott's office in the lodge. The door was open, so she peeked inside and said, "Hi."

He looked up from the computer and smiled at her. "Perfect timing. I could use a break."

His smile melted her heart. It always had. She moved into the office and asked, "Can

I use your SUV?"

"Um, sure, why?"

"I need to make a trip into town for groceries. Otherwise it will be franks and beans for supper."

"If you can wait a little bit, I'll take you," he offered.

"No, I can do it myself."

He frowned. "Are you sure?"

Beth laughed at him. "The town isn't that big. I won't get lost."

"All right. But I don't have the keys with me. They're at the house."

"Then I could have just called." She blew out a breath in frustration. "I should have thought of that."

Scott stood and stretched. "I really do need a break. I'll walk you back to the house."

It felt good, walking with Scott, holding hands, the sun shining on their heads as they walked toward his house — their house. She was getting used to the sound of that. It was a good thought.

Inside, Scott showed Beth where he kept his keys. "Are you sure you don't want me to go with you?"

"No. I'll be fine." She didn't want to raise false hopes in him, but she meant to see if she could feel comfortable on her own in the community. Grocery shopping seemed like a good way to test the waters. "I'd better get going. I told Shannon I wouldn't leave Risa with her too long."

"All right." He pulled her close for a quick kiss. "Call me when you get back."

"I'm only going into town, not overseas or something." She almost reminded him that she'd managed to get along just fine for three and a half years without him, but stopped herself. It was a touchy subject, and to mention it might bring on another bout of guilt in Scott. She wouldn't do that to him.

Once she was settled in the SUV, she adjusted the seat, changed the position of his mirrors slightly and started off. She got confused on a couple of the turns and had to backtrack, but she made it into town okay.

In the grocery store, Beth grabbed a cart and pushed it past the checkouts and into the first aisle. Then she paused for a moment to read her list. The conversation from the checkouts drifted to her ears.

"Hey, isn't that Scott Lund's SUV out front?" asked a woman.

"Yeah, but you can relax. He wasn't driving. That new wife of his was." The second voice was also a woman's, a note of

252

disgust in it.

"I hear she's not new. They were just separated."

Beth heard the second woman reply with a note of triumph in her voice, "Scott never told me he was married. Well, that explains it."

"Explains what? Why he never succumbed to your powerful charms?" There was more than a hint of sarcasm in the voice.

"I never said that," the first woman snapped.

"But you thought it, I'll bet. He's the one who got away," the woman chuckled.

There was a note of anger in the other woman's voice. "Maybe, but don't you think it's strange that this wife showed up so soon after he inherited the resort? I'll bet she's a gold digger."

Beth covered her mouth to muffle the gasp that escaped when she heard the woman's assumption. Why hadn't she agreed to let Scott come with her? But if he had, these women wouldn't have said anything and she wouldn't have known there was gossip going around about her. Did other people think the same thing?

Anger flooded through her, causing her heart to pound and her pulse to jump. What should she do now? Finish shopping and pretend she hadn't heard the clerks talking about her? Walk out and let them know they'd upset her? Confront them and cause more talk? It didn't seem there was a winning solution. Her grip on the cart tightened.

Another cart pulled up beside hers and an arm went around Beth's shoulders. She looked up, surprised. It was Linda Gilly, the Early Childhood teacher.

"Don't let them bother you," she said, keeping her voice low.

"You heard?" Beth whispered back.

"Honey, this store isn't that big. Everyone in here must have heard."

Beth groaned.

"And everyone knows that it's sour grapes with those two. Ann's biggest accomplishment in life was being elected Prom Queen. And Jean can't stand to see anyone happy since her husband left her."

"Does anyone else think. . . ."

"Maybe. I never met your husband until our meeting, but I did hear there were quite a few broken hearts when it came out that he was married. They'd probably jump on any idea that put you in a bad light."

"Oh, great." Wait a minute. What was that about Scott being a heartbreaker?

"Hey, it's not that bad. Once people get

to know you, they'll see that you're a nice person."

"How do you know that? Maybe I'm as bad as they say." Was this woman just trying to make her feel better? She didn't want anyone to feel sorry for her.

"I've met a lot of moms in my day, Beth. I found you can usually judge a parent by the child. Risa is delightful. It's obvious she's loved and well-cared for."

"And a gold digger wouldn't take care of her child?"

Linda laughed. "Maybe, but I think a real schemer would be too self-centered to take such good care of a child like Risa."

"They must have known I'd overhear them. I'm going to go talk to them," Beth decided.

"And give those two the satisfaction of knowing they upset you? It would cause even more talk. Just finish your shopping and when you check out, be as sweet as pie. It will drive them crazy."

Beth smiled. She liked that idea. "Thank you, Mrs. Gilly."

"Call me Linda, and it's no problem. One more thing. You haven't signed Risa up for school this fall. You were going to do that, weren't you?"

Beth didn't want to tell Linda that she

hadn't decided. Instead she told her, "I've been so busy lately. I guess I forgot about school."

"I'll be watching for the paperwork, then. I'm really excited about having Risa in my class this fall."

With a wave, Linda pushed her cart down the aisle and left Beth by herself. She took a deep breath and forced herself to put the checkout girls and their gossip out of her mind. She focused on her list: bread, milk, orange juice. . . . She could do this.

Beth went through the store and filled her cart. She didn't know where everything was, but it was a small store, so it wasn't long before she had everything on her list. She double-checked it, and then took a deep breath and prepared to face the spiteful women at the checkout.

They were lounging against the counter and paging through a fashion magazine. When they saw Beth, they straightened up, and one of them shoved the magazine back on the rack. Beth pushed her cart up to the first checkout and began to unload it. The younger of the two women, a blonde with dark roots and too much makeup, began scanning each item. The other woman, with no makeup and a surly expression on her face, bagged her groceries. Neither woman spoke to her. So much for small-town friendliness, Beth thought.

Forcing a smile, she said with all the pleasantness she could manage, "I haven't been in town very long but I really like it here."

"Yeah, I'll bet," mumbled the blonde. The other woman snorted.

"The people are so friendly. Everyone I've met has been so welcoming."

The clerks exchanged glances. "I hear you're Scott Lund's wife," the older woman said.

"Yes, I am. Oh, do you know Scott?"

The blonde scanned the last item and handed it to her coworker. "A little."

Beth turned her smile up a notch and made her voice as sweet as honey. "I know that in small towns people like to look out for each other. That's so kind of you, but I don't think Scott needs your protection. He's a smart guy. I think he can handle any gold diggers that come his way."

The women stared at her, mouths hanging open. Beth handed over her debit card and waited while the blonde fumbled through the transaction.

"Have a nice day," she said before picking up her groceries and walking out. Beth felt a great deal of satisfaction from making those two speechless.

She remained calm and collected as she loaded her groceries into the vehicle and pulled out onto the road. Once she was out of town, she pulled over to the side of the road and rested her head on the steering wheel.

She couldn't believe her behavior. Those two women at the checkout had been nasty, but did they really deserve that? She should feel bad about being mean to them, but instead a giggle slipped out. They'd looked so silly with their mouths hanging open like that.

She could dismiss the clerks from her thoughts but it was harder to accept that there were, according to Linda, a number of women who'd been interested in Scott. Even if he hadn't dated, was there someone *he* was interested in? Interested in enough that he would have happily accepted a divorce from her before he knew about Risa? Certainly not the bottle blonde from the grocery store, but someone else?

She'd hoped the trip into town would help her decide if she should stay here or not. Instead, it had just made things more confusing. She couldn't sit here by the side of the road and figure it out while her frozen food melted. Checking the mirror for traffic, Beth pulled back onto the road, wondering just how many broken hearts there had been when it was discovered that Scott Lund was married.

Scott took another look out the window. There was no silver SUV coming down the road, no sign of Beth. He'd tried calling her, but her cell phone went right to voice mail, meaning that it was shut off. How long did it take to get a few groceries?

He took a deep breath and tried to calm down. He was overreacting, surely. Beth was a grown woman. How much trouble could she get into in Spruce Point? He took another deep breath. He was being ridiculous. He should just forget about it and go back to work for a little while. But he didn't, because he hadn't gotten one thing done since Beth left. So he'd come home early to wait for her. But having nothing to do was worse than not being able to concentrate on what he should be doing.

He spotted the SUV just as he was about to dial her cell phone again. With a sigh of relief he went out to greet her.

"Are you okay? What took so long? Why didn't you have your phone on?"

Beth smiled at him, but her eyes looked sad.

"Nothing happened, but I'm glad you're here. You can help me carry in the groceries."

Scott grabbed two bags from the back of the SUV and headed into the house. She took the last bag, a light one with only a few items in it, and shut the SUV door.

Scott set the bags down on the counter in the kitchen. "Now what's wrong?"

"The ice cream is going to melt, that's what's wrong," she answered flippantly as she dug through the bags and brought out the slightly soggy carton and stowed it in the freezer.

"I saw it in your eyes when you pulled up. Something happened, Beth."

She continued to unpack and put away the groceries, avoiding his gaze. "I took a couple of wrong turns and had to find my way back, that's all."

He grabbed the can from her that she had been holding, and put it down on the counter. She wouldn't tell him what was bothering her, but he was glad she was home safe. He had a lot of pent-up energy from worrying and he knew exactly how he wanted to get rid of it. He pulled her into his arms and kissed her.

Beth gave a soft cry of surprise and her hands clenched the front of his shirt. He ran his hands down her back and then lower, pressing her into him. His mouth moved from her lips and down her throat. He nuzzled at her collar bone and she shivered.

He knew that waiting for Beth to be sure about him was the smart thing to do, but right now his self-control was crumbling. Beth was his wife and he wanted her, needed her. The sofa was only a few feet away. . . .

But he vaguely felt her pushing him away. "Scott, there's someone at the door."

It took a moment for her words to sink in. Then he heard the knock.

"That must be Shannon," said Beth, her voice rough with emotion. "I told her I wouldn't leave Risa with her for long. She's going on a date."

That was enough of a surprise to distract him. "A date? Is she old enough for that?"

Beth flashed a shaky smile. "She's seventeen. Weren't you dating when you were that age?"

Scott shrugged and backed away from her, with a sigh of regret. He strode to the front door, opened it and got another surprise. Troy stood there with Shannon and Risa.

"Can you take Risa, Scott?" asked Shannon. "Beth said she wouldn't be long, but. . . ."

Beth peeped from behind Scott's shoulder. "I'm sorry Shannon. I got lost, otherwise I would have been back sooner."

"Oh, you're home, Beth. We wouldn't mind keeping Risa longer, but we have plans."

"We?" echoed Scott. "Plans?"

"We're going to Rhinelander to see a movie," Shannon explained.

"If we don't make the first show we won't be home by her curfew," Troy added.

Scott seemed to be at a loss for words. Beth squeezed in beside him and took over the conversation. "You'd better get going then. Have a good time."

"Thanks, we will." Troy handed Risa to Scott, and then the two headed back toward Shannon's house, hand in hand.

Scott closed the door and faced Beth. "Shannon is going out with Troy? Do Cindy and Ben know about this?"

"Of course they do. What's wrong with him?" asked Beth.

"I like Troy, but that kid has a chip on his shoulder the size of Mount Rushmore. I'm not sure he's boyfriend material."

"Don't be so quick to judge," Beth admonished him. "Besides, it's just one date, Scott."

"Do you know where they're going?"

"To see a movie in Rhinelander," she replied.

"In Rhinelander? Is Ben out of his mind?"

"Scott, calm down. Shannon is a smart girl and I gave her my cell phone. She can call if she has any trouble."

"You gave her your cell phone?"

"Yes."

He relaxed a little. "No wonder you didn't answer when I called. You could have told me. Shannon is like a niece to me. And Troy is dealing with a lot in his life, according to Fred. I just don't see him making good choices right now."

"You mean like you and I?"

"We weren't seventeen, Beth," he responded forcefully.

"No, but we weren't much older. And now you're stuck with me."

Scott was surprised by the sudden harshness in her tone. His instincts had been right. Something had happened to upset her while she was in town. "What is that supposed to mean?"

"Nothing." Beth turned away from him and went back to the kitchen.

Scott followed her, still holding Risa. "What do you mean 'now I'm stuck with you'?"

"I bought chicken for dinner. Do you want it grilled or baked?"

Risa squirmed to be let down. Scott set her on her booster seat at the table and opened a box of animal crackers for her from the groceries Beth had bought. With his daughter settled, he turned his attention back to his wife.

"Beth, answer me. What did you mean by that?"

"I didn't mean anything. I need to put the groceries away."

Right now, Scott was feeling just a bit tired of Beth's tactics to evade meaningful conversation. He stepped in front of her. "First, you need to tell me what's wrong."

She glared at him, crossing her arms. "Why do you always think something's wrong."

"Because something always is."

"Oh, so now you're saying I complain too much."

"More like too little," Scott shot back. "For once I'd like to know what's really going on with you."

"What's going on with me? What about what's going on with you?"

"I've been completely honest with you."

"Oh really? Then you somehow forgot to mention your fan club in town."

She'd lost him. "Fan club?"

"Yes, I heard about the legion of broken hearts you left behind in town when they discovered you were married." Beth's voice rose and became shrill as control over her emotions slipped.

"That's ridiculous," he shouted back. "Where did you hear that?"

"From the same place I heard about your gold-digging wife."

Suddenly Risa burst into tears. It was only then that Scott realized how loud and angry their voices had become. Both he and Beth instantly turned their attention to her. Beth reached for the little girl first and scooped her up, hugging her tightly.

"I'm sorry, sweetheart," she crooned. "I didn't mean to upset you."

Scott put one arm around Beth and rubbed Risa's back with the other. "It's all right," he told her. "Mommy and Daddy won't shout anymore."

After a few minutes of soothing, Risa's cries decreased and eventually wound down to sniffles.

Beth looked up at Scott, guilt permeating her expression. "Scott, I'm sorry. I . . . I didn't handle that well."

"I'm sorry, too," he admitted. "I didn't mean to yell."

They stayed huddled together a little longer. Finally Risa grew restless and demanded to be put down. "I'll take her up to her room and let her play for a while," Scott volunteered.

"Great," Beth replied. "I can finish putting the groceries away and make supper."

"Or I can make supper if you want," he countered. "Just let me know when everything's put away and I'll switch with you."

She opened her mouth for what he expected to be a protest. But she hesitated and then said, "Thank you. That would be nice."

"You're welcome. Just call me when you need me."

She nodded. "I will."

Scott made a point of seeking out his friend the next day. "Hey, Ben," he asked. "Are you free anytime today?"

Ben looked up from the computer in the cramped office he shared with Cindy. "Not likely," he said. "Not if you want all the bills for the restaurant paid and fresh supplies ordered."

"You have to eat," Scott pointed out. "How about lunch?"

Ben sighed, his giant-sized frame shaking with the force of his exhalation. "I should probably have a sandwich at my desk, but why not?"

"Taking a break will do wonders for your disposition," suggested Scott.

"All right, let's grab a booth before the lunch rush arrives."

"Sounds good to me."

The men gave their orders to one of the waitresses and then settled into one of the wooden booths near the back of the dining room.

"So, I hear Shannon went out with Troy last night." It wasn't exactly the subtlest opening Scott could have made, but it was good enough.

"Yeah, she did." Ben grimaced. "I hate to think of her being old enough to date. It was bad enough with the boys, but. . . ."

"But Shannon is still your little girl," teased Scott.

"You'll understand someday," warned Ben grimly.

He didn't want to think about that. "I know Shannon is old enough, but seriously Ben, do you think Troy is a good choice?"

The big man shrugged. "It's not my choice. I trust Shannon. I think Troy may have some issues, but I don't think he's dangerous. And she's a big girl. She can tell him to get lost if she wants to."

"I'm not trying to make Troy out as the bad guy here," Scott said. "I do like him. I just . . . I just think he has a lot to deal with right now."

"Maybe being friends with Shannon will help him."

"If he's like I was at seventeen, he's not exactly thinking about friendship," Scott grumbled.

"This is hard enough already," Ben snapped. "Don't make it worse."

"Sorry."

Silence settled over the men for a few minutes as they finished their lunches.

"Was there anything else you wanted to talk to me about?" Ben asked. "Somehow I don't think you'd drag me away from work for that."

"Well, no. But you know how I feel about Shannon. I don't want to see her get hurt."

"Neither do I, Scott. Unfortunately, that's part of being a parent. You can't shield your children forever from all the hurts. Sometimes, even when you can see it coming, all you can do is let them make their own choices and be there for them when they fall."

Scott pondered the wisdom in Ben's words. He didn't much like the idea of stepping back and letting Risa get hurt. He wondered how his own father had felt about some of his choices. Shaking his head, Scott brought himself back to the matter at hand.

"Actually, I wanted to talk to you about Beth."

Ben's serious demeanor dropped away and mischievous gleam shone in his eyes. "You know, I don't much like that guy *she's* been hanging around with. I think he's a bad influence if I've ever seen one."

"Funny."

"Okay, what about Beth?"

"She hasn't decided if she's going to stay or not."

"She seems happy here."

"I don't think she trusts me. I guess I deserve that."

"She loves you, though." Ben softened his tone. "Even I can see it in her face when she looks at you."

Scott chose not to answer that. "I'm thinking about offering Beth a job."

He laughed out loud at that. "You think you can keep her around by putting her on the payroll?"

"She told me that if she stayed, she'd want to feel like she was a part of things around here."

"Oh, I get it now." Ben chuckled. "You're reversing it. You give her a job, make her feel a part of things, and then she won't want to leave."

"Something like that," admitted Scott. "Do you think it will work?"

"What kind of job are you going to offer her?"

"You know how when Henry remodeled, he added those meeting rooms to the lodge? He wanted to attract some corporate customers with a place where they could have business meetings, or hold workshops or maybe entertain clients while negotiating a deal."

"Yeah. So?"

"Beth has a background in sales. I wonder if she could get us some corporate customers."

Ben was quiet for a moment, rolling the idea around in his head. Then he said, "I think that might just work."

"You don't have to sound so surprised," complained Scott. "I do come up with a good idea every now and then."

"It may help her make up her mind."

"What if it helps her to decide she doesn't want to stay?"

Ben reached over and clasped Scott's shoulder. "Then at least you wouldn't be wondering anymore."

Scott nodded. "I guess there's that."

Maybe if that was how it was going to be, it'd be better to know as soon as possible.

"Just ask her," Ben urged.

"I plan to. Thanks, Ben."

CHAPTER 14

Scott continued to mull over the idea of offering Beth a job. He'd need to come up with a title for her and a place for her to have a desk. How many hours would she want to work? What would they do about salary and benefits? There were a lot of details to consider, but they could iron those out when — and if — she accepted the job.

By the time he quit for the day, he had made his decision. He would ask her. But his shoulders were tight with tension. He wasn't sure what he would do if she changed her mind and said she didn't want to stay after all.

On his way home he asked Shannon if she would babysit that evening. Home at last, he bounded up the steps of the deck and slipped in through the sliding door. He could hear Beth talking on the phone.

"Yes, I know it's been a while, but I'm not ready to come home yet, Hal. Things are . . .

going well."

Scott smiled.

After a pause, Beth spoke again. "I'm not quite ready to send you a resignation. Just give me a little more time, please."

Well, at least it was progress, thought Scott, trying not to be disappointed.

"I know that's a lot more than two weeks, but Hal, this is important. There's a lot at stake here. I have to be sure. Say hi to Margie for me. Thanks. Bye."

Scott stepped into the living room as she hung up the receiver. "Who was that?" he asked, hoping she'd tell him about the conversation.

"Oh, Scott. It was your father. If I'd known you were home, I would have let you talk to him."

"Maybe next time. I have something better in mind. Let's go out for supper."

"I already have some meat thawed."

"It'll keep until tomorrow," he replied. "Shannon said she'd babysit."

"Babysit? You mean it would be just the two of us?"

He realized they hadn't done much of anything as a couple since Beth had arrived. Maybe this was the right direction to go in. "Yeah, just the two of us tonight."

"Oh. Well, sure, I guess. Since you already

asked Shannon." She tried to sound non-chalant, but he could tell she was pleased. "Do I need to change?"

Scott studied her slim figure in denim shorts and a red camp shirt. "You look good, but the place I had in mind requires that we dress up a bit more. We have time to change before we leave."

Beth wore khaki pants and a soft yellow blouse. She brushed her hair and decided not to re-braid it, instead letting it curl around her face and shoulders. She scooped up Risa, who had been playing on the floor nearby, and went downstairs.

Scott was just coming out of the bathroom. He'd changed into dress pants and put on a polo shirt — one without the Pine Away Resort logo on it for once. When Beth breezed past him she could smell his cologne. "I'm going to make supper for Risa before we go," she called.

She was just dishing up macaroni and cheese when Shannon knocked on the sliding door. Scott pushed it open for her. "Hi, Shannon. Thanks for babysitting," he greeted her.

"No problem," she answered, sitting in the chair next to Risa's. "How are you tonight, Miss Risa?"

Risa giggled in reply.

"Have you eaten, Shannon?" asked Beth. "I know it's only mac and cheese and applesauce, but there's plenty."

"No, thanks," Shannon replied. "I've eaten."

Scott showed Shannon the paper by the phone where he'd written the restaurant's number and his cell-phone number. Beth put away the leftovers from Risa's supper.

"We won't be too late," Scott reassured her.

"It doesn't matter," said Shannon. "I don't work the early shift tomorrow. Stay out as late as you like."

"Did you hear that, Beth," said Scott, waggling his eyebrows suggestively. "We could paint the town red tonight."

Beth laughed at him and rolled her eyes. "In a town this size, that would take how long? Until eight-thirty?"

"Don't be silly," said Scott as he ushered her out. "They don't roll up the sidewalks until nine o'clock at least."

Scott took Beth to a supper club hidden on a back road on the other side of Spruce Point.

"How does a place like this stay in business?" asked Beth. "How does anyone find it?"

"Well, the locals all know where it is and

275

they advertise for the tourists," Scott told her. "The tourists think it's unique to eat in such a rustic place."

"Everything up here is rustic," insisted Beth, "but I'm starting to get used to it."

"Maybe you could even learn to like it," Scott said.

"It could grow on me," she replied, smiling at him.

He slipped an arm around her waist. She seemed more relaxed than usual. He wished they could have more times like this. If tonight went well, maybe they would.

The hostess came to take them to their seats. She favored them with a big, friendly smile. "Hi Scott. I haven't seen you out and about lately."

"It's summer," he replied, "our busy season."

"Don't forget the saying about all work and no play."

Beth cleared her throat and Scott realized they were leaving her out. "Have you met my wife, Beth?"

The wattage in the hostess's smile faded briefly, but she recovered. "Wife? I hadn't heard that you were married. Congratulations . . . to both of you."

She left them with menus and went back to seat the next couple. Beth was looking at him, a question in her eyes.

He raised his eyebrows. "What?"

"Oh nothing," she said, her voice much cooler than it had been minutes ago. "I just wondered if she were a member of the broken-hearts brigade."

"Of what?" Then it dawned on him. Beth was referring to that idiotic story she'd heard in town yesterday.

"Never mind," she mumbled and picked up her menu.

"I don't know where you heard that," Scott told her, "but it is absolutely untrue. I haven't dated anyone since you."

"Maybe, but you seem to have attracted more than your share of feminine attention." Her face was hidden behind the menu. He reached over and pushed it down.

"Please don't let this spoil our evening," he said as gently as possible, remembering that losing his temper hadn't gotten him anywhere last time.

Her eyes searched his face and finally she relented with a smile. "All right. I do want to enjoy having you all to myself tonight."

Scott felt like he'd dodged a bullet there. "What are you going to have?"

Light conversation followed and it felt like their date was back on track. He was planning how to lead up to the job offer in his head when their waitress arrived. She was young and cute and a former resort employee.

"Hey, Scott," she cried when she saw who was at her table. "How are things at the resort? I hear you're the head honcho there now."

"Yes, I guess that's right," he replied, torn between not wanting to hurt her feelings and reluctance to rile Beth up again.

"I was sorry to hear about Henry," the waitress continued. "I know you two were close."

"Yes," Scott admitted. "It was rough at first."

He glanced at Beth to see how she was taking this. She was studying her menu intently.

"I'd like you to meet my wife."

"Oh, so this is . . . your wife."

Scott wondered what she had been about to say. It was obvious that "wife" wasn't her original word choice. "Yes, this is Beth. Beth, this is Liz. She worked at the resort a couple of summers back."

"Nice to meet you," Beth murmured.

Liz stared at her for a moment and then said, "What can I get you folks tonight?"

They placed their orders for soft drinks, steak and baked potatoes and the waitress quickly retreated.

Beth was quiet after she left and Scott wondered what she was thinking. Was this evening doomed already, or did he still have a shot at talking to her about the job at the resort?

"I think I'll go freshen up," she said abruptly and rose. "I'll be right back."

In the ladies room, Beth took a few moments to comb her hair and freshen her lipstick. She felt strange and out of place. At the resort, she was starting to feel at home, but out in the community it was a different story. Everyone knew Scott, but not her, and now that she knew a few things about how people saw him . . . how women saw him . . . she was confused.

She wanted neither to be unreasonably jealous nor naively unaware. Was there a middle ground? Beth made a decision. She had the chance for a pleasant evening with a person she cared about. If everything fell apart tomorrow, she still wanted this one night to enjoy with Scott. She wasn't going to let her mother's dire warnings or cute waitresses take that away from her.

She walked out of the ladies room and saw their waitress chatting with Scott. Beth could see that she'd just delivered their drinks, but she wasn't making any effort to go on with her work. The restaurant was packed. Surely this woman had something to do besides visit with her husband.

Maybe she'd have to retreat to the ladies room and have another chat with herself, Beth thought. And then Scott looked up and saw her. He smiled, his attention shifting away from Liz, the waitress, and fully onto her, his wife.

The knot in her middle loosened and Beth felt herself returning his smile. She moved through the maze of tables and back to Scott. To her surprise, Liz smiled at her, too.

"Scott has been telling me about your daughter," she gushed. "She sounds beautiful. I love children. My fiancé and I plan to have lots."

Now Beth noticed the sparkling ring on Liz's finger. She stifled the urge to laugh out loud, she was so relieved. Her fears had been totally unfounded — at least in this case.

"Lots of children," she echoed. "That's wonderful. I wish you both the best. Children are blessings."

"Thanks. I'll send you both an invitation to the wedding. It's next summer, after we graduate from college."

"We'll look for it," Scott promised and she went away to wait on her other customers.

"She seemed nice." Beth drew her soda toward her and took a drink.

"Yeah, she was a good employee at the resort. I suppose she makes better tips here."

Beth noticed that Scott seemed a little preoccupied now. He fidgeted, rubbing the sparkling clean silverware on his cloth napkin.

"Are you nervous about something?" she asked.

He flashed a sheepish grin. "I guess I'm pretty transparent."

"Mmmmhmm."

"I wanted to ask you something tonight."

Beth raised her eyebrows in surprise. "So you took me out to butter me up, huh?" she teased.

Scott gave her a crooked grin that did more to soften her heart than the most elite supper out. "Maybe a little. I also thought you might be getting bored hanging around the house."

"Don't try to change the subject. What did you want to ask me?"

"Well, I was going to wait until after we'd eaten. . . ."

"Too late. Spill it."

"All right, all right." Scott took a deep breath. "I had an idea. I want to create a new position at the resort." He spent a few minutes explaining what he had in mind.

"That sounds reasonable," Beth responded. "I mean, you have the facilities. You may as well go after the clients."

"Good, then it's settled. What do you say, Beth? Will you take the job?"

Beth's jaw dropped and she stared at Scott. After a moment she managed to close her mouth. "You're creating a job for me?"

Scott became more animated as he continued. "Yes. You said if you stayed, you'd want a job. I want you to stay and I think you'd be good at this. The clients would bring in a nice stream of income."

Beth turned a wary eye on him. "Would you create this position if you weren't trying to convince me to stay?"

Scott nodded. "Henry always intended to find some corporate clients. It just sort of got pushed to the back burner for a while."

Suspicion made her cautious. "And now it's suddenly time to bring it up again?"

"Yes, because we have the perfect person to fill the job," Scott replied.

"What makes you think that?"

He shrugged. "You're good with people. You have a background in sales. You're organized and dependable."

Beth held up her hand. "That's enough, Scott. I'm convinced you've thought this through."

"So what do you say?" Scott's eyes were pleading and she didn't want to let him down. But she also didn't want to say yes just to make him happy. She closed her eyes to shut out the sight of Scott's face. What should she do?

"What does the job entail?" she asked, hoping to buy herself some time.

This seemed to work because Scott happily launched into a more detailed description of the job. The more Beth heard, the more she thought she would enjoy the job.

Their waitress soon came with the food. Eating offered a good excuse to put off answering Scott and when they did talk again, Beth managed to change the subject.

The rest of the evening was carefree and casual. They sat and talked long after their meals were finished. He paid the bill, and together, hand in hand they walked out to his silver SUV.

"It's not that late," he said as he turned the key in the ignition. "Are you ready to go home?"

"I don't know. What did you have in mind?"

"I know a great place for stargazing."

"Stargazing? I've never done that before."

He shook his head. "City girl."

"Hey, I spent a lot of time in the country when I was growing up."

"And you've never gone stargazing before?"

"No one's ever asked me."

"I'm asking you now," he replied.

Beth shrugged, not caring where they went as long as they were together. "All right. Let's go."

Scott drove back to the resort and parked in the main lot. After spraying insect repellent on both of them, he led Beth along one of the hiking trails.

"How can you see any stars through all these trees," she complained.

"Just wait. We're not there yet."

"Where are you taking me?"

Scott held back a low branch and motioned for her to go ahead. "Just here."

Beth stepped out into a clearing. They were on a bluff looking out over the lake. Above the lake a field of glittering stars unfurled. Beth gasped, "It's beautiful."

Taking her hand, he steered her to a picnic table situated for the best view. The moon hung low over the lake, its reflection a twin in the water. They sat on top of the table, their feet resting on the benches.

"I admit, I was skeptical at first, but this is absolutely gorgeous." Beth sighed and leaned against him. Scott wrapped his arms around her and held her close.

Beth felt contentment wash over and gratitude filled her heart for this moment of complete peace. She wasn't sure how long they sat there, drinking in the beauty of their surroundings and enjoying the simple companionship of each other.

"Thank you, Scott, for this moment."

His lips nuzzled at her ear. "I love you, Beth. I'd like you to stay and be able to enjoy this whenever you want."

Scott jolted her back to the real world. "Will you accept the job, Beth?"

"Is it important to you?"

"I think you'd be great at it and the resort would benefit."

Beth remained silent. It was a wonderful offer. Scott had listened to her and was giving her what she'd asked for. But if she took it, she would have to give up everything she had in Green Bay.

"I'd like to, Scott, but. . . ."

He pulled away and turned Beth so he could look in her eyes. "You want to do this, I can tell. What's holding you back?"

Beth closed her eyes and summoned up

her courage. She'd promised herself that she'd try. She couldn't give up at the first little bump in the road.

"If I take the job it would mean I'm staying. It's not that I don't want to stay, but the idea of giving up my job, my home, everything I've come to depend on is . . . a little frightening. Please try to understand."

"I understand," he replied in a grim voice. "I let you down and now you can't trust me."

He looked so hurt, Beth felt moved to explain further. It was hard for her to admit these things, but she was as honest as she could be about it. "It's not that. It's . . . it's remembering my parents and how bitter they were toward each other. I'm afraid you'll feel that way about me someday. I know you want to do the right thing by staying married, but what if the right thing doesn't make you happy? I'd rather let you go than have you come to hate me."

"I don't really know how things were with your parents. You never told me."

A lifetime's worth of emotions rose in her — hurt, betrayal, guilt. The rush of feelings almost choked her and she couldn't reply.

"Beth, tell me about your parents," Scott urged.

She stared straight ahead, her voice suddenly measured and lifeless. "They got married because my mom was pregnant, just like us. They stopped loving each other sometime . . . if they ever loved each other in the first place. There was fighting and screaming and Dad would leave for days. Then finally he left and didn't come back."

"That's a horrible way to grow up. I'm sorry," Scott whispered, pulling her close to him again.

"They said all the things they were supposed to, that it wasn't my fault and that they still loved me. But after the divorce I never felt that either of them wanted me. They both remarried and started new families. It didn't seem like there was a place for me."

"That's when you became close to your grandmother."

She nodded. "So you understand why this is hard for me. I can't bear the thought of putting Risa in the same position, or of being stuck in a marriage gone bad because I have no way to support myself."

"Just because it happened to your parents doesn't mean it will happen to us," Scott argued.

"It did happen to us," Beth reminded him, her mind returning to the matter at hand. "We argued and fought and were miserable.

I told you to leave, and you did. You were gone for more than three years. Now you want me to leave the life I built and depend on you for everything — food, a roof over my head, even a job."

"But things are different now."

"No they're not. You're still pushing me. You want everything to be your way just like before."

"When did I ever do that . . . ?" His words trailed off and she knew he caught her meaning. She'd been timid and naïve and let him make all the decisions in their relationship before. Including the one that led to a marriage neither one was ready for.

Scott got up abruptly and walked away. "So you're blaming me for everything."

She closed her eyes and tried to regain a hold on her fragile control. "No, that's not fair. I could have said 'no.' 'No' to sleeping with you, 'no' to marrying you. But I wasn't strong enough then and now I am. Maybe you're still in love with that Beth, but not with me. Why don't you think about that for a while."

She got up and walked away, leaving him in the clearing. She'd been at the resort long enough to know her way around, so she didn't bother to wait for him at the SUV. She just went home.

Only it wasn't her home, it was Scott's.
So why did it feel more like home than her
house in Green Bay?

Scott had gotten back before her. He was
just sending Shannon off through the front
door while Beth was coming in the back.

They met in the family room, staring at
each other warily.

"Where's Risa?" Beth finally asked, need-
ing to end the silence.

"She's asleep."

Beth nodded. "Thank you for . . . dinner.
I'm sorry the evening didn't turn out the
way you planned."

"Me, too." His face was stony but his eyes
betrayed the anger still simmering inside.

"I'm going upstairs now," she told him.
"I'll talk to you in the morning."

Scott didn't respond but she felt his gaze
on her until she was out of sight upstairs.

It didn't seem as if rest were a possibility.
She checked on Risa, found her sleeping
peacefully and retreated to the piano. But it
reminded her of Scott and she couldn't look
at it tonight.

She turned and went to the bedroom after
all. Sleep or no sleep it looked like she was
stuck there until morning.

Around three A.M., Beth decided anything
was better than staring at the ceiling for

another minute. She crept downstairs, hoping to sneak into the kitchen for a cup of herbal tea to soothe her nerves.

Scott was there, peering into the refrigerator. She tried to back out quietly before he saw her, but she tripped over one of the stools at the counter with a loud thump, and fell right on her backside.

Before she could move, Scott was there. "Beth, are you all right?"

She groaned and sat up. "Yes. So much for a graceful exit. I didn't mean to disturb you. The kitchen is all yours."

Scott pulled her to her feet. "You disturbed me all right, but not by coming into the kitchen."

"What are you talking about? I'm too exhausted to handle cryptic. Just give it to me straight, Scott."

He pulled out a chair at the table and gestured for her to join him. Reluctantly, she did.

"What you said tonight . . . it hurt. I can't deny that. But you have a valid point."

"I do?" She was too surprised to give a more intelligent response.

"Yes. Maybe we need a little more time together before we decide what to do."

Oh no. Had she made such a good case that he was convinced he didn't want her anymore? And wasn't that what she'd told herself all along? That he didn't really love her. Why did she have this sinking feeling in her stomach now?

The fear of losing him suddenly became stronger than the fear of a marriage going bad in the future.

"I'm sorry. So sorry. I was . . . mean. I'm sorry." You sound crazy, she told herself and bit her lip so she wouldn't say anything else.

"You were honest," Scott replied. "And I'm glad, even though I didn't like what you said."

She felt the urge to apologize again and fought it.

"I want you to know that I've noticed how much you've changed. And I like the new Beth, the more assertive one."

"You do?"

"I've changed, too. Maybe you need more time to get to know the new me. If you need to go back to Green Bay for a while, we'll work it out. I just want you to know I'm not giving up."

Beth wondered if she'd finally managed to fall asleep and was dreaming. "I don't understand," she protested. "I yelled at you. I said you had to have everything your way. I blamed you. . . ."

"Husbands and wives argue sometimes.

That doesn't mean they don't love each other."

"I can stay a while longer," she found herself saying in a deceptively calm voice. "I could . . . I could look at your idea for this position at the resort, help you create a job description, maybe even outline a campaign to attract corporate clients. Then . . . then even if I don't stay, someone else can step in and follow through."

"Thank you," Scott said quietly. "I accept your offer."

"Does that mean we're not fighting anymore?"

"I don't want to fight anymore, Beth."

She burst into tears. Not quiet, ladylike tears but huge, choking sobs. She should be smiling and making up with him, but the sudden release of guilt and regret opened the flood gates instead.

She was grateful to Scott for not asking what was wrong, not asking for an explanation. He simply led her to the sofa — even though the bed was folded out — and sat with her, held her until her sobs subsided.

"I'm so glad we aren't fighting anymore," she told him.

"You have a funny way of showing it," he replied.

Scott carried her up to bed and tucked

her in much like he would have with Risa. She felt him kiss her, so softly and tenderly that it almost made her cry again. Then he left and she slipped into a deep, exhausted sleep.

Once she agreed to try the job, Scott wasted no time in getting a computer installed in their living room. They'd decided that for now, Beth didn't need to be at the resort. At first she'd be doing research and planning her campaign.

She kissed Scott good-bye Monday morning and, once he'd left, settled herself at the computer, with Risa playing nearby. Beth put her fingers on the keyboard, ready to go.

Ten minutes later she was still staring at a blank screen. Should she research some area companies on the Internet? Work on an ad? Make a to-do list? What was wrong with her?

Beth sighed. She couldn't even pretend to kid herself. She knew why she was so nervous. She didn't want to disappoint Scott. She didn't want to embarrass him in front of his resort family.

And speaking of family, she hadn't called Hal yet to tell him she'd be staying even longer.

Beth dreaded that call. Hal would not appreciate her continued absence at work or being kept from his granddaughter all summer. With determination, she pushed herself to work.

By the time she stopped to make supper, Beth thought she had made a creditable start, although she felt more like she'd spent the day running a marathon than sitting at the computer.

Scott came home looking anxious, but he didn't ask her about what she'd accomplished. She could tell he was wondering, so she gave him a report over supper.

"That's a good start, Beth," he told her. "I knew you would be perfect for this job."

She tried to tell herself that Scott would say that no matter what she said because he wanted to keep her here at the resort with him. Still, she couldn't help feeling good when he praised her.

After supper Scott began clearing the table. "First days are always hard. You go put your feet up while Risa and I clean up here."

"I spent the whole day in the living room. I shouldn't feel this tired," Beth protested.

"But you do," Scott finished for her. "Go ahead, relax."

"Since you offer so nicely," said Beth with a smile, "I think I'll go have a soak in the tub. My back is sore from sitting at the computer all day."

Scott grinned at her. "Just let me know when you want me to come in and wash your back for you."

Beth wrinkled her nose at him. "Don't hold your breath," she called over her shoulder as she left the kitchen.

Her foot was at the bottom of the steps when the sound of shouts were heard followed by a scream.

"What's going on?" asked Beth, but Scott was already outside. She grabbed Risa and rushed to follow him.

Ben and Cindy's cottage was close to Scott's, but hidden by the trees. Scott raced down the path and Beth was right behind him. She pulled up short when she saw Troy and Shaun punching and wrestling with each other on the ground, a distraught Shannon standing nearby.

Ben and Scott reached the teens at the same time. Scott grabbed Troy and Ben grabbed Shaun. They hauled the boys apart and to their feet.

"What's going on?" demanded Ben.

"This jerk was kissing Shannon," Shaun yelled as he swung again. Ben's hold kept the punch from hitting its mark.

"Settle down," he roared, and Shaun stilled.

Ben directed his question to Shannon this time. "Tell me what happened."

Between sobs Shannon explained that she and Troy had been sitting on the deck talking, when Troy had kissed her. "It was a nice kiss. There was no . . . no groping or anything else going on, Dad. Shaun had no reason to hit him, really."

By this time, Cindy was on the scene with an ice pack for Troy's jaw, where a bruise was already starting to show.

Seeing that everything was in hand, Beth took the opportunity to return to their cottage. The night air was chilly and Risa was in shorts and a T-shirt.

A few minutes later, Scott came in. "How did things turn out?" Beth asked.

"Ben made Shaun apologize, but he couldn't force any sincerity. Shannon was fussing over Troy and that upset him more than getting punched, I think. So Ben sent him home."

"Is Ben mad at Troy for kissing Shannon?"

"He said he wasn't, but he didn't look too happy either."

Beth shook her head. "Poor Shannon, she must be so embarrassed."

"So is Troy."

"Ah, well," Beth intoned, "the path of true love never runs smoothly."

"Don't I know it," Scott agreed. The words were light, but there was a strange look in his eyes when he said them, so Beth didn't add anything.

"I'm going to try again to take my bath," she said. "Then I'm ready for some sleep." A quick glance back showed Scott standing at the foot of the steps watching her as she reached the top and turned into the bathroom.

CHAPTER 15

"Hello, Hal." Beth gripped the phone so tightly her knuckles showed white. She was not looking forward to her father-in-law's reaction to her news.

"Beth, finally," Hal's gruff voice rang out through the phone. "I thought maybe you'd gotten lost in the woods up there."

She laughed nervously. "Not exactly."

"So, when are you coming home?"

Beth gulped, took a deep breath and told him straight out. "Not for a while. Maybe not until the end of August."

"What?"

"Scott offered me a job and I said I'd try it for a while."

"You still think you're coming back?"

There was a long pause, then finally she asked, "Will you hold my job until then, Hal?"

"If it were anyone else, no. But I'll do it for you, Beth."

"Thanks, Hal. I do appreciate it, you know."

"I know. How's Risa?"

"She's doing great." Beth launched into a description of picnics, swimming, walks in the woods and all the other activities that Risa had been doing. "I was worried about her missing her therapies while we're here, but she's so active I don't think it matters."

"That's great. I miss her."

"You'll be here for her birthday," Beth reminded him. She felt a stab of guilt at the wistful tone in his voice.

"How's . . . how's Scott?"

"He's fine. He's doing great actually. Wait until you see him in action here. He loves this place and he's doing a wonderful job with it."

"Glad to hear that. What's this job he's given you?"

Beth launched into a description of her new responsibilities.

"Hmmm," said Hal when she'd finished. "It sounds like the job's a good fit for you."

"It makes me happy to know that I'm contributing."

"Well, thanks for calling, Beth, but I have to get back to work now."

"All right. Say 'hello' to Margie for me."

"I will."

Beth hung up the phone and heaved a sigh of relief. The call hadn't gone as badly as she thought it might. Hal didn't even get mad, but what if she didn't come back in September? What if she really did decide to move up here for good? She didn't want to think about it right now.

Instead, she worked on her ad campaign aimed at corporate customers, practiced piano, played with Risa, and did some laundry. She was folding towels when Scott came in, finished with work for the day.

He greeted her with a kiss and a hug. It felt good, warm and safe, to have him come home and kiss her every day.

"How was your day?" she asked.

"Fine. How about yours?"

Beth didn't have a chance to say more than "fine" before Risa realized her daddy was home and flung herself into his arms. Scott lifted her up and swung her around, making her giggle.

"Would you like to hang out with Shaun and Sam tonight?" Scott asked Risa. She nodded enthusiastically.

"What? Why would Shaun and Sam be hanging out with Risa?" asked Beth.

"There's a street dance in Spruce Point tonight," Scott explained. "I asked Shannon to babysit so we could go, but she and Troy

300

have a date. Sam volunteered to watch Risa and Shaun offered to keep him company."

"We're going to a dance?" asked Beth.

"If you want to," Scott replied. "I thought it would be fun."

"I'd love to. I'll go change."

The main street of Spruce Point was blocked off for the dance. A country music band was playing when they got there and the street was filled with dancers. One of the local businesses had volunteered its parking lot so food vendors could set up their stands. Scott pulled Beth into the crowd and they danced until they were both breathless and thirsty.

"Let's take a break," suggested Beth at the end of a song.

Scott nodded and taking her hand again, they threaded their way through the crowd to the food stand where they picked up cups of iced tea. Picnic tables had been set up and they found an empty one to sit at while they cooled off.

Several people came by when they saw Scott and stopped to talk. He introduced them to Beth and they were friendly and welcoming to her. Mostly she just listened to Scott talk. She leaned against him and he put his arm around her.

After a while, the last of his friends drifted

off. "Are you ready to dance again?" he asked her.

Beth shook her head. "In a minute. It's nice just to sit with you for a bit."

Scott hugged her to his side and dropped a kiss on her head. "Everything is nice when you're around."

Beth's mouth curled into a teasing smile. "Just nice? That's it? Not fantastic or wonderful. It's just 'nice.' "

"Are you fishing for compliments?" he teased back.

"Would I catch any?"

"Definitely."

The way he looked into her eyes when he said it was at odds with his teasing tone. Beth shivered with anticipation.

"Are you cold?"

"Maybe a little. We'd better dance so I can warm up."

Among the dancers, they spotted Shannon and Troy. Shannon smiled and waved, and Troy raised his hand in a brief acknowledgement. They were with some other teens, Shannon's friends most likely, Beth thought, so she and Scott didn't approach them. She saw a few couples that were guests at the resort and Scott introduced her to them. She suspected that a few of the women he introduced her to were the ones who'd been disappointed when they found out Scott was married. But they didn't seem to hold a grudge, at least not in front of Scott, and Beth found that it didn't bother her as much as she thought it would.

It was a fun night, much better than just "nice." But too soon she had to admit she was getting tired. "I think it's time to go home," she told Scott.

"I guess so. Shaun and Sam have to work tomorrow at the restaurant. We shouldn't keep them up too late," he agreed.

They walked down one of the side streets to where the SUV waited. About a block from where they parked, Beth noticed Troy's truck. As they got closer, she saw someone was inside.

Scott saw it too and quickened his pace. He walked up to the truck and knocked on the window. Now Beth could see it was Troy and Shannon inside, locked in an embrace.

Both teens jumped when they heard the knock at the window. When Shannon saw Scott and Beth standing outside, her face turned red and she pushed away from Troy. Looking grim, Troy rolled the window down.

"Isn't it past your curfew, Shannon?" asked Scott.

"Is it?" Shannon checked her watch,

squinting to see the time in the dim glow from the streetlights. "Oh no. Troy, I have to go home."

"We can give Shannon a ride if you like," Scott offered. He didn't look any friendlier than Troy did just now.

"No, I can take her," insisted Troy.

"There's no reason for you to drive all the way out to the resort and then back into town to Fred's house."

"It's my responsibility to see Shannon home."

Scott and Troy stared at each other, surrounded by a hostile silence. Shannon and Beth exchanged glances.

Finally Scott stepped back. "All right, but make sure you take her right home. No detours."

"I will." Troy looked as if he would like to say much more, but held back. "Good night."

"Good night." Scott took Beth's hand and they moved down to his SUV.

"Wow," said Beth, "things are really heating up between those two."

"Yeah," said Scott grimly. "I don't know if I should tell Ben and Cindy or not."

"I would hate for Shannon to think she couldn't trust you. I'll try talking to her tomorrow to see just how serious this is getting," Beth offered.

"Thanks," he said and started the SUV. "I won't say anything yet."

Beth laughed. "And definitely don't say anything to the boys tonight or they'll be out after Troy's hide."

Scott smiled but stayed quiet.

The next morning Beth was sitting at the kitchen table, sipping her tea and trying to think of a way to get Shannon alone. Beth groaned and wished she hadn't offered to talk to her. But if she hadn't, Scott would have gone straight to Ben. She didn't think that would actually help the situation.

Just then there was a knock at the kitchen door. Beth glanced up to see Shannon standing on the deck, waiting to be invited in. She smiled and motioned to come in. Shannon slid the door open and walked into the kitchen.

"Hi, Beth," she said, quietly.

"Hi, Shannon," Beth replied. "What brings you over?"

She stared at the floor. "I was wondering if you had anything for me to do today."

"You mean like babysitting? No, I'm fine today."

"Oh. Okay. I guess I can go then." She continued to stare at the floor.

Realizing that there was more on the teen's mind than making a little extra money, Beth said, "Would you like to stay for a cup of tea?"

Shannon looked up and smiled. "Yes, thanks."

Beth started to rise, but Shannon stopped her. "I can put the kettle on. You don't have to get up."

While the water heated, they talked about the weather, the resort and this week's guests. Risa heard Shannon's voice and toddled in from the next room where she'd been playing. Beth got out a coloring book and a box of crayons and settled Risa at the table.

When both women were seated at the table with steaming mugs of tea, Beth said, "Did you enjoy the dance last night, Shannon?"

"Yes." There was a long pause, then Shannon asked, "Where's Scott?"

"I know, it's Saturday, but he went over to his office. He had a little paperwork to finish up."

"I just wanted to ask if. . . ." Shannon bit her lip. "If you were going to tell my parents about me and Troy last night."

"You mean about you two making out in his truck?"

Shannon nodded, her face redder than her hair.

Beth stirred a bit of sugar into her tea. "Well, we did talk about it. Do you think it's something they would approve of?"

Shannon shook her head. "Probably not. I mean, I think it's okay to kiss your boyfriend, but. . . ."

"But there, in his truck, things could have easily gone too far."

"We were right in town," protested Shannon. "Anyone could have walked by. Nothing was going to happen."

"If you believe that, why are you worried about me telling your parents?" asked Beth.

Tears shone in Shannon's eyes. She grabbed a paper napkin from the holder on the table and swiped at her eyes. "I don't know. It's just that I'm not sure what my mom and dad think of Troy, and you know what my brothers think of him."

Beth reached out and took Shannon's hand. "I think you're worried about more than what your parents are going to say. What's going on?"

Now Shannon started to cry for real. Risa looked up from her coloring. Seeing her friend cry, she slid out of her chair and went to Shannon who picked her up and hugged her tightly. The child touched Shannon's wet face. "Cry?" she asked.

Beth took Risa from Shannon. "Yes, Shannon is crying. She's sad right now."

Shannon took a deep breath and wiped her eyes one more time. "I'm all right, Risa," she said. Beth waited while her friend got herself under control.

"Do you want to tell me what's bothering you?"

"I don't know what to say exactly," began Shannon. "It's all so confusing."

"Just a minute," said Beth. She took Risa into the living room and popped a DVD in. Risa was instantly mesmerized. She didn't move and Beth could still see her from the kitchen.

She sat down again. "Okay, tell me."

Shannon was nervously shredding her damp napkin. "I don't know where to start."

"Start with Troy. How do you feel about him?"

"Well, I like him obviously. I like him a lot."

"What do you like about him?"

"I like talking to him. He's different when we're alone. He doesn't have the bad-boy attitude and we can talk about anything — our families, school, our friends, movies. Oh you know, just anything."

Beth nodded. "What else?"

"The way he treats me. He opens doors for me. No one has ever done that before. Last weekend, when we went to a movie, some guys from school started teasing me, and Troy made them stop. It was kind of scary because I thought they were going to get in a fight, but they didn't and it was nice to know I could depend on him to stand up for me."

"I'm glad he didn't get into a fight, but I can see what you mean," Beth said. "So what's the problem?"

"I don't know. It's just that everything is moving so fast."

"Like in the truck last night?"

Shannon nodded, and stared down at the table. "We didn't intend to sit there and park. Troy was going to take me home, but then we started kissing and . . . and we sort of lost track of time."

"I can see how that would happen," Beth commented dryly.

"Now I'm in trouble for being late and my parents are starting to wonder if they can trust me. I want them to be able to trust me, but. . . ."

"But what?"

"But sometimes I *don't* trust me."

"Physical attraction is a powerful force," Beth admitted. "I guess I can't tell you that

I've never been carried away by it. But there are a lot of reasons not to give in to it."

"I know," Shannon nodded. "Troy is leaving at the end of the summer. How could we start a serious relationship?"

"I'm glad to hear you think you'd have to be in a serious relationship to consider sex with someone."

Shannon's face burned red. "I didn't say we were going to have — to do it."

"You'd better think about it. If you don't and let one thing lead to another, that's what's going to happen."

"What do you mean?"

"You two need to think about some boundaries," Beth explained. "You need to agree on how physical your relationship is going to get and when to stop. If you don't talk about it, you're more likely to get carried away and do something you'll regret later."

When Shannon didn't say anything, Beth continued. "I wasn't much older than you when Scott and I got pregnant. I was very lucky it was with Scott. I didn't really know him well enough to be sure I wanted to spend the rest of my life with him. What if he'd turned out to be a real jerk? If I'd had a child with someone like that, I'd be linked to him forever whether we got married or not."

Shannon was silent for a long moment. "Thank you, Beth. I thought you'd just tell me 'you're too young' or something like that. I appreciate you talking to me like I'm an adult."

Beth didn't know what to say so she settled for a simple "You're welcome."

"I don't want to have sex with Troy." She stopped and rolled her eyes. "Well, I mean I do . . . sometimes . . . but I know it would be a bad idea for me right now."

"I'm sure you could talk to your mom if you have any questions."

"I know, but it would be hard. She'd be disappointed in me if I made a mistake. You're more . . . objective, I guess. I'm glad you came here this summer."

"Thank you. I'm glad I came, too."

"Are you going to stay, Beth?" asked Shannon.

It was Beth's turn to stare at the table. How could she explain this to Shannon? Funny that it would be harder to talk about marriage than sex. "I haven't made a final decision yet."

"Why not? You said yourself that Scott's a great guy. Or you implied it anyway. And we all love you and Risa. You should stay."

"I have a job back in Green Bay."

Shannon rolled her eyes. "Well, quit."

Beth forced a smile. She wished it were that easy. She'd love to stay here at the resort forever. But would Hal take it out on Scott if she quit? Would Scott be angry with her if he did? "I'll think about it. I'm going to be here until September anyway, I guess. I don't have to make a decision yet."

The phone rang and Beth, glad to end their conversation, jumped up to answer it. The caller ID showed that it was Scott. As soon as she answered he spoke. "Beth, I'm going to the hospital. Troy's with me."

"The hospital? Why? What happened? Why is Troy with you?"

"Fred had a heart attack."

Beth gasped and glanced at Shannon. Obviously she'd heard one side of the conversation. "Troy's all right," she hastened to reassure her.

"What's going on?"

"Beth I have to go." Scott's voice reminded her that she was still on the phone.

"I'm sorry," she said. "Call me later, when you know something."

She hung up and reached out to a clearly agitated Shannon. "I'm sorry. Fred's had a heart attack."

Chapter 16

It was late when Troy and Scott left the hospital that night. Together they walked out to Scott's SUV in the parking lot.

"Thanks for staying with me," Troy said quietly as Scott turned the key in the ignition.

"I've known Fred for a long time. I was glad I could be there," Scott replied. Troy had dropped his tough-guy image pretty fast when he thought he might lose his grandfather. Now he looked tired, but mostly he looked young and vulnerable.

"You know your grandfather's going to be okay, don't you?" The heart attack had been fairly severe and it had been frightening to see Fred in that hospital bed, hooked up to monitors and an IV. It must have been infinitely worse for Troy.

Troy nodded. "The doctor said so. I guess I should call my mom." He didn't look happy about that.

"Do you want me to call her?" Scott found himself offering.

"No, I should do it." Troy stared out the window into the night. "It's just that things have been hard for her lately. I don't want to give her more bad news."

"You mean because of your dad leaving?" asked Scott gently. "Fred told me about that."

For a moment, Scott thought Troy would resurrect the hostile attitude he usually wore. But then he nodded. "Yeah."

"I'm sure it's been hard for you, too."

Troy shrugged. "I don't need him. It's just that money's been tight since he left. I'll get a job at home after the summer and help out."

Scott didn't know why he felt he had to push it. They were both tired. But Troy was being open for a change and he may never get another chance like this.

"You don't miss him at all?"

"My dad's a jerk. He was having an affair and he ran off with a woman. He doesn't care what happens to me or my mom. I wish I had a family like yours," Troy admitted.

Scott glanced at him in surprise. "You do?"

"Yeah. I bet your parents have always been there for you." The look in Troy's eyes was

314

wistful and Scott thought he should probably just let the subject drop.

Instead, he found himself saying, "Actually, not. My . . . my dad and I haven't seen
eye to eye on anything for a long time."

Troy's head bobbed up. "Really?"

"Really," Scott answered softly. "I guess
that's why the people at the resort mean so
much to me."

"What's your dad like?" asked Troy.

"He's a perfectionist. My older brother
Dave was the ideal son to him."

"Wow. That must be hard to swallow."

"It wasn't so bad until Dave died. He
drowned in a boating accident when he was
eighteen."

"Man," Troy exhaled softly. Scott could
feel the compassion in that one syllable.
"I'm sorry."

"It was a long time ago." This was Scott's
standard answer to the sympathy people offered when they heard he had a brilliant
brother who had died young. He didn't say
it because the hurt had lessened over the
years. It was only that saying "it was a long
time ago" tended to stop the conversation
from continuing.

"But . . . but what does that have to do
with you and your dad?"

"After my brother died, my dad pushed

hard for me to become like my brother. Dave got the best grades, was always MVP of whatever sport he played, was a leader with the youth group at church. He was the all-around American boy as far as my father was concerned. And I loved my brother. But we're not interchangeable."

"Your dad wanted you to be just like your brother?"

"I tried. I managed okay. I even got a basketball scholarship to our hometown college. But then I hurt my knee and couldn't play anymore. The worst part was that I didn't even do it playing basketball. I had a summer job building houses and it happened on the construction site. I don't think my dad has ever forgiven me. I don't know why, but I still hope he will someday."

Troy shrugged. "I've never told this to anyone before, but even though I know my dad was wrong and a total jerk, there are times when I wish he'd come back."

"I can understand that."

"If I have a kid someday," Troy said, "I won't run out on him . . . or her."

Scott put a hand on Troy's shoulder. "I know you won't." He thought of all the long conversations he'd had with Henry and how the older man had listened and guided him but hadn't pushed. He'd given Scott things to think about but never told him *what* to think. Was he doing the same for Troy now? He hoped so.

Scott pulled into Fred's driveway but it occurred to him that Troy may not want to stay at his grandfather's house alone. "Will you be all right? You can come back to the resort if you want. We have plenty of room for you."

Troy shook his head. "I'm fine. I'm used to being on my own."

Scott closed his eyes. Troy wasn't such a tough guy after all. He was still only a kid, really. Before he could change his mind he said, "Go get your stuff. You can stay at my place tonight."

"But I have to call my mom."

"We have a phone."

"But it's long distance."

"Troy, you have three minutes to get your stuff together. Get moving."

Troy stood undecided for a moment, then he said, "Okay," and sprinted for the house.

Beth was in bed, but only dozing when she heard the door open downstairs. The sound of voices floated up to her and she realized Scott wasn't alone.

Grabbing her robe, she headed downstairs. Troy was pulling out the sofa bed.

"Hi, Beth," he said. "Scott said I could stay tonight."

She tried not to let her surprise show. "Oh. That's fine. How's your grandfather?"

"The doctor said he's going to be okay. But he has to stay in the hospital for a few days, I guess."

Scott stepped in from the laundry room with sheets in his arms. "What are you doing up? Did we wake you?"

"I wasn't really sleeping," Beth said. "I wanted to wait up for you and hear how Fred was doing."

"He's doing fine. They'll take good care of him."

"That's a relief. Troy said he's staying here tonight."

"Yeah, you don't mind, do you?"

"No, but where will you . . . ?"

He cut her off. "Beth, why don't you go back to bed? I'll be up in a minute," Scott said.

Well, that answered that question. "Okay. Good night, Troy."

After Beth had gone back upstairs, Troy grinned at Scott.

"What?"

"You've been sleeping on the sofa. She was going to ask where you were going to sleep."

Scott was too tired to deny it. He started to put the bottom sheet on the bed. "So?"

"That means Beth hasn't really taken you back yet, has she?" Troy grabbed a pillow and started stuffing it into a pillowcase. "Shannon told me about you guys."

"We haven't finalized everything, so no. And we didn't want to rush things."

"So you're not. . . ."

"Troy, I'm not going to discuss my personal life with Beth with you," Scott warned the teen.

"Okay, okay. It's just that . . . you're already married. Why not?"

How did he explain this to a seventeen-year-old? "I want to rebuild a relationship with Beth."

"But you love her, don't you?"

"Love and commitment isn't the same thing. I've learned it's better to have both before you get into bed with someone."

"You mean like being married?"

Scott sighed. "Beth and I are married but we aren't one-hundred-percent sure how things are going to work out for our future. Until she's ready to commit to me again, I don't want to complicate things."

Troy shrugged. "I don't get it."

Scott wondered if he should be talking to Troy about this. He wasn't the kid's parent.

But then again, Troy didn't have anyone else on hand to give him advice. Scott finished placing the sheets while he pulled his thoughts together. "Sex is an important part of a relationship between a man and a woman. But that doesn't mean it's the best way to show your feelings for someone. Making love changes your relationship. It also has pros and cons."

"You mean like getting pregnant or getting a disease?"

"Yes. If you're going to have sex with someone you have to be sure you're ready to deal with things like that. But there are also emotional consequences. Making love with someone forges a sort of bond with them. It's more painful to break up after that." Thinking of Shannon, Scott couldn't help but add, "So if you aren't planning on sticking around, it's really kind of selfish to start that sort of relationship."

As they finished making up the bed Scott could tell Troy was thinking things over.

"What if you both know it's only temporary, but you still want to do it? If you both feel the same way. . . ."

"I guess that could be okay, but you never know what's going to happen. What if she gets pregnant? And don't say it couldn't happen if you use birth control. I can tell you for a fact, it can. If you're not ready to accept the consequences, you're not ready for that kind of relationship. Believe me, I found that out the hard way."

"So you should just wait, like forever, until you know you've found *the one?*"

Scott considered his words carefully. If he pushed his point too hard, Troy would certainly head in the opposite direction. "That's your choice. But you should understand that it's a big deal, because it is."

"Man, I can't believe we're talking about this. My mom freaks if I just mention sex. And my dad . . . well, I don't talk to him about anything anymore."

"It's late. I think we'd both better go to bed."

"Where are you going to sleep?"

"Upstairs. And that's all I'll be doing — sleeping."

Scott stripped to his boxers and T-shirt and slid under the covers. It felt good to be in his own bed again, but not half as good as the idea of holding Beth in his own bed. He pulled her to him, cradling her body with his.

"Scott?" she whispered.

He heard the uncertainty in her voice. "Don't worry, Beth. I'm only here to sleep.

I'm too tired to try anything else." There were certain parts of his body that denied that, but he was willing to ignore them. He felt her relax and soon her even breaths told him that she was asleep.

Scott wished he could sleep, too. His body was tired, but his mind couldn't shut down. He had to admit, he was glad for the excuse to be back in his own room and to hold Beth close again. He would keep his word — he was there for sleeping only. But Scott couldn't help wondering how Beth would respond if he'd asked for more. She might have said yes.

There were times in the past few weeks when she'd seemed more than willing. But she hadn't made up her mind about him yet. Scott didn't want to risk doing something that would damage the trust he was trying to build with her again. Regret for the decision he'd made three years ago made his stomach clench. Where would they be today if he'd stayed?

On the other hand, if he'd stayed he'd never have met Henry and come to the Pine Away Inn. Being here, knowing these people had changed him, helped him grow up.

He thought of Troy and hoped he'd said the right things. He wasn't that much older than Troy. He felt like he was, but in years there wasn't so much difference. Beth sighed in her sleep and snuggled closer to him. That put an abrupt end to all thoughts of anything but her. He let himself travel back in his mind, thinking about when he first noticed her.

She was always with other cast members, but somehow she'd seemed set apart. She had an aura of loneliness about her and Scott could relate to that. Maybe that was what first drew his attention to her, but it was her personality that had kept it. He'd watched her backstage and noticed how nice she was. She went out of her way to make someone feel better when they were having an off night. She was always willing to help other cast members memorize lines. Most amazing of all, she didn't like to gossip and seldom had a bad word to say about anyone. This was what had convinced him that she wouldn't be interested in and didn't deserve what Jeremy Fletcher had in mind for her.

But he had to admit, he soon wasn't any better than that two-bit Romeo. After they started dating, all Scott could think of was how to get her alone. Her sweet, shy personality was a balm to the raw places of his soul. Beth didn't care if he wasn't on the basketball team anymore. She didn't care if he didn't get straight A's or if he didn't know what he wanted to do after graduation. She simply loved him for who he was.

And she was beautiful. He loved the way she looked, the way she felt, the way she smelled. He couldn't get enough of her. Memories of those nights — and mornings — and afternoons — had kept him awake more than once in the past years.

What an idiot he was. He couldn't think beyond the next time he would see her. Things got too hot, too fast.

Granted, Beth could have said no like she had to Jeremy. She could have told him to get lost. Instead she'd offered up her innocence, his for the taking. But she'd been so timid then that later he wondered if she was as willing a participant as he'd thought.

Scott eased himself away from Beth and sat up. He wasn't going to sleep while his brain was on overload. He walked down the hall to check on Risa.

Moonlight streamed in through the window, highlighting the soft, childish curve of her cheek. He reached out and brushed her bangs back from her face, wishing she could stay little forever.

He prowled restlessly around her room, picking up a toy here and there and putting a T-shirt in the hamper.

He couldn't sleep and he couldn't go

downstairs to watch TV without waking Troy. What was he going to do with himself? Scott sat down in the rocking chair by Risa's bed. He'd just have to sit and wait for morning.

Beth found Scott in the early hours of the morning, his head thrown back, snoring in the rocking chair. "Scott," she whispered, shaking his shoulder. "Scott."

His head snapped up. "What?"

"What are you doing in here? Was something wrong with Risa?"

He shook his head. "No. I couldn't sleep."

It was cool in the room and she shivered. "Well, for heaven's sake, come back to bed now. You can get a few hours in anyway."

"No, I think I'll just go take a shower and go to work. I never finished that paperwork yesterday."

"But it's Sunday," Beth protested. Why would he want to go to work now?

"Yeah, well, with Fred in the hospital, I really won't have time for it this week."

"What about church later?"

He yawned and stretched. "I can get a lot done before then."

"Whatever you say, Scott. I'm going back to bed."

Beth crawled back into bed, choking down

her disappointment. It seemed Scott couldn't even stand to be in the same bed with her. The way he'd reacted when she woke him up, you'd think he didn't even want to be in the same room as her. Why did he act so sweet one minute and push her away the next? Was this the proof that he was trying to keep their marriage together for Risa and not because he loved her?

How can I put my trust in him until I know for sure? Beth wondered.

CHAPTER 17

"If you don't eat, you'll never get out of this place. Is that what you want, Fred?" Ronnie asked, staring down at him, hands on her hips.

"I'd eat if they gave me something edible," grumbled Fred. "Have you ever tasted hospital food?"

Ronnie scooped up a spoonful of gelatin. "Stop being such a baby. Open up."

Fred stared at the green blob quivering on the end of the spoon. He rolled his eyes and opened his mouth.

Watching the scene from the sidelines, Beth stifled a giggle. She was sure Fred was loving the attention from Ronnie, but if he let her know it, she'd back off. Instead he argued and complained like a five-year-old. Maybe he *was* feeling better.

She was glad someone's love life was working out. Hers certainly wasn't. Scott had avoided her all day Sunday. When she'd hinted that he could join her in bed that night, he'd declined and went back to the sleeper sofa. Troy had decided to go back to Fred's and Scott let him.

Maybe it was time for her to go home, too. She wouldn't stay if she thought Scott was trying to keep their marriage intact for Risa's sake. The idea of staying scared her. The idea of clinging to Scott if he didn't love her was pathetic. But the thought of leaving made her heart ache.

Ronnie wiped Fred's chin with a napkin.

"If Ronnie keeps taking care of you like that, you'll be home in no time," Beth said encouraging them.

"Yes, but he'll have to take it easy for a while," insisted Ronnie.

Fred scowled. "Don't try to coddle me, woman."

"Don't call me 'woman' you old coot. I have a name."

"Well, I have a name, too, and it's not 'old coot.' "

"Yeah, yeah, finish your gelatin."

Beth checked her watch. "Yes, do finish eating, Fred, so I can take Ronnie back to the resort. I have work to do this afternoon."

"I don't know," Fred leaned back against his pillows. "I'm getting tired. I don't think I can eat any more."

Ronnie picked up the spoon again. "Just a few more bites, then you can rest."

After another round of spoon-feeding and pillow-fluffing, Beth was able to pull Ronnie away. As they got into Scott's SUV, Beth was surprised to see tears in Ronnie's eyes.

"What's wrong?" asked Beth, digging through her purse for tissues.

"Oh, nothing," the older woman mumbled. "I just hate to think we almost lost him."

"Ronnie, I do believe you're sweet on Fred," teased Beth, as she handed her a tissue.

"No, no I'm not," she insisted. "It's just that it hasn't been so long since we lost Henry. I hate to see our little family diminished again."

"Right."

"But we've added Troy, and you and Risa, of course."

"Of course," echoed Beth.

"You are going to be staying permanently, aren't you?"

Beth stared straight ahead, avoiding Ronnie's eye contact, not entirely because she was watching the road. "We haven't made any final decisions."

"Well, take it from me," Ronnie advised, "a good man is hard to find. I was lonely for years after my Jim passed away. You have a good man, Beth, so hold on to him. Don't waste any time."

"That's interesting advice from someone who spends all her time arguing with a good man who adores her."

Ronnie smiled. "It adds a little spice to things. Keeps him interested. I don't have a killer figure or a pretty face anymore. I've got to do what I can."

Beth laughed. "I'll remember that."

She patted her blue-grey curls and looked satisfied. "Yes, you'd better remember that."

Scott looked up when Beth came in his office. Her hair was windblown and her cheeks were pink from the sun. She looked good to him — too good.

Since Saturday night, he'd had a hard time keeping his thoughts out of the bedroom. Things had to be resolved between them soon. He couldn't handle the uncertainty anymore.

"Troy showed up bright and early to open the boat house. He's determined to do Fred's job as well as his own," Scott told her.

"That's commendable," said Beth.

"Yes, and it keeps him out of trouble."

She laughed. "There is that, too."

Scott watched her face light up with the laugh. His stomach tightened and he decided to throw out a challenge. "Mrs. Gilly called today. She reminded me that we need to officially register Risa so she'll be ready to start school in September."

Beth's smile disappeared. "Surely we have lots of time before we have to do that."

"It would be better to do it early. That way Mrs. Gilly can schedule her for an evaluation. All the therapists have to evaluate her as well, you know."

"I see," said Beth.

"Is there any reason we shouldn't register her?" Scott watched her expression carefully.

"I might still want Risa to go to school back in Green Bay."

"You might, or *you do?*"

She avoided his gaze. "M— might."

He stood up and walked around the desk. "What is it that's holding you back from making a decision here, Beth?"

She was uncomfortable, looking away from him and twisting her hands. Too bad, because Scott was getting uncomfortable himself.

"I thought we were going to wait until the end of the summer to decide."

"Not if we want to register Risa, and I

don't think I can wait that long, Beth. Not knowing is killing me. We have to plan for Risa's education. We can't do that unless we know where she'll be."

"I — I owe your father. He gave me a chance, he helped me. . . ."

"Let's not make this about my dad."

"Scott. . . ."

"Don't you owe me anything as your husband? Do you remember the vows *we* took?"

Her head jerked up and there was fire in her eyes. "Yes, and I don't remember hearing anything about one of us deserting the other for three years."

"That was a mistake. I apologized and I thought you forgave me."

"I . . . I do, but. . . ." She dropped her eyes again and inched away.

Scott's hands shot out and captured her arms, holding her near him. "Beth, I can't take much more of this. I want to know where I stand."

"You want to know where you stand? How do you think I feel? You couldn't even be in the same room with me the other night. When did I become so repulsive to you?"

"What do you mean?"

"You slept in the chair in Risa's room! You didn't want to be with me. I'm starting to think the only reason you want Risa to be enrolled in school is so that you'll get to keep her here."

"Is that what you thought? That I left because I didn't want to be near you?" He laughed, a harsh humorless sound.

"Why else?"

"Beth, you've got it completely backwards. I had to put some distance between us because. . . ."

"Because why?"

Scott let her go abruptly and strode to the office door. He closed it firmly and turned back to her.

"What are you doing?"

He could see uncertainty in her eyes. He had her off balance and that was fine with him.

Scott reached for her. He held her body close to his with one hand and brought the other hand to the back of her head, tangled his fingers in her hair and brought his mouth down hard on hers, releasing some of the passion he'd been holding in check for weeks.

At first, she was rigid in his arms, resisting him. He felt a burst of triumph when she relaxed and kissed him back. In response, he pressed her closer to him, until he could feel her wildly beating heart against his.

He lifted his head, but kept her tight against him. He'd been prepared to be patient, to give Beth time to get used to the resort before she'd agree to stay permanently. He'd even been prepared for her to change her mind and return to Green Bay. But there was no way he could stand her waffling anymore. "Say you'll stay," he whispered to her.

She was shaking. "Why didn't you kiss me like this before?"

"Because I promised myself I'd do things right this time. Because I wanted your commitment more than I wanted a good time."

"So if I told you I'm willing to stay for good, you'd come to bed with me tonight?"

"Is that all you want from me?" he said in mock horror.

She shook her head. "But I thought maybe . . . maybe you weren't attracted to me anymore. Maybe you just wanted to keep Risa here. . . ."

"I see. Maybe I've been going about this the wrong way. I've been trying to tell you how much I love you when I should have been showing you."

The couch in his office was only a step away. He backed up to it and let himself fall, carrying her with him. They tumbled onto it and he began kissing his way down her neck to her shoulder, all the time whispering to her, "Stay with me, Beth. I love you. I need you here with me."

Her hands cupped his face and brought his lips back to hers. He forgot where they were or why he should use restraint as he explored her body. He was as lost with her as he'd been years ago. One thought surfaced in his brain. It was amazing that his brain was working at all. It wasn't as if there was a lot of blood flowing to it right now. She hadn't said yes to staying yet. He needed her to say yes.

He eased back and stared into her eyes. "Will you stay?" he asked.

She blinked and frowned in confusion. "What?"

"Are you ready to make things permanent between us?"

"This isn't the way to make a decision."

"Talking hasn't worked so far. I thought this was what you needed."

"I . . . I don't know." Wide brown eyes stared back at him. She was frightened, but was she frightened of him, or of her own emotions? Scott wasn't sure, and before he could decide there was a knock on his door. Beth jerked away from him and straightened her clothes. Reluctantly Scott rose and opened the door.

"Scott, why was your office door closed?" asked Cindy as she breezed in. "You almost never shut. . . ." Her voice trailed off when she saw Beth sitting there. Her lips twitched into a smirk. "Ah, I see."

Scott ran his hand through his hair. "What did you want, Cindy?"

"Far be it from me to ruin your fun, but I was going to invite you two over for supper tonight. Risa, too, of course."

Scott looked at Beth, who still seemed a bit dazed. He couldn't help smiling at her. "That sounds good. Is that okay with you, Beth?"

"Um . . . sure. Can I bring anything, Cindy?"

"Not a thing. And since Shannon already has Risa, she can just stay with us until supper. That will give you guys a little time together."

"Oh no, that's not necessary," Beth protested, rising from the couch.

"Don't worry about it. You two are like newlyweds. It's been a while, but I still remember what that was like." Cindy exited and, with a wink, closed the door behind her again.

Beth stared at the closed door. Then she looked at Scott and read trouble in his expression. She started inching toward the exit. "I'm going back to the house. I need a shower before we go over to Ben and Cindy's."

Scott was right behind her. "Great idea. I'll come, too."

"No, you won't," Beth snapped. "You must have stuff to do here."

"Nope. I'm finished for the day."

They walked to the house in silence. Beth was fuming, but Scott seemed very pleased with himself. She stormed up the stairs and, shutting the bedroom door behind her, opened the closet door and stared at her clothes. She should be picking out something to wear, but all she could think about was what had happened in the office — and what almost happened.

She had to figure out what to do. Her head was telling her one thing, her heart another. Which did she follow? It seemed that Scott wouldn't give her any time to think about it alone as he slipped into the room behind her.

"Now, where were we before Cindy interrupted us?"

"I don't remember." Beth grabbed the first thing that came to hand from the closet. "We'd better get ready for supper."

Scott put an arm around her waist. "I'm

sure Cindy won't mind if we're late."

Beth was beginning to get angry. She pushed him away. "Aren't you the one that said we needed to wait until we were sure we were staying together?"

"I'm trying a new tactic."

"What? You're trying to seduce me into staying?"

"Is it working?"

"Scott, be serious!"

Instead, he pulled her close and started to nibble on her ear. Beth wanted to push him away but her willpower melted with the first kiss he planted on her lips. "I've tried being serious," he told her between kisses. "Isn't working. I've tried being open and honest, giving you space, talking to you. Where have I gotten? Nowhere. If seduction works I have nothing against it."

She wanted to laugh at his teasing and scream at him at the same time. Head or heart? Which should she follow? He kissed his way down her throat and nuzzled the hollow by her collar bone. His hands slipped under her shirt and his thumbs grazed the sensitive skin above the waistband of her shorts.

"Don't you love me, Beth?"

"That's not the problem."

"Don't think about all the things that

could be wrong. Think about what's right with us."

Her arms came up and circled his neck. "I'm afraid," she admitted. "I'm afraid of making the wrong decision and hurting everyone."

"You can't have it both ways. You have to make a decision. Isn't it better to try and fail than to wonder what might have been?"

His words stirred something within her. In a moment of clarity she realized that nothing that happened between them could be worse than a lifetime of looking back and wondering. Her head and her heart agreed.

He stopped, took a step back and looked into her eyes. "Do you want me to stop, Beth?"

"No," her voice came out hoarse and breathy.

"Then you know what I want to hear."

"I love you, Scott. I'll stay with you. I'll enroll Risa in school here. I'll get rid of my house and quit my. . . ."

She didn't get any farther because Scott scooped her up and carried her to bed. He put her down gently and lay beside her, holding her close.

"Promise me," he demanded.

"I promise," she whispered.

And she meant it. Relief coursed through

her at finally having made her decision and she responded freely to Scott's touch. He was her husband. She loved him, and she accepted his love for her. This was the right decision.

Chapter 18

Scott was miserable. He couldn't admit it to Beth, but he felt horribly guilty for the way he'd convinced her to stay. She said he always had to have things his way and he'd gone and proved her right. He'd acted exactly the way he had resolved not to.

She'd been constantly busy since that evening. The next day she enrolled Risa at the Spruce Point Elementary School. She began to make lists of things she needed to do to transfer her life from Green Bay. She worked extra hours on her ad campaign to bring corporate clients into the resort and went shopping with Cindy to prepare for Risa's birthday party. He took her need for activity to be her way of hiding her regret from him.

A promise extracted under pressure like that couldn't be valid, could it? Would she really follow through on it?

■ ■ ■ ■

Beth sat at her desk and looked over her plans again. Since she'd made her decision to stay, she'd thrown herself into her new life and was content. Just now she was not working at her job, but rather at her course of action for transferring her life from Green Bay to the Pine Away Inn. It was all pretty straightforward except for one thing — Hal.

How would she handle giving him her resignation? She doubted he'd be surprised, but he'd still probably be angry. After a great deal of thought, Beth decided the best way to handle this was in person — alone. She didn't want Scott to be there in case Hal decided to blame her leaving on him.

And she was going to give Hal the full details on the argument she and Scott had the night before he left, how she'd practically thrown him out. More than likely Hal would be furious with her, but it might take some of the heat from Scott and that was all she was concerned about at this point.

The pain of her own ruined relationships with her parents convinced her that she should spare Scott that ordeal if she could. There was still a chance that he and his father could work things out.

Now the only problem was how to convince Scott she needed to go to Green Bay by herself.

That night at supper, Beth broached the subject.

"Scott," she said, "I need to go to Green Bay and do a few things. I was thinking I'd go sometime this week."

He shook his head. "I can't get away this week. Maybe I can clear some time in my schedule for next week."

"I don't need you to come along. I'd hate to drag you away from the resort at the height of the season. I'll just be gone a couple of days."

Scott set his fork down. "It's a long trip. I'm not sure I want you to go by yourself."

"Don't be silly. I'll be fine. And I'll have Risa for company."

He stared at her for a moment. "You want to take Risa?"

"You can hardly watch Risa all day and work. Plus this will give your folks a chance to visit with her."

"Why can't you wait until I can go with you?"

"It just seems like a waste of time for you. There are a lot of things I have to do by myself, like close out my bank accounts." Beth worked to maintain a serene expression on her face. She had to convince Scott she could take care of this herself.

"If you take the SUV, then what am I going to drive while you're gone?"

"I already talked to Cindy about that. She said you can use one of their cars if you need to."

"If I came with you, you could drive your car back."

He had a point. She scrambled to find an argument.

"That's a great idea. It'll take a few trips to get all my stuff up here. Let me go by myself this time and the next time you can come with me and we'll bring my car back."

Risa chose that moment to upset her plate, the fish and rice pilaf that Beth had prepared hit the floor.

Cleaning up the mess distracted Scott from the argument. After supper he did dishes while Beth gave Risa her bath.

Beth loved "after bath" time. She loved the fresh scent of shampoo and clean pajamas. She loved the way Risa clung to her, trying to warm up, while Beth combed her hair.

Downstairs, they found Scott sitting on the couch and joined him there. He was looking through Risa's baby book again.

Glancing up when they sat down, he

asked, "When were you thinking of leaving, Beth?"

She shrugged. "Maybe the day after tomorrow."

Scott raised his eyebrows. "That soon?"

"Now that we've decided that Risa and I are moving up here, there are things I need to do. I thought this was what you wanted."

He frowned at her. "I didn't mean that you should do it all yourself."

Risa had grown restless as they talked and was trying to pull her baby book away from Scott. She loved to look at pictures of herself.

"Let's talk about it later," Beth suggested. "It's almost time for Risa to go to bed. How about we spend this time with her instead of arguing?"

Scott slipped an arm around her, drawing both of them closer to him. "That's fine with me. Let's go through this book again."

The rest of the evening was peaceful, but when bedtime came around, Risa chose to be stubborn. Bedtime and naptime had often turned into a battle of wills between her and Beth when they lived in Green Bay. Here at the resort Risa had become more willing to go to bed. Beth figured all the activity and the fresh air tired her out and just accepted it as a blessing. Tonight, however, Risa returned to her old habits.

Beth tucked her in and gave the little girl her usual kiss and hug. Risa didn't want to let her go. Gently she pried Risa's arms away and gave her one last kiss before leaving the room.

Beth didn't make it down the stairs before she heard the sound of little feet behind her. Risa flashed her a big smile as if she didn't know she was being naughty.

"No, honey," Beth scolded. "It's bedtime. You need to stay in your bed."

Beth walked Risa back and tucked her in again. They repeated this pattern three more times before Scott came to see what the problem was.

"Risa won't stay in her bed," Beth explained.

"Let me try."

Scott didn't have any more luck at getting her to stay in bed than Beth did. She seemed to think this was all a big game. Finally he volunteered to sit with her for a while.

"Thanks," Beth said, and went downstairs. It was good to have someone else to rely on when it came to parenting. And Scott seemed to be a natural with children. He'd adjusted to being a father pretty quickly, she thought.

She sat down with the copy of *Persuasion* that she'd brought with her. She'd been rereading it bit by bit over the last few weeks. Opening the book, she pulled out the embroidered bookmark her grandmother Jane made for her. Beth ran a finger over the letters that made up the saying "Love never fails," thinking she should have put more stock in Grandma Jane's advice than in her mother's words all along.

Beth made herself comfortable and began to read, but soon her eyelids were closing and her head was nodding. She lay down and drifted into a dream.

She was remembering the first Christmas after Grandma Jane had passed away. Reluctantly she'd left Scott and the campus to spend Christmas with her dad and his family. He and her stepmother were obviously not getting along. Beth had never felt at home there before, but the tension increased her discomfort exponentially. After a week of polite conversation, thinly veiled insults and frigid silences, she was more than ready to go home, and even a dorm room felt more like home than her father's house.

Of course she could not go to her real home anymore, to Grandma Jane's farm. It had been sold and a new family had taken up residence. The thought had made her want to cry.

She opened her door and staggered in with her luggage. Then suddenly her bags were taken from her and she looked up. It was Scott. She'd never been so glad to see anyone. And he looked incredible in a new blue sweater that matched his eyes.

"What are you doing here?" she blurted out in surprise.

"I knew you were getting back today."

"Yes, but not what time."

"It didn't matter," he said. "I'd wait all day just to see you."

"How did you get in? My roommate won't be back for two weeks yet."

He grinned at her. "That's my secret. Don't I get a kiss?"

He got a kiss. And a lot more. Since they'd started dating a couple of months before, things had been heating up between them, and Scott had let her know that he was ready to move their relationship to the next level whenever she was. But Beth had always asked Scott to stop before they went too far. That night she didn't say stop.

It had been their first separation and Beth had missed him terribly. And even if she hadn't, she needed something to fill the hole that loneliness had eaten in her heart.

The dream was so vivid, she felt as if she

were reliving the memory instead of dreaming it. She could actually feel Scott's lips on hers.

She started to wake and discovered that Scott really was there with her, kissing her.

"I was just dreaming about you," she said as soon as he gave her a chance.

"A good dream, I hope."

She smiled and stretched. "Very good."

"Want to tell me about it?"

"I have a better idea," Beth told him. "Let's go upstairs and I'll show you how it went."

For an answer he picked her up and set her on her feet, then led her up the stairs to their room. Beth was very glad he wasn't sleeping on the couch anymore.

Scott lay awake that night long after Beth slept. He was worried about this trip she wanted to take to Green Bay. It was obvious that she didn't want him along. Why? There was something she wasn't telling him?

He continued to be uneasy about the trip, right up to the morning that Beth and Risa left. He hovered in the doorway of the bathroom as she packed her toiletries. "Are you positive that you don't want to wait until I can go with you?" he asked once again.

349

"For the hundredth time, yes," Beth replied, clearly irritated with him. "Do you really think I'm incapable of going by myself?"

"If this is no big deal, why didn't you just drive up here in the first place instead of having me come down to get you?"

"Because you offered. And now I know where I'm going."

"It wasn't so long ago," Scott reminded her, "that you got lost on your way into town."

"It was my first time out on my own," she countered. "Now I can do it without even thinking about it."

She zipped her bag shut and attempted to walk past Scott but he refused to let her by.

Exasperated she asked, "Scott, what is wrong with you? I'm usually the worrier, not you."

"I just want to know . . . are you really planning on coming back."

He studied her face, watching for a sign that she was lying. All he saw was shock.

"How can you even ask that?"

He knew how difficult it was for her to make that decision. He'd watched her agonize over it for weeks. "It just seems odd to me that you're so anxious to go with Risa, but without me. You promised that you were going to stay, remember?"

Irritation gave way to a wave of anger. Her hands clenched around the handle of her case. "I'm not likely to forget the way you got me to make that promise."

"I admit I went about that the wrong way, but I'll still hold you to it."

"And just what will you do if I don't keep my promise?" She didn't mean it, but his lack of faith hurt enough to make her want to lash out at him.

Looking her right in the eye, he replied, "If you leave, I'll fight you for custody of Risa."

Beth gasped, and took a step back. "You wouldn't."

"Yes, I would. I'll do whatever I have to, to keep my family together."

Pushing past him she rushed down the stairs. He was right behind her but she refused to acknowledge him as she put the bag with her toiletries into her suitcase. She took it out to the SUV and he didn't offer to help. Then she came back in to get Risa.

Scott was holding her. Should he insist that she stay here at the resort while Beth was gone? What would she do if he did? Were they already putting Risa in the middle?

He handed Risa over to her.

"I'll call you tonight," Beth said, keeping her voice low and steady. "Until then, you'd better do some thinking, Scott. I meant it when I said I would stay but now I'm having second thoughts."

That's what he was afraid of.

Upon reaching Green Bay, the first thing Beth did was stop at Hal and Margie's house. Hal was working, as she expected, but Margie was home and thrilled to see Beth and Risa. Margie hugged Risa instantly upon seeing her.

"Can you keep Risa while I go and talk to Hal," Beth asked.

Margie agreed at once. "Of course I will. Is this about your job?"

Nodding, she replied, "Yes. I'm turning in my resignation."

"I thought so. You *are* going to stay with Scott."

"Yes, we've managed to work things out."

"I'm happy and sad at the same time," Margie admitted.

"Me, too," Beth said with a sigh. "But I think this is the best choice for us." At least I did, she added to herself.

"I do, too. That's why I can stand to let you and Risa go."

Margie's understanding gave Beth the

strength to face Hal. She pulled up in front of the dealership, her heart pounding. She was hoping surprise would give her the advantage.

Jared was the first person she met. He was talking to a pretty young blond woman. And they were holding hands. This was interesting.

He was obviously startled to see her. "Beth," he cried. "What are you doing here?"

"I need to talk to Hal. Is he in his office?"

"Um, yeah. Let me walk you down." To his companion, he said, "I'll be right back."

Curiosity was eating her up. When they had moved out of earshot of the woman, Beth asked, "Who was that?"

The tips of Jared's ears turned red. "That's the new accountant Hal hired. Her name is Janie Anderson."

Beth bit back a smile. "How well do you know her?"

"Actually. . . ." The red color spread down his ears and neck. "Actually we've been seeing each other for a couple of weeks. No hard feelings, I hope."

She managed to reply with a straight face. "Not at all, Jared. You make a cute couple."

"Thanks."

Jared knocked on Hal's door and opened

it without waiting for a response. "Someone's here to see you," he said, moving aside
so that Beth could walk through.

Hal looked up. He didn't seem surprised
to see her. "Margie called. She said you
were on your way."

"I've got to get back to . . . um . . . work,"
said Jared, still in the doorway. "See you,
Beth." He closed the door behind him.

So much for the element of surprise,
thought Beth dismally. "Did she tell you
why I wanted to talk to you?"

Hal shook his head. "Either you're here to
tell me you're quitting or that you'll be in
to work tomorrow. Which is it?"

There was no sense in prolonging this.
"I'm quitting. I've decided to stay at the
resort with Scott and Risa."

Hal nodded, not betraying any emotion.
"I hope you made the right decision."

She pushed this morning's argument out
of her mind. "I know I have."

"Then why did you bother to come all the
way over here. Why didn't you just call?"

Beth pulled up a chair and sat down.
"Because I have something else to tell you.
Do you have a few minutes?"

Hal leaned back in his chair and nodded.
The familiar squeak made her want to smile
even while she was dreading the conversa-

tion. She took a deep breath and began. "I want to tell you about the night before Scott left."

He fixed a steely eye on her and gestured for her to go ahead.

"After the miscarriage I struggled with some heavy depression. Believe me, I was not a fun person to live with."

"That's understandable."

Beth nodded. "I was horrible to Scott. I took out all my misery on him. I don't know how he put up with me."

Hal shrugged his big shoulders. "Marriage is no picnic. All couples go through rough patches. It's no excuse for leaving."

"No, but this is. The night before he left, we had a nasty fight. I don't even remember what it was about, something silly. But, by the end, we were both yelling, and I told him to leave. I told him I didn't want to live with him anymore. I was very hurtful to him. The truth is I practically kicked him out. He packed his stuff the next day and was gone before I got home from my doctor's appointment. I hadn't meant to say the things I did to him but I can't take back what I said that night. I did really want him to go. And he thought by his leaving me that I would get back into my parents' good graces and return to school. You shouldn't blame him for leaving me."

Silence fell between them and they stared at each other for a few moments. Beth wondered what would happen now.

"Why didn't you tell me this before?" he asked her, a calmer answer than she'd expected.

"I didn't tell you at first because I was afraid you wouldn't give me the job. It was tough enough to get you to agree even when you thought I was the victim."

"I should have known you were a good salesperson then," Hal remarked with the hint of a smile. "You sold me on hiring you."

"And the longer I waited to tell you the harder it got." Beth paused and then forced herself to finish. "But I was wrong and selfish for not telling you. It made you think the worst of Scott and he didn't deserve it. I'm sorry, Hal."

A troubled silence followed. Hal was usually so decisive, so quick to say what he thought. His stillness frightened Beth a little.

"Do you hate me now?" she ventured to ask.

Hal looked up, now showing surprise. "Of course not. In fact, if I had been in your shoes, I may have done the same thing to get on my feet. You were alone and frightened. And even if you told him to go in the heat of an argument, Scott should have stayed."

"Does that mean you're still angry with him?" Beth held her breath, waiting for his answer.

"He made a really big mistake, a terrible mistake, when he left you," Hal replied and Beth's heart plummeted.

Until he spoke again. "But I've been thinking about it a lot since you left. It took a lot of courage for him to come back and make everything right. I respect that. I don't hold a grudge against him anymore, Beth."

"That's wonderful. Scott will be thrilled." She wanted to clap her hands like a child, she was so happy and excited.

"I don't think so. Scott and I haven't seen eye to eye on much of anything long before you came into the picture."

Beth's heart ached at the regret she heard in his voice. "There's more to this than you know."

"He's told me some of it, Hal. Did you really push him so hard after your other son's death? Scott thinks that you wished Scott would have died instead of Dave."

"What? Never. I could never choose between my sons like that."

"Then why were you so hard on him, Hal?"

There was more raw emotion than she'd ever seen in the big man's eyes. "I just wanted him to have everything that Dave missed. Dave was cheated out of so much, dying so young."

Beth reached across the desk and took Hal's hand. "You need to tell this to Scott."

He shook his head and squeezed her hand. She suspected he couldn't answer for fear of his emotions getting the better of him.

"Remember when you accused me of leaving my own parents out of Risa's life?" Beth asked, gently.

He nodded.

"Well, I called my mother after you said that. I thought maybe you were right and she'd missed me. But she didn't. She was . . . awful to me."

He cleared his throat. "I'm sorry about that, Beth. I shouldn't have said anything."

"But it's not too late for you and Scott to fix things. Talk to him, Hal," Beth urged him.

Hal shook his head. "I don't know."

"You're coming to the resort soon for Risa's birthday. Do it then."

"I can't. You don't understand," Hal protested.

"I understand that Scott wants everything to be right between you two. Don't leave it until it's too late, please."

CHAPTER 19

Scott did a lot of thinking after Beth left. He didn't know where that threat had come from. He was as surprised as she was when he'd said it. She was right. He was trying to impose his will on the situation, just like he'd done when he'd gotten that promise from her.

What was he doing? Things had gone from bad to worse because of him. How could he show Beth that he loved her and respected her when he was threatening to take Risa away from her? This wasn't going to be an easy road, he acknowledged.

After work, he went home to a dark, quiet house, and it emphasized how much he missed Beth and Risa.

He regretted his hasty words that morning now more than ever. But if he took them back, would she think she could go back on her promise?

The phone rang while he was making a

sandwich for supper. He saw Beth's cell-phone number on the caller ID and waited for two more rings before he picked up. No use in letting her think he was waiting by the phone.

"Hello."

"Scott?"

He could hear voices in the background. "Beth, where are you?"

"I'm at your folks' house. It seemed easier for us to stay here than to juggle things with Margie's cousin."

It didn't escape him that she was a welcome guest in his father's house and he'd been forbidden to stay there on his last visit. "Did you get a lot done today?" he asked abruptly, wanting to distract himself from bitter thoughts.

"Just a minute." The background noise receded and then disappeared. He heard a door shut. "That's better," said Beth. "What did you ask?"

"I asked if you got a lot done today."

"I told your dad I was quitting. That was the hardest thing on my list."

"How did he take it?"

"It went well. Really, really well." He could hear the excitement in her voice. That was a strange emotion to have upon quitting a job she'd been so reluctant to give up. Once again he was filled with suspicion about the reason behind her visit.

"When are you coming home?" His question sounded harsh and abrupt even to him. He added, "I miss you and Risa. It's too quiet here without you."

"I think I'll have everything wrapped up by tomorrow evening. We'll come home the day after that. It will give me just enough time to get ready for Risa's party."

"All right. Call me before you leave."

She hadn't said anything about this morning. Maybe she'd forgotten. Maybe he was off the hook.

"There was one more thing," Beth said. "About this morning. . . ."

So much for that hope. "What about it?"

"You didn't really mean what you said about . . . about fighting me for custody of Risa."

"Why? Are you planning on leaving me?"

"I wasn't. But if you're going to start making threats, I may have to reconsider."

"Then plan on seeing me in court." That was definitely the wrong thing to say. Her horrified gasp echoed in his ear.

"Scott . . . there are just so many things wrong with this. Why would you start talking like this after I agreed to make our relationship permanent? Why would you think I was going to go back on my promise? Are you trying to manipulate me? Don't you *trust* me?"

He didn't know what to say to that. "Listen, Beth . . . I admit I may have overreacted. I shouldn't have said those things. It's just that I know there's something about this trip that you aren't telling me. It's hard to trust someone who's keeping secrets."

"And that's how you invite me to confide in you?"

"I said I overreacted. I'm sorry. Are you going to tell me why you really wanted to go there without me or not?"

There was a long pause and then what he suspected was a sob. "No. I'm not telling you anything if you treat me like this."

"Beth. . . ." Before he could respond, she hung up. When he called her back, her voice mail came up immediately. She'd shut her phone off.

He considered calling his parents' house, but that would cause his parents to wonder, making things more complicated for him, and for Beth. Besides, what could he say? He'd acted like a jerk and she had a right to be mad at him.

"How can I make this right?" he asked himself over and over. Later, he fell into a troubled sleep.

■ ■ ■ ■

Beth wiped her eyes and stuffed her phone into her pocket. She couldn't return to the living room until she'd gotten herself together. There was no way she was going to let Hal and Margie see she'd been crying.

Had she been wrong not to confide in Scott about her reason for coming? She thought most likely he would tell her not to talk to his father, that their problems were between them. That's why she'd decided not to say anything.

How had he picked up on that? Why would that immediately lead him to assume that she was planning on leaving him?

She'd given up her house to Margie's cousin. She'd quit her job and now worked for her husband. What would she do now if things didn't work out with Scott? With horror, Beth realized she was in the situation she'd feared most. Her marriage was floundering and she was stuck with nowhere to go and no means of support if it failed altogether.

Panic clutched at her and she forced it down. She had to get a hold of herself. She had to go back out to the living room and visit with her in-laws. She couldn't let them know anything was wrong, not now that she'd come so close to convincing Hal it was time to mend things with Scott.

With tremendous effort, Beth forced a smile and went back to play the good guest. She wouldn't make any decisions until she got home and had a chance to talk to Scott face to face.

Two days later, she left Green Bay with mixed feelings. After all that had happened between her and Scott in the last few weeks she'd been sure they had as good a shot at making their marriage work as anyone else, maybe better than some. Scott's sudden threat had definitely shaken her confidence, but hadn't extinguished hope.

She and Risa got home around mid-afternoon. She knew Scott would be at work, so she pulled up to the lodge before going home. He was definitely surprised to see them walk into his office.

Scott was on his feet and around the desk before she'd taken more than a couple of steps into the room. He enveloped both her and Risa in a huge hug, and Beth felt a surge of optimism. Surely things couldn't be that bad. They would talk this through and everything would be all right.

"I didn't expect to see you so soon," he

said, dropping a kiss on her cheek, and then on Risa's.

"We were anxious to be home, so we got on the road early," she replied.

"Home? Is this really home to you now?" His eyes searched hers.

"Yes, it is." That was the truth. Beth had come to love the resort in the short time she'd been here. It would be hard to leave now. Not that she was going to.

Risa broke in with a string of unintelligible syllables.

Beth smiled. "She's telling you about her visit with Grandma and Grandpa."

"Why don't I go home with you and help you carry in your luggage. I'd love to hear all that Risa's got to say."

The conversation remained light and pleasant throughout the afternoon and evening. Beth almost brought up their argument several times, but didn't. Things were going so well she was afraid to resurrect what had been said. She knew it was cowardly, but she wanted to enjoy their family time.

Once Risa had been put to bed it was different. They didn't talk about the argument, but there were too many awkward pauses in the conversation. Scott was probably thinking about it as much as she was.

Why didn't he bring it up? She was ashamed of herself for letting it go.

Beth knew it would be even harder to bring the subject up tomorrow. But he *had* apologized. Sort of. Maybe it was okay to let it drop. She hoped so anyway.

Again Scott was surprised by Beth's silence on his affront. He shouldn't have used seduction to gain her promise to stay, and she hadn't called him on it.

He'd threatened to take her child away from her and she'd gotten angry. They'd argued but never resolved the problem.

Before she'd come home Scott had decided to apologize and take back his threat. But he didn't have the courage to bring it up. When she didn't he was surprised, and then relieved, and now worried. The Beth he'd known in college would have let it go, but not the Beth he knew now.

Maybe he should come totally clean and apologize for his tactics in winning her promise as well as his inappropriate suggestion about Risa's custody. If it came down to it, he could never allow Risa to be used as a pawn in his relationship with Beth. The thought sickened him.

But if he admitted her promise had not been won fairly, it would mean he had to let her back out of it if she wanted.

On the surface their relationship seemed fine, but the unresolved issue between them was eating at him. He had to do something soon. Something that would make up for his behavior, but not cost him his family.

Fred wasn't strong enough to come back to work yet, but he was up to making short visits to the resort. Usually he visited with Ronnie who was being almost nice to him these days. But today was her day off and he'd decided to tag along with Scott while he did some minor repairs to the cottages — broken window cranks, doors that stuck, etcetera.

The older man asked questions about everything that had happened since he'd last been there. Scott was not feeling up to one of Fred's counseling sessions, but he put up with it. He did care about the elderly man even if he didn't want to hear Fred's no-fail method of getting rid of some of the weeds that sprang up around the cottages.

Scott's mind wandered. He had a lot to do today and began composing a list in his mind as Fred went on about old-fashioned methods that his grandfather had used and how the old ways were always best. Because he wasn't listening, Fred caught him off guard when he changed the subject by asking:

"So how are things going with you and your wife? Did you convince her to stay?"

"Hmmm? Oh, yes. She's working on getting herself and Risa settled."

"Working on it? What exactly does she have to do besides pack her things?"

Scott found himself a bit irritated by Fred's assumption that Beth didn't have a life before him, so he went into more detail than he normally would have. To give details was to encourage Fred to comment on them.

"She had to quit her job and give notice to her landlord. Then she has to pack up her house. And put her things in storage until we decide what to do with them. She had to arrange for all of Risa's records to be sent up here so she can attend school. . . ."

Fred laughed. "That sounds like a lot of work. I can't believe a beautiful, intelligent woman like Beth would do all that for a sorry so-and-so like you."

Fred was constantly ribbing him and Scott knew it didn't mean anything, but today he had a point. "You're absolutely right. I wish I could figure it out myself."

"I know my daughter is having a hard time right now. I could never figure that one out either. She was bright, had a good job. But she has to fall in love with a guy who's never been any good for her. She left Spruce Point and followed him down there by the Cities. While they were married, he made her miserable. Now that he's gone, she's left high and dry with a mortgage and a stack of bills to pay every month. I wish there was something I could do to help her. She couldn't afford to take off work to come and visit me in the hospital, even though she wanted to."

Scott had a sudden flash of insight into Beth's point of view. She'd said much the same thing to him. If she moved up here and things didn't work out, she'd be left with no job, no home and even no friends, since everyone she knew here was his friend.

It did require a lot of trust for her to stay with him after just a few short weeks' trial. He'd been too impatient with her, too pushy.

All of a sudden he could see, and he was touched by the faith she'd chosen to put in him. Especially since he didn't deserve it.

"Fred," Scott broke abruptly into the older man's monologue on the failings of his son-in-law. "Don't you think Troy must be looking for you? You know the doctor wants you to take it easy still."

He waved a hand dismissively at Scott. "Don't worry about me. Those doctors want to keep a fellow down as long as they can. That way they can keep sending him bills."

In spite of what he said, Fred did look tired. Scott had been too wrapped up in his own problems to pay attention sooner. He wouldn't have noticed now if it hadn't suited his own purposes, Scott realized with a hint of guilt. But he promised himself he'd do better in the future, just as soon as he got everything worked out with Beth.

It didn't take much more convincing to get Fred to agree to go home. They went back to the office and called Troy to drive him home, since that was one of the things his doctor hadn't cleared him for yet.

Once the two had left, Fred happily complaining all the way, Scott picked up the phone and began punching in numbers. Now he knew exactly what he was going to do.

"Hand me another balloon, will you?" asked Beth.

"Pink or white?" Shannon replied.

"I need more tape," Shaun hollered out.

They were decorating one of the conference rooms at the lodge for Risa's party.

Pink and white balloons and streamers hung from the ceiling. White plastic tablecloths with pink ponies covered the tables.

Cindy looked up from the cardboard castle she was putting together for the table centerpiece. "This is beautiful Beth. It's a little girl's dream."

"Really?" she asked anxiously. "Do you think she'll like it?"

"She'll love it," Cindy assured her. "What time are Scott's parents supposed to get here?"

"Um, probably this evening sometime. I'm sure Hal wanted to work as many hours as he could before they left."

"I can't wait to meet them. Scott must be excited that they're coming."

"Do we have any more streamers?" Beth asked so she didn't have to answer. She didn't know how Scott felt, but she was nervous about Hal and Margie's visit. She hoped that Hal had listened to her and would initiate a talk with Scott that would set things right between them.

"What's going on in here?" Scott walked in carrying Risa.

"Oh, Scott," cried Beth, hurrying over to the door. "Take Risa out of here. I don't want her to see all this yet."

■ ■ ■ ■

Scott found himself pushed out of the room and the door slammed behind him. He turned to Risa, still in his arms. Her face wore a puzzled expression that made him laugh. At the sound of her father's laughter, Risa laughed too and Scott hugged her. "Let's go wait for Grandma and Grandpa at the lodge. I think Ronnie's working and she hasn't had a whole lot of time to spoil you lately."

Risa nodded in agreement, though Scott knew she'd only understood a few words. But Grandma, Grandpa, and Ronnie were all good words to her.

They'd only been in the lobby for a few minutes when his parents' car pulled up, much earlier than he'd expected. The moment they stepped inside and Risa saw them, she rushed forward. Hal scooped her up and hugged her tightly. Margie was close behind, pulling Risa out of his arms to shower her with kisses.

"Hi Mom, Dad." Scott stepped forward to greet them and was surprised that his father offered a hand for him to shake. Okay, it wasn't a bear hug like Risa got, but it was definitely a friendly gesture.

"Nice place you got here," said Hal.

"Yes, honey, it's beautiful," Margie agreed.

"Thank you, but you've hardly seen any of it yet," protested Scott. He turned and gestured toward the desk. "This is Ronnie. She'll get you checked in."

Ronnie held out her hand to each of his parents in turn. "I'm so glad to finally meet you," she told them with warmth evident in her voice. "We all love Scott and we're so glad he's taken over the resort."

Margie beamed with pleasure at this compliment and even Hal smiled.

Ronnie continued, "And this summer, Risa has just stolen everyone's hearts. We're so happy she could be with us. Oh, and Beth. Beth is wonderful, too."

"I can see why Scott loves it here," Margie said. "The scenery is beautiful, but more importantly, so are the people."

Soon Margie and Ronnie were lost in conversation about children and grand-children, Risa still content in her grand-mother's arms.

Scott shrugged, went around Ronnie and grabbed the keys for his parents' cottage. "We'll take the luggage down and get you settled, Mom."

She caught him as he came back past her and kissed his cheek. "Thank you," she said before returning to her conversation with Ronnie.

Together Hal and Scott walked out to the car. "You're in number three. If you pull up around here we won't have to carry anything very far," Scott told his dad.

When his father opened the trunk, Scott did a double take at the amount of luggage. "This is just for the weekend!"

Hal pulled out one of the bags. "You know how your mother is. She doesn't know the meaning of the words 'traveling light.' Besides, we thought if the cottage wasn't booked for next week, we might stay a few extra days."

"Really?" Scott tried not to get his hopes up, but this was already more than he expected.

"Is the cottage available?"

"If it isn't, I'll fix it so it will be." He reached in and pulled out a suitcase. "What did Mom pack?"

"One whole suitcase is just presents for Risa."

"No way."

Hal just rolled his eyes and repeated, "You know your mother."

Once they had everything squared away, Scott gave his dad a tour of the cottage. He didn't want to leave his mom alone for too long, but he thought she was in good hands with Ronnie.

The tour ended on the deck which had a perfect view of the lake, like all the cottages. It amazed Scott that he and his father were able to talk to each other for almost half an hour without a single harsh word exchanged between them.

And he told Beth so when they were getting ready for supper.

"I'm glad you and your father had a good visit today. Did you talk about anything special?" She pushed her hair over one shoulder as she fastened the catch on her necklace.

With her neck exposed, Scott took the opportunity to kiss her there. She smiled but didn't encourage him further.

Things hadn't been bad between them lately, but still. . . . There seemed to be a distance between them that he couldn't broach. Tomorrow he would resolve everything, he promised.

They ate out at the restaurant that night, and the whole resort family, minus Fred and Troy, joined them. Fred was getting stronger every day, but Troy thought that Risa's party would be enough excitement for a while without adding a dinner party the night before.

Everyone talked and laughed and ate too much. Even Hal seemed caught up in the moment. With his parents and his resort family, with Beth and Risa beside him, Scott couldn't have been happier. A great wave of gratitude filled him and he was quiet amidst the noisy bunch.

It was one of those rare moments when his life was in harmony and he chose to appreciate it. Beth was seated next to him and he reached for her hand. She turned toward him, still laughing over something someone had said. She must have sensed something of his mood because she leaned in and asked quietly, "What is it? Is something wrong?"

She was wearing a light, fruity scent and Scott thought she smelled like summer. He couldn't resist drawing her closer to kiss her soft, sweet mouth. "No," he whispered back. "Absolutely nothing's wrong."

CHAPTER 20

The next morning, Scott was giving Hal an extensive tour of the grounds while Margie, Beth, Ronnie and Cindy had coffee together. Risa was with Margie, who'd hardly let the little girl out of her sight since she arrived.

They stopped at the dock and Scott introduced Hal to Troy. "This is Troy's first summer here. You'll meet his grandfather, Fred, at the party this afternoon. He recently suffered a heart attack and Troy stepped in and took over Fred's job. We're very proud of him."

Troy lit up at Scott's words of praise. He stood straighter and offered his hand to Hal. "It's good to meet you, sir."

Hal shook the younger man's hand. "Good to meet you, too. There's not many kids your age who'd take on responsibility like this."

"It was good of my grandfather to invite

me to stay this summer. I really needed the job. So I don't want to let him down now that he needs me."

"That's commendable of you."

"Thank you," Troy hesitated as if unsure what to do. Then, he lifted his head and met Hal's gaze. "I'm also grateful to Scott for giving me the job and for not giving up on me this summer. I did a lot of things wrong at first and I . . . I had a real attitude when I got here."

Hal lifted his eyebrows in surprise. "Most people wouldn't admit that to a stranger."

"I wanted you to know. Scott went out of his way to help me and I'm very grateful." Scott knew what the speech must have cost Troy in terms of pride. He was touched that Troy would make the gesture for him.

He laid a hand on the younger man's shoulder. "Thank you. You didn't have to say those things."

Troy nodded. He'd said what he wanted and didn't seem to have any words left.

"We'll let you get back to work." Scott led his father away. "See you at the party this afternoon."

Scott took Hal to see one of the cottages he'd remodeled when he first came to the resort with Henry. His father had never been impressed with his carpentry skills, but Scott still felt the need to show him what he'd done. He gave him the "grand tour" ending up on the deck built to show off the spectacular view over the lake.

Hal ran his hand along the rail of the deck Scott had added. "That was a very impressive speech that kid made."

"I didn't ask him to say those things."

"I know. He may be a good kid, but I have a feeling acting isn't one of his talents." Hal flashed him a crooked smile.

"If I helped him, I'm glad," Scott replied simply.

"It seems like your employees all think highly of you."

"I've become close to the employees that work here all year round."

"I can see that," Hal replied. "That says something about a man, when his employees both like and respect him."

Was this a compliment or was he going to throw a "but" in there? Scott found himself holding his breath as his father continued.

Hal stuck his hands in his pockets and stared out at the lake. "I've been doing a lot of thinking since you came back. I'm real sorry for the way things have been between us for the last few years, even before you left."

Scott was speechless.

Hal continued, "I know you think that I loved Dave better and that you disappointed me but the truth is after we lost Dave, I was afraid of something happening to you, too. I wanted to make sure you were strong, that you made smart choices. I worried about you all the time."

"Really? That's what was behind . . . everything."

"Yeah. I guess that fear translated into anger. I didn't mean for us to grow so far apart."

"What about all those things you said when I came back?" Scott ventured to ask.

"When you left, I thought it was my worst nightmare come true," Hal confessed. "For the first few weeks I kept waiting for the police to call, to say you'd been in an accident or gotten into some kind of trouble.

"After the first year, I figured you were never coming back and I was sorry for everything I did to chase you away. But then when you showed up at the dealership, all I could think of was what you'd put me through."

"I'm sorry, Dad. I wish I would have understood."

"I should have told you. I'm just not good at all this touchy-feely stuff."

Scott grinned. "Yeah, I know."

Hal didn't offer to give him a hug and it would have been so out of character that Scott would have been horrified if he did. His father's words were more than enough for him.

But still he wondered . . . "Why are you telling me this now, Dad?"

"When Beth came to Green Bay to tell me she was quitting, she also asked me to talk to you. She convinced me that things weren't so bad between us that they couldn't be made right."

"Beth did that?"

"Yes," Hal replied.

"After she came back to Green Bay?" That couldn't be right, could it?

"I told you it was the same day she resigned."

Beth had worked to make peace between him and his father, even after he'd treated her so badly. Suddenly the surprise he had planned for her didn't seem like nearly enough.

"Have I ever told you what a good job you did in choosing a wife?" Hal asked.

"I seem to remember a time when you weren't too thrilled about it."

"That was before I really knew Beth. I judged you both too quickly."

"I can't believe she would do this after. . . ."

"After what?"

"I pressured Beth into agreeing to stay."
He wasn't about to give out the details on
that one, even with the new goodwill between them. "Instead of trusting her, I
threatened her on the day she came to see
you because I knew something was going
on that she wasn't telling me. I thought
maybe she was planning on not coming
back. I never imagined that her secret was
something like this."

"You owe her an apology."

"I owe her a lot more than that. Come
on." Scott started out at a brisk pace.

"Where are we going?" asked Hal, attempting to keep up.

"To the lodge. I want to talk to Beth now."

Hal was a little breathless when they got
there. He'd had to hurry to keep up with
his son, but Scott wouldn't slow down. He
was too eager to talk to Beth and settle
things between them.

The women were still in the restaurant,
gathered around their table with Risa in
their midst, like a little queen holding court.
She was in Cindy's lap presently.

He dropped a kiss on Risa's head. "How's
the birthday girl?" he asked.

"She's getting an overload of attention,"

Beth confirmed. "She's going to be so spoiled after this party, I don't know what we'll do with her."

"And I don't know what I'm going to do with you."

Surprised by her husband's words, Beth looked up and was caught in the intensity of his gaze. "What do you mean?"

"Can I talk to you in my office for a minute?"

"Sure." Beth pushed her chair back and rose.

"Excuse us," he said to the rest of the group. "We'll only be a few minutes."

Beth was baffled. What was going on?

Once they were in his office, Scott pulled the door shut behind them. Beth turned to him, ready to talk but found herself swept into his arms instead.

Scott kissed her. "I love you," he said.

She stepped back from him so she could see his face. "I love you, too. But surely you didn't call me in here to tell me that?"

"No. There's something we do need to discuss, but, first, I want to tell you that my father just . . . well, just came as close to apologizing to me for all our problems as he'll likely ever get."

"He did? That's wonderful!" She'd hoped

Hal would come through on this but didn't expect it so soon.

"Yes, and I know exactly who to thank for it — you."

She felt her cheeks grow warm. "Me? This is between you and your father."

"Don't be modest. He told me that you talked to him about it when you went to Green Bay."

"I didn't really do. . . ."

Scott cut her off. "That was why you didn't want me to come. You weren't sure how things would go with my dad."

Beth nodded. "I was afraid he'd be angry when I told him I was quitting and I didn't want him to take it out on you. I told him about the fight we had before you left and that he shouldn't blame you for leaving."

Scott stroked her cheek. "I think that's the nicest thing anyone has ever done for me. Thank you, Beth."

"I'm just glad you and your dad are all right."

"It was more than I deserved after the way I acted."

Her gaze shifted from his face to the floor. She didn't want him to see how much that still hurt her. But his hand cupped her chin and lifted her head back up.

"I'm sorry I made you promise to stay

here in the way I did. Because I felt like I'd forced you to say what I wanted to hear, I wasn't able to believe you'd keep your word. That's why I panicked and made that completely stupid threat."

She felt tears pricking at her eyes and blinked them back. "Oh Scott, thank you for telling me that. But no matter how it came about, I did mean it when I said I was staying. I knew that was what I wanted but I was afraid to take that final step. Your 'method' may have been out of the ordinary, but it did encourage me to finally say the words."

"Will you say them again?"

"Say what?"

"That you love me and you want us to stay together, to be a family with Risa?"

"Why?"

"I need to hear you say it but only if that's what you truly want."

"I love you, Scott Lund, and I want us to stay together."

"And be a family with Risa," he prompted.

Beth couldn't help but smile. It felt like she was reciting an oath. "And of course be a family with Risa."

"Thank you," Scott replied, his voice sounding suspiciously rough.

"You're welcome. I'll say it every day if

you want. Now let's get back to our guests."

He shook his head. "That's not all."

Beth raised her eyebrows. "Really? More than that?"

"Yes." He moved around his desk and took a file from one of the drawers. "I had my lawyer draw up papers putting the resort in both our names."

"Really? I can't believe this." Surely she heard him wrong.

"I was going to do it anyway. But the other day Fred was telling me about how his daughter is struggling now that her husband has left her. It made me understand what you meant when you said I was asking you to give up everything to move here with me, and it made changing the deed seem more urgent."

"Scott, you didn't have to do this. I knew you didn't mean what you said about fighting for custody of Risa."

"No, you didn't. You've been distant since I said that. I acted like an idiot. Honestly Beth, I would never put Risa in that situation."

"Thank you Scott. I believe you this time."

"That's what I had planned before I found out that you'd talked to my father. Now I've changed my mind."

"Changed your mind? Why?"

"Talking to my father was such a selfless act on your part, especially considering what I'd just done. It made me realize how much you were giving to this marriage and how little I was. Like you said before, I was trying to have everything my way."

He took both of her hands in his. "So I'm going to offer you a choice. Either I'll have your name added to the deed of the resort or. . . ."

"Or what?"

"Or we'll sell the resort and use the money to start over. In Green Bay or anywhere you'd like."

"Scott, are you sure? I know how much the resort means to you. Your friend left it to you."

"Yes, but you and Risa mean more to me. I know Henry would understand that and approve."

Tears flooded her eyes. "Scott, this is a beautiful thing you're offering."

"Do you want some time to think it over?"

She managed a smile. "I don't know. I've heard California is a great place to live."

His expression solemn, Scott said, "Anywhere you want to go, I'm there."

"Don't start packing yet. I'm happy right where I am."

"You don't have to say that for my sake,"

he insisted.

"I'm not. I love it here. And you'd better be careful about putting the resort in both our names. If you leave me, I'll fight you for it."

She saw him processing that. It took a few seconds, and then he realized she was teasing him. A smile spread across his face and he laughed, a rumbling laugh that started deep inside him.

There really was no more to say, so she held out her arms to him and met his embrace. He held her tightly, as if he'd never let her go.

Too soon there was a knock on the door and Cindy called, "Are you two almost finished in there? It's time to get ready for the party."

"The party!" Beth exclaimed. "I completely forgot about it."

Cindy's voice, even muffled by the door, sounded clearly. "I thought you might have."

It was a good thing that Cindy was there to help her. Beth was floating in a daze of happiness.

Hal and Margie took Risa while the rest of them transferred the food from the restaurant into the party room. Cindy and Beth had made a selection of finger foods and had made pizza from scratch. Ben had made the cake, a decadent creation with gobs of gooey pink frosting adorning it. Sam and Shaun hauled in all of Risa's gifts, which was no small feat. Margie hadn't been the only one to go overboard on the little girl.

Scott shook his head when he saw the towering pile on one table. "Are you sure we bought that many things for Risa?" he asked, examining the gifts.

"You may not have actually been along when I bought some of them," admitted Beth with a smile and a shrug.

"Just tell me if the credit card's maxed out."

She gave him a playful jab in the ribs. "Of course it's not."

Shannon and Troy arrived with Fred and Ronnie in tow. Everyone rushed to hug Fred and tell him how good he looked and how happy they were with his recovery. Scott introduced Fred to his parents. Hal seemed to like him as much as Margie liked Ronnie.

Once all the guests were settled, everyone ate until they were full. Beth groaned and pushed her plate away. "Cindy, it's dangerous living with you. Pretty soon you'll have to roll me down the hill to the restaurant."

Her friend laughed. "Yes, but don't forget we have miles of hiking trails so you can work it off."

Risa was, of course, the star of the party. She was kissed, hugged and passed around. Everyone wanted to have a chance to talk to the birthday girl. Even Shaun wasn't embarrassed to be seen playing with such a young child.

"I swear that girl has grown three inches this summer," Margie fussed to Scott.

"Isn't that what she's supposed to do?"

"Yes," Margie sighed. "But I missed it."

"I'm sorry, Mom."

She smiled and patted his cheek. "It's okay. This is a wonderful place for Risa to grow up. If the school has a good program for her, I'd say there's no better place she could be."

"But you'll miss her."

Margie shrugged. "This is also a great place to visit. You may get tired of seeing your father and me."

Scott leaned over and hugged his mother. "I'll never get tired of you, Mom."

Across the room, Scott noticed Sam and Shaun talking to Troy and Shannon. The atmosphere was casual and at least marginally friendly. He was glad that the twins had finally learned to get along with Troy. Risa pulled on Shannon's shirt and she picked her up. The three boys talked with her for a second, then they all headed for Beth.

"Risa says it's time for her to open her presents," Shaun announced.

Beth arched an eyebrow. "Risa says so?"

"Yes," Sam affirmed. "Didn't she say that, Troy?"

"I'm sure I heard her say that," Troy answered with mock seriousness.

"Well, what are we waiting for, then?" Beth rose and took Risa from Shannon. She led Risa to the table that was heaped with gifts. Scott went to join them, while the boys announced loudly that Risa was going to open her presents.

Beth smiled at Scott and handed over Risa. "You help her open gifts and I'll write down what she got and from whom."

The business of opening presents took quite a while. When they were finished, there was a pile of colorful paper and bows on one side of Scott and an assortment of gifts on the other. "What can we possibly get her for Christmas?" he joked. "There can't be anything left in the stores."

His parents had given her the most gifts. There were several new outfits ranging from dresses that were all ruffles and lace to pastel-colored sweat suits and snuggly pajamas. There were plenty of toys and books as well. The one gift that stood out was a scooter in the shape of a car. Scott was sure his father had picked that one out.

Cindy and Ben bought clothes for Risa. Fred and Troy gave her a soft, cuddly doll. Ronnie bought her a DVD and Shannon gave Risa a big fluffy teddy bear. Sam and Shaun each gave Risa a book — *The Big Red Barn* and *Red Fish, Blue Fish* — their own favorites from childhood.

"Now it's time for cake," Shaun announced, leaping to his feet.

"No," Scott shook his head. "Not yet."

He plopped back down. "Aaaawwww."

Handing Risa to Beth, Scott stood and cleared his throat.

"Oh no," whispered Sam loudly. "He's gonna make a speech. We'll never get to the cake."

Scott laughed at the boys' antics. "Don't worry. I won't take that long. I just want to thank all of you for coming today and for bringing such wonderful gifts for my daughter."

"All right," Shaun exclaimed, rising from his chair again. "That didn't take long. Let's have cake."

"Wait." Beth stood up. "I have something to add."

Sam sat down with a groan.

"For a long time, I dreaded this day when

Risa turned three because it meant big changes for us. In the last few months, my and Risa's lives have changed far beyond what I was expecting at this point. Today, instead of dreading the future I'm looking forward to it. I'm sad that I can't see Hal and Margie every day anymore, but I'm very happy with my new home and my new friends. And I'm especially happy with my old husband. Thanks for giving *me* a second chance, Scott."

Scott, his heart swelling with happiness, surrounded Beth with a bear hug and swung her in a circle, to applause from their guests. Especially Shaun, when he realized it was time for cake. Ben lit the candles and they all sang "Happy Birthday."

Everyone cheered Risa on when it was time to blow out the candles. In the end she needed some extra help. Cindy and Ben cut the cake and passed out slices and everyone ate it enthusiastically. Soon everything was finished except the cleanup.

CHAPTER 21

Scott put an arm around Beth. "You don't have to do this if you don't want to," he assured her.

"No, I want to. I'm just nervous."

"It doesn't matter. I love you. Mom and Dad love you. Risa loves you. You don't need him, you know."

"I know. I just feel like I need to give him another chance, like you gave me when you came back."

"All right. Go ahead then."

Beth stared at the paper in her hand for a moment, then picked up the phone and punched in the number written there. Scott didn't move from her side.

She held her breath and counted the rings. One. Two. Three. And then he picked up.

"Hello."

"Daddy?"

A pause . . . and then — "Beth?"

"Yes, Daddy, it's me."

There was another pause and then, "Where are you? How are you? It's been so long since I heard from you." There was no mistaking the joy in her father's voice and her own heart leapt in response.

"I didn't think you wanted to hear from me."

"I'm sorry," he said quickly, as if rushing to get the words out. "I'm really sorry for the way I acted when you told me about getting married. When I wanted to apologize I realized I had no idea where you were, or how to reach you. Your mother didn't know either when I asked her. I'm so, so sorry, Beth."

A lump rose in her throat. She swallowed and said, "I should have given you the chance to apologize. I'm sorry I didn't."

"Where are you now and what are you doing?" His voice was as full of excitement as a little boy's at Christmas.

"I'm still married to Scott. But I didn't have the baby. I miscarried."

"Oh, Beth."

She didn't want to dwell on that so she quickly moved on. "We have a daughter now though. She just turned three."

"I have a granddaughter?"

"Yes. Her name is Risa. She's starting school soon."

"At three?"

"Risa has Down syndrome; she'll be in a special Early Childhood program so she'll get all the help she'll need."

"Oh. Well, that's good. That she's getting help."

"It's okay. We couldn't love her any more than we do, even if she didn't have this disability. She's the sweetest child you can imagine."

"I'm sure I'll love her, too."

Hearing her father say that brought tears to Beth's eyes. "How's Melanie?" she asked, referring to her stepmother.

"We divorced shortly after the last time I saw you," her father admitted. "She took the kids and moved to Washington, near her parents. I've been alone since then."

"I'm sorry to hear that, Dad." She hated thinking of her father spending the last few years alone. If only she'd known.

"It's okay. I wish I could see your brothers more, but I'm better off without her."

Beth had to agree there, but she didn't say so. Instead she changed the subject. "Dad, would you consider coming for a visit, maybe at Thanksgiving?"

Silence.

"Daddy, are you still there?"

"I'm still here, baby. I can't believe this.

I'd love to come. Where are you?" His voice was thick with emotion.

"We're in Spruce Point, not far from Rhinelander. Scott and I own Pine Away Resort and we'd love for you to come see the place." She looked to Scott who gave her a thumbs-up.

"I'm so glad you called," her father said.

They talked for a little longer. She assured him that when he did his lodging, it would be on the house. He thought he might try to visit much sooner than Thanksgiving. After promising her dad she'd call again soon, Beth hung up.

She turned to Scott and hugged him. "I should have called him this spring instead of my mother."

"Your mother is the one that's losing out," he told her.

"Do you think we should send her an invitation to Thanksgiving anyway?"

"That's entirely up to you," Scott told her.

"Maybe I'll send one to my half sister. I do feel sorry for her. Now she's stuck trying to live up to my mom's expectations. That can't be easy. Think of all the years you spent trying to please your father."

"Definitely send her the invitation." Scott grinned.

They both laughed.

■ ■ ■ ■

It seemed to Beth like she just turned around and summer was over. She'd gone back to Green Bay and spent a week packing up her house. Then Scott, Ben and the twins had come down and loaded up all her things to take back to the resort. Actually it turned out to be not much of a load, since she sold most of her furniture to Margie's cousin.

Margie and Hal stayed for most of the week after Risa's party and had come to visit on a couple of other weekends. Beth couldn't have been more surprised when Hal announced that he and Margie had bought some land near the resort and intended to build a cottage of their own. "I'm going to retire in a few years," Hal told them, "and we'll move up here at that time. Until then, we plan on spending all the days we can here."

"What about the dealership?" asked Beth.

"I've been giving Jared more responsibility there. I figure by the time I retire, he'll be ready to take over." Then Hal turned to Scott. "I know that the two of you didn't exactly have a great reunion this spring, but I hope you'll give your cousin a chance. He and I have grown close over the years. I always hoped you'd take over the dealership, Scott. But when you left I started grooming Jared for the position. You've done so well for yourself with the resort, that I have a feeling you won't mind."

"Selling cars was never my thing, Dad," Scott assured him. "I'm happy for Jared."

They got another surprise when Troy's mother quit her job and announced that she intended to move back to Spruce Point. She wanted to be there to take care of her father, she explained. The deal benefited her and Troy as well. Living in Fred's house would cut their expenses. Scott immediately offered to keep Troy on all year instead of just in the summer. Troy's mom applied for and got a job at the restaurant on the resort. She didn't start until after the high school and college students left to go back to school, but that was okay since she needed time to settle her affairs in Hudson and get moved.

Shannon was thrilled that Troy was staying and they could be seen together, often holding hands and talking about the upcoming school year. Beth didn't know if Shannon and Troy's romance would last through their senior year, but she was glad Troy and his mother were going to stay in

Spruce Point.

The week before school started, Beth spent a day in Wausau with Risa, Cindy and Shannon. They did all their school shopping. Shannon was excited about starting her senior year, but Cindy looked less than happy.

"One more year and she'll be gone just like the twins. I'm losing my baby," she complained.

Shannon rolled her eyes. "Oh, Mother."

Beth gave Cindy a sympathetic smile. She felt the same way about sending Risa to school. She was losing her baby, too.

But she couldn't hold back time.

Before she was ready, the first day of school dawned.

"I can't believe I let you talk me into allowing Risa to ride the bus," Beth grumbled at Scott. They stood at the end of their driveway, Risa between them, waiting for the big yellow school bus.

"Relax, Beth. Risa will love it. And it will save time. Now that you're working, too, we don't really have time to be running into town twice a day." Beth had started her advertising campaign and already had three companies signed up for tours of the resort. She was trying to organize her work schedule around the time Risa was in school.

"Maybe I shouldn't be doing this. Maybe I should stay home."

"You were the one who wanted a job," Scott reminded her. "Besides, you're home even when you work. Most of the time, at least."

Beth bit her lip. "I'm worrying again, aren't I?"

He leaned over and kissed her cheek. "You're only doing what all mothers do."

Risa began to jump up and down. Beth looked around and saw the bus rumbling down their road. It pulled up to them with a squeal of brakes and the door opened.

"All right, kiddo," said Scott, taking Risa's hand and leading her to the steps. "You go ahead and get on."

Risa stared at the huge vehicle, her eyes wide. Beth felt her stomach knot. This was all wrong. How could she put her baby on this noisy, smelly machine and send her. . . .

The aide came forward and held out her hand to Risa. "Come on, sweetie. I have a seat waiting for you."

With a giggle Risa moved forward. Scott lifted her up and set her on the bus. "Bye, Risa. We'll see you after school."

"Wait!" Beth rushed in to kiss Risa. Then the aide whisked her off and buckled her into a seat. The bus pulled away and Risa smiled and waved at them from her seat at the window. Scott and Beth waved back, then stood and watched the bus until it was out of sight.

As soon as it was gone, Beth burst into tears. Scott, who didn't seem the least bit surprised, led her back into the house and onto the sofa. He held her until her sobs subsided.

Grabbing some tissue from the coffee table Beth wiped at her face and blew her nose.

"Better now?" asked Scott.

She nodded. "Thanks for staying. I know you have to get to work."

"No, I don't. I cleared my schedule for the whole morning."

"The whole morning? Why?"

"So I could spend it with you."

"You don't have to do this, Scott."

"Yes, I do," he insisted. "If I don't, you're going to spend the whole morning moping around. I'm not going to let you do that."

"You think I'm overreacting on Risa's first day of school," Beth accused.

"I think you're a good mother and you're anxious about putting your child into a new situation, that's all."

"It's just that . . . Risa was all I had for so

long. And she needed so much extra help. Up until a little while ago, she was my whole life. The only reason I went to work was to provide for her. The only reason I got up every morning was to see her smile."

"I know." Scott pulled her close again. "It will get easier."

Beth snuggled into his embrace, grateful for Scott's comforting presence. How different would this day have been if she were still a single parent?

"You know what you need?" asked Scott suddenly. "Something besides Risa to keep you busy. You need a hobby — knitting, or something."

Beth wrinkled her nose. "Knitting?"

"You never know, you could learn to like it."

"I don't know. What other ideas have you got?"

He kissed the top of her head. "How about planning a wedding."

"What? Whose wedding? Are you thinking of renting out space at the lodge for that?"

With a laugh, Scott shook his head. "I was definitely not thinking of that."

Beth considered, her mind caught by the suggestion. "It's not a bad idea. The same space you had planned for our corporate clients could be used for weddings and family reunions and other events."

"You're right, it could. But I wasn't talking about the resort. I was talking about us."

"Now you've lost me."

He pulled a small velvet box out of his pocket and handed it to her. Beth felt her eyes widen as she opened it and revealed a beautiful platinum ring, set with three sparkling diamonds.

"I wanted to buy you an engagement ring because I couldn't afford one before. But the salesperson at the store told me the three stones on these rings represent the past, present, and future. I thought it was perfect for us."

She drew in a sharp breath, unable to look away from the beautiful ring he'd picked out. "Thank you, Scott. This is beautiful. Past, present, and future. We've got all of those, haven't we?"

"Yes, but it's our future that I'm mainly concerned about now. I want to get started on the right foot this time. I want us to have a wedding, with guests and cake and all of the things we missed out on the first time. Will you marry me again, Beth?"

She peered up at him, overwhelmed by his gift and suddenly feeling very shy. She realized he was waiting for an answer. "Yes,

I'll marry you." After a moment she added, "As long as you bring me roses again."

"You know I will." Scott took the ring from the box and slipped it onto her finger. "And then after the wedding. . . ."

"Then what?" He'd certainly been busy thinking all this up.

"Then I think we should look into building a new house."

"But I like your house," Beth protested.

"That's just it. It's 'my' house. I want to live in 'our' house."

"Hmmm," she murmured, feeling playful now that she'd recovered from her surprise. "I suppose *our* house will be built in a rustic, log-cabin style."

"I don't care about that as long as it's a big house with a music room and four or five bedrooms."

A giggle escaped her. "What would we do with all those bedrooms?"

"Fill them with brothers and sisters for Risa, of course," he said with a grin.

"My, you have been thinking ahead." She snuggled closer. "But I like the way you think, so go on."

"Actually," Scott said, turning her toward him so he could kiss her. "I'd rather not 'go on' by myself. If there's any more planning to do, I want us to do it together. I love you, Beth."

"I love you, too, Scott, with all my heart." She turned toward him and placed her lips on his. He joined in the kiss, and it was so intense, so passionate she tried to pour all the love she felt for him into this one moment. But she didn't have to. She had her whole lifetime to show him.

ABOUT THE AUTHOR

Kara Lynn Russell lives with her family in a small village in the heart of Wisconsin's dairy land, but enjoys the occasional escape to the northern woods. She serves as her town's library director and enjoys reading, crochet, jigsaw puzzles and community theater. She is fortunate to have a husband who is very supportive of her writing habit, even if it means a messy house or late suppers. Kara Lynn is also the mother of four wonderful children, one of whom happens to have Down syndrome. You can visit Kara Lynn on the Web at karalynnrussell .googlepages.com.